PENTALOGY

BOOK ONE

HALE

CODY MAY

INKWATER
PRESS

PORTLAND • OREGON
INKWATERPRESS.COM

Publisher: Inkwater Press | www.inkwaterpress.com

Paperback
ISBN-13 978-1-59299-748-0 | ISBN-10 1-59299-748-1

Kindle
ISBN-13 978-1-59299-749-7 | ISBN-10 1-59299-749-X

Printed in the U.S.A.
All paper is acid free and meets all ANSI standards for archival quality paper.

3 5 7 9 10 8 6 4

Dedicated to those who think they're alone.
You're not.

Consequence is the Blind Man's only cure.

PENTALOGY OF THE BECOMING

WELCOME, READERS AND FUTURE FANS, TO PENTALOGY OF THE Becoming, Book One of Five, HALE. This is just the beginning to a five book, two million word pentalogy that will be sure to thrill, sadden, anger and inspire you all the way through from page one, to the final period of book five.

I began this five book compilation in the summer of 2009, and will put forth all my words, my conception and perception, and share, with you, a part of myself in this pentalogy.

Each book will introduce new characters (to either nod your head with or oppose against), a fresh plot even more exciting than the last, and another expression of defending, or, if your perception tells you otherwise, offending morality.

Through the first four books in the pentalogy, a main character—whether they are a merciless vigilante, an unconquerable idea, or a dignified rebel—will rise and compromise their own identities to fight crime with their own bloody motives. And in the fifth, concluding book of the pentalogy, all four heroes will join to reestablish our society as we know it, and leave the deepest scar on Earth.

Let their stories, their personas and identities, inspire you and widen the perspective you hold to the crime of our world. Choose your side, shine your light, establish your own perception of morality and justice, and allow yourself to become.

Here is Alexander Hale's dark tale of his own, merciless becoming...

Thank you to...

Arlin Tawzer for your ideas and thoughts,

Kimberly Waters for your unending love and support,

Jeramie Greene for being the first ever to read HALE,

Ms. Evans for, inadvertently, making my knowledge bloom,

And every reader who will lay their eyes upon this book.

Thank you.

HALE

PROLOGUE

RAGGING ACROSS THE SAND AND BETWEEN THE PRESSES OF HIS footprints was the deceitfully water-like gasoline pouring from the pepper-red container. The ground behind him ended, and the edge of the wooden planked dock looked over several feet of air, then the black, wobbling water of the Pacific. Over the passive lapping of the waves, the kid could hear the echoes of voices calling after him.

They sprawled over easy sloping hills embedding the port in isolation from the distant city. He dropped the tub at his feet, and felt for a matchbox in his coat's pocket. When he reclaimed his gloved hand from the pocket's depth, he separated one matchstick from all the others and held it by the tips of his fingers.

As if the voices had skipped a great distance closer to the kid, their echoes were suddenly intensified in volume. His eyes twitched up from his black palm, to the short-cut field of stubby buildings sitting in the dip of a cove at the start of the dock. He could see the bright, circular scopes of flashlights sliding across the sides of buildings and the sandy ground of the beach. But when the shine of a single flashlight trailed the kid's path to the dock's far end, he was blinded by white glare.

A voice howled loudest of all, to the moon of shallow eyes and the men of eyes even shallower, "He's over here!" The darkly dressed man—armed with not only a flashlight, but a loaded rifle slung by a strap across his back—called out to the hooded figure backed to the dock's last wooden plank. "Hey!" he called. "Stop right there! Don't you dare make a move!" He focused the circular aim of his flashlight to the kid's vague figure.

Slowly approaching, the man continued throwing orders across the great distance between him and the hooded kid. Soon, the other men still on the port's beach were quickly marching to the end of the dock. And still, the kid held a single matchstick in his grip. Although alone the matchstick was harmless, the aid of bloody motives, utmost provocation, and a roughly textured surface could spark a flame hot enough to burn an entire empire to ashes, and hot enough to burn those ashes far beyond nothing.

The hood on the kid's head threw a shadow across his face like oil. Even within the flashlight's continuous stare, the kid's face, and identity, was completely shrouded. His heart was pounding uncontrollably in his chest, like a beast caged within a prison of bone and cartilage. The night's humidity was sticky, and touched the skin of his neck like syrupy sweat, his breaths were drunk with exhaustion, drowning in swampy oxygen.

Slowly, the kid brought the match to the side of its box, threatening, and ready, to scrape it along. "Stop!" pleaded the man who increased the speed of his march and replaced his flashlight with a rifle, undoubtedly loaded with lead bullets.

When the man had shrunken the distance between him and the hooded figure to only a few meters, he brought a transmitter radio close to his mouth. "Sir," he spoke, "I have the intruder in sight. He's not going anywhere."

A voice muffled by the radio spoke back through. The man, with an obvious amount of jurisdiction, asked, expecting nothing less than an absolute answer, *"Who is he?"*

The guard, again, held a flashlight in his hand while gripping the handle of his rifle in the other. He kept the kid in the aim of both his flashlight and firearm. Bending down, the man sent a cone of light up the kid's face, and when he saw who it was beneath the hood, his expectation fell with a great amount of oppression. His surprise was set aloft.

This time, more carefully bringing the radio to his mouth, the man spoke slowly, with words dry of intensity or anything close to anxiety. He readied a breath, and said to the man through the transmitter, "It's your son..."

"*What?*" the voice barked back abruptly. *"Are you sure?"* he asked, angrily.

"Yes, sir," the man replied without needing to affirm his observation. "I'm sure."

The exposure of his identity didn't water-down the bloody pool of his objective. With no missing intent to finish what he had started, the kid slid the matchstick across the sandpaper strip, and a small flame hissed, then burst to life.

"Sir," the man continued his dialogue with his boss, "he has a match. What should I do?" he asked, nervously anticipating a spread of flames. His boss never responded, and the man asked again, "What should I do?"

After a second hiatus of speech, the boss called back, *"Stop him!"* he answered bluntly. *"Do whatever you need to do. Don't let him light that fire!"* The boss's apathy was potent enough.

The man placed both hands upon his rifle, and brought the butt of the gun to his cheek, readying an aim. "Extinguish the match, kid," said the guard, warning him about his permission to pull the trigger. "Extinguish the match," he advised again.

But the kid let his flame slowly fall down the limb of his match, allowing it to grow hotter, brighter, bigger. "Burn to hell," he said, not to the guard, but to his father who was deaf to his own son's suffering. The kid extended his arm, and began loosening the small grip he had on the matchstick.

The guard screamed, while all the approaching others were clogging behind him, "Don't do it, kid! Don't do it!"

He parted his fingers, and the match began a decent which, to the guard and his disbelief, was a slow, agonizing fall of both the wick, and the empire he was slaving under. Almost instinctively (as it is for every member of mankind to seize the opportunity of permitted injustice) he pulled back on the trigger of his rifle.

A programmed burst of bullets fired from the gun's barrel. The three, thick lead darts dug themselves into the kid's chest. He was forced backward, off his feet and the edge of the dock on which he stood. And while he fell closer and closer to the fragile surface of the ocean, the match was landing in the wetted trail of gasoline.

Its flame ignited the fuel, the gun shots' echoes thinned away completely, and the kid sunk beneath the watery mouth of man's childish corruptibility.

ONE

I**T FELT GOOD TO KILL HIM.**

My hands were wrapped around his neck, inescapable like the grip of a marble statue. Slowly, the color in his face dimmed and died as he did—the veins in his face drying to shallow streams of red dust.

And it was amusing knowing that the man's last ever sight would be of my angry eyes.

For a while he thrashed about the choke I had on him. He swiped at my face and tried to gouge out my eyes. When he had the strength, the man tried to use his legs and pry me off of him. At one pathetic point, I could hear a single sentence fight its way up his throat and through his teeth like a fleeing fool, chasing a distant, uncatchable freedom.

It was a plea for his life: he told me not to kill him.

But I couldn't help to wonder why he thought mercy was on his side. From his very birth and seed of existence, until the moment he let mankind's cruelty rot his skin, I was always going to decide the length of his life.

I didn't want him to taste my mercy or kindness in the last moments of living; mercy's sweet breath of air and its laughable tolerance. I didn't want him to die happily or with absolution. He couldn't be content. He had to die wanting to live, wishing he could change something. There was no room for mercy. There never was from the very beginning.

Beneath the grip of my hands I could feel his esophagus break and his windpipe collapse. I knew he felt pain just as I felt the snap of his bones, and the pleasure which rose from that. His eyes widened just before they shut. Before he died I could see the pulse of his heartbeat lifting and lowering his chest in rapid little spurts that never seemed to slow down.

Isn't it humorous? Isn't it amusing that when a person has no time left to live, they come alive?

"If crime is merciless," I whispered into his ear, hoping there was something in him left that could hear, "justice must be too." I leaned away from his face and pulled back a spotless fist.

When I charged my knuckles into his face, it was like breaking through a pumpkin to the gushy guts inside.

With heavy releases of air, panting breaths, I reclaimed my fist from the man's skull. Pasty blood dripped from my knuckles, and the determination behind my blood and his was indefinable. For a while I stood over him, looking at his mutilated head and trying to believe my mutilated innocence. There was no face, no structure, no shape to the man's shell. It was broken and shattered.

I ripped the dead man's sleeve from his right arm, and looked for the tattoo. On the muscle of his shoulder was a fresh coat of sunflower gold, ruby red jewels, balled tips, and the nasty crack tearing a scar down the center of an ink crown. The man, as I expected, was a bird under the wing of Big Rich.

I stood, looking down at the body. My first kill; perfectly revengeful, heartlessly necessary.

Clothes stiff from the dried saltwater, and fists bloody from the baneful murder, I walked onward, not sure where to go, but knowing what to do. Ed's apartment was near there, so I walked myself through the rotten neighborhood until I came knocking weakly on his door.

The entire trip seemed to be a chapped cobblestone street walking its way right through the core of an oven. Not even the passing shade graced you with one less degree. I couldn't look up at the sky, burnt orange, for the bleeding light of the sun was strangely blinding.

Ed's apartment was nuzzled in the middle of a crumbling complex. The grass was dead, though no different from any other yard. A pool had once been filled with crystal like water and the splashes of kids treading. Those days had passed, and the pool was then just a pit, a grave already dug for a loot of corpses.

I took my fist to the wooden door of Ed's apartment, and each time I knocked, I left a bloody mark shaped like the side of my curled hand. His arrival to the door was unwarned and unexpected. And to him, my presence slumped at the mat of his door was equally strange.

He placed his eyes upon me and firstly asked, "You okay, bud?"

"I'm going to kill him, Ed!" I lifted my head so he could see the pair of steaming eyes under my hood. "I'm going to kill that son-of-a-bitch!"

Ed's response was immediately alarmed. "Whoa…" he repeated several times. "What the hell happened?"

"They killed him! They just…" I looked for a deeper explanation. I failed. "They just fucking killed him!"

"What are you talking about, Hale?" My friend couldn't make sense of the scrambled, distraught speech dripping from my mouth. Verbal rabies.

"Big Rich! His men murdered Jay…" I wanted to scream it! But never found the strength in such a sentence.

"What?" he asked me. "How do you know? I mean…are you sure?"

"I killed the man who murdered him."

Ed's voice dropped, and he spoke to himself with slow, sticky words. "Oh, God…"

"I'm going to kill Big Rich," I slugged Ed with the sentence again. "I swear."

"Oh, God…" he apostrophized again. After looking both ways down the hall outside of his particular apartment, Ed looked back at me and said, "You'd better come in."

The only furniture in Ed's boxy, square-roomed apartment was stacks and tipping piles of cardboard boxes. In some, there were papers scarred with ink words, and in others, Ed's actual furniture that had never been unpacked since his recent move. Though, Ed didn't own many things worth removing from the boxes.

He sat me down on the one couch sitting before a small, out of date television on the floor. Ed handed me a cup of water to sip at and asked, "What exactly happened?"

"I told you...Richard's men killed Jay. I strangled one of them, and now I'm after Big Rich himself." I took a brief sip.

Ed was taken aback by the morbidity. "What? What the hell do you know about killing? You just took one, pathetic life out of anger, and you'll probably pay for that. Regardless, you can't go around killing people you think are...evil."

"These aren't just thoughts," I told Ed. "He killed Jay..."

Ed took a seat next to me and leaned into the back cushion. He exhaled through the gaps between his teeth and thought. I was silent with my own racing mind. "What are you planning to accomplish?" he finally asked. It was at our very first bit of dialogue when I knew he would ask the inevitable.

"The Drug Trade is a tree...all I have to do is burn it down." It was justice I was seeking, justice that I would have to sift out of the ashes from Big's operation.

"You don't even know if this Drug Trade exists. You have a *feeling* that it exists; you have a *feeling* that Big Rich is in charge. You can't just suspect that of someone like Richard Lucifer," Ed said to me.

"And why not?" Ed's statement, to me, was airheaded.

"He's Los Angeles's angel!" he exclaimed excitedly, though speaking from the public's mouth, not his own. "He's its savior! If it wasn't for Big Rich, neither of us would have had a home to grow up in."

"That orphanage spit me out just as quickly as it took me in!" I snapped.

"Oh..." Ed said inquisitively, but sarcastically. "So the orphanage, the place *we* grew up in, is a conspiracy too? It's also part of the Drug Trade?"

"Believe me or not Ed," I spoke, "it is, and if you can't see that, then you're just as blind as everyone else."

"Or maybe you're the blind one," Ed bravely treaded.

His offensive dialect brought silence over the room. The two of us sat there in the musky aroma of our own thoughts. Or maybe it was just the apartment's scent…

"I can't let him finish Project Home," I said softly, holding my match just close enough to Ed's fuse that it wouldn't light, but he could still feel its heat.

"Jesus Christ, Hale!" Ed shot to his feet and stood over me. "Is everything an enemy to you? Project Home is nothing to condemn! It's charitable!" Ed tramped over to the tiny kitchen behind us and filled his own glass with water, then just as rapidly chugged it down.

I too stood, combating Ed's rising logos. "It's a God damned cover up, Ed! Everything! The orphanage, his God damned smile, Project Home!"

Shaking his head, Ed set down the glass and asked, quietly, trying to arouse any logic within me, "How? How is it a cover up? And why aren't you just paranoid?"

"I…" I was stuck in my own paste. For a long, dematerializing moment I remained silent, collecting any sort of answer. "I…" Giving it one last chance, I soon realized something: "I don't know." Behind the counter of his kitchen, Ed was nodding his head, for once agreeing with me. I *didn't* know. "But there's something more to it than either of us know…" I couldn't give it up, nor did I want to. Otherwise my hands would have been dirty purposelessly.

"You're seventeen, pal," Ed began to speak as he walked out from around the counter. He stood next to me with a hand on my back. "I understand you're furious and heartbroken…truly. I've experienced tragedy too." His own sentence brought Ed's eyes to the floor, watery with two salty tears. "Just...just don't act in the moment. I think we both know that won't get you anywhere."

I did, honestly, listen to Ed's words. I could tell that Ed had nearly stepped off the edge of catastrophe. He crept so close to the temptation before he realized the doom it held in its hand. My friend's only motive was to be a friend. His sentences, even those that were completely opposing to mine, were meant for protection. Nothing else.

But when Jay's face crept back into my head, and when I pictured the old man being murdered in the middle of the boiling street, I couldn't help but let my rage speak for me.

"I'm going to kill him," I finalized, seemingly ignorant toward what Ed had just said.

He had been waiting for me to say so. Ed asked, "What if you die trying?"

"I have nothing to lose..." I said surely.

"Really?" Ed took a white jacket over his arm and headed toward the door of his apartment. "What about Raine?" He looked at me for a second before opening the door and walking through.

What about Raine? I asked myself. And then I felt the one thing that was worth sitting in my pocket. Other than my bane and the mercilessness I felt clawing inside of me, a rusted gun with one, single bullet was my only possession.

I held it in my hands and traced my eyes across it several times.

"Here," Jay said and began to pull something from a deep pocket, "take this. I know it's not much, but I want you to have it. It's my only source of protection—I feel that one day, you can put it to true, valuable work."

With his old, shaking hands, Jay handed me the deadliness of a handgun. I looked at it then back to him. It was a cycle I continued to repeat. When I looked at the barrel and its textured handle, I couldn't—no matter how hard I tried—imagine my innocent, young hands holding such a fatal thing to someone else's life.

"Don't let it work you up too much," Jay comforted me and my anxiety. "I'm confident that one day you'll know what to do."

My ripe voice said to the old, silver-haired man, "I...I don't understand, Jay..."

"In time, you will," Jay said back with very few words, though wise words.

I looked at the gun, turning it and flipping it in my hands. Even when I felt no reason to thank the old man, I climbed my eyes up to his and spoke, "Thanks, Jay."

He smiled, and laid one arm across the back of my shoulders. "You're welcome, son."

"You know..." I bounced alongside him and looked up at his sunlight traced silhouette. "Someday, I'm going to make you proud."

Jay smiled and said, "Someday, I know you will."

TWO

HER HOUSE (THE BARE AND BALD STRUCTURE SHE WOULD NEVER dare to call home) was a few blocks south of the orphanage, planted like a dried plant on a street running east and west. Ed's complex was only a few blocks from Raine's house as well.

When he left me standing alone in his apartment, I caught, from the air, the whizz of a fresh aroma, the taste of sugary syrup. *What about Raine?* I asked my thoughts. *What about Raine?*

We had always recognized our adolescent love for each other. Though, our days of bonded friendship with Ed, spent on the streets frying beneath LA's sun, seemed to make us content. Her and I—we were alike, yet so different. It was the comfort of similarity, yet the thrill, the intrigue of differentiation that drew us closer each time we met. And each time we met, it was like a bright flash allowed me to see her face for the first time.

I knew that if a person was strong and potent enough to completely build or destroy my own, then they were worth keeping. Her opinion, I found, could either break me or make me. Through the decaying eyes of my own optimism—those that lose sight more and more each day—, I found it pleasing to believe that more people like Raine existed. Though, beneath reality's jurisdiction, beneath its law and rules, Raine was a single light pushed far into the corner of a blackened room. Her species, it seemed, was a dying breed.

For a long while, I was standing just off the property of the house she lived (and only lived) in. I considered putting one foot on the uplifted first slab of a concrete path drunkenly leading to a front door, struggling to stay on its hinges. I looked at the door that I believe was once blue, and waited for it to open and Raine to step out so I didn't have to step up.

And then the reason for my arrival outside of the shack settled over me like a fog of lead. What was I going to tell her? My true motives, my most raw objective was much too gruesome to flog someone like Raine with. And there was no way to soften the blow if I expected her to understand what I was going to do. Jay had just been murdered, and I was already dead.

My head was empty of an answer, my hands shaking with the tremors of necessity—the necessity of what I had to do to preserve as much of the angel's virtue as I could. Even through my nearly blind eye of optimism, I never thought virtue was truly attainable. But I could cut the extent of her guilt short. I could chop it like a stub, and burn the end so it could never grow long.

I began walking slowly toward the front door, stepping over the lips of concrete slabs that had been lifted over time. The hood on my head covered my face and the identity that I was pretending to still possess. Raine couldn't know about what happened to *me* either. It was unbearable to comprehend my own truth, my own making.

A crack of the most golden sunlight burst over the shadow of my hood. She sent her light sailing across the darkened slime like a solid golden ship, until it hit my own eyes and made an effort out of not returning anything back. It was innate for Raine to smile, even in the presence of a mouth bent in the opposite direction.

"Alex!" Raine sang and spread her arms out to hug me. "It's so good to see you!" she said with her chin on my shoulder.

She separated from me and stood in the doorframe of her house. Raine waited for me to speak, but my head was tipped, and the hood over it threw away the sight of any expression. She lowered her head to catch a glimpse of my face.

"Hale?" Raine asked in the emptiness of my quietude.

"I'm going away for a while…" I said—quite a disheartening first sentence. I suppose the entrance was more of a dodge.

"What do you mean?" Raine asked over a slight laugh. Her electrical eyes studied me, looking for a smile or at least a hint of one. "And take that hood off!" she requested politely, then gently removed it from my head. She pushed her fingers through the black strands of my hair and returned her arm to her side.

"I'm leaving California for a while. I thought I'd stop by before I left."

"Are you taking a vacation?" she asked me, convincing herself that there was nothing permanent happening.

"I'm just...I need to get out of here. I can't stand the heat and the..." There was a word I was looking for, but nothing that could be said before such a blissful person. "...dirt," I completed.

She wrinkled her eyebrows at what I had just 'explained'. "Here," she stood aside the doorframe, "come inside."

"No." My response was curt. She flinched a bit at the aggression in my voice. "I mean...I just came to say goodbye. Listen..." I took her hands in mine. "There's something I need to do, okay? And I can't expect you to understand it...but I have to leave for a little while. It's just...you mean a lot to me, and I couldn't leave without seeing you first." A brilliant smile formed in her lips. Her pearly teeth flashed at me. "So here I am...I'm here to say goodbye for now."

So far, all my words defied the personality of mine that Raine had grown up with and known. She stumbled a bit by the different person standing before her in a shadow, when, in the past, I stood in as most light as I could. I thought myself invincible under the weight and influence of cruelty.

The sun was setting in the west, to my right and her left. Half of my face was shrouded in the shadow cast by the sinking sun. While noon lived under a mildly toasted orange color, evening was doused in fiery, blazing orange, an intense blast of colors that only came from the hottest palette.

Clouds were only splashes of brown smeared in the empty spaces of the hazy sky. There was a constant, dusty layer that threw itself like a transparent drape over Los Angeles. Everything had been stained by that damn *orange*. Greens were suddenly warm colors, and blues fell black. It was relentless!

Some days I would feel claustrophobic in the most open space. And I could have been sitting in a pool of melted ice only to feel like I was bathing in lukewarm water. Every breath had to be the deepest, otherwise your head would become light, and you would topple over.

But it seemed, no matter the circumstance of her environment, Raine remained vivid. Not the golden hair on her head, curling to fine, bobbing tips, nor the electrical turquoise color of her eyes seemed to give in to the fire in the sky. It seemed the air around her was fresh, like it had just blown in from the skin of a glacier. And yet, even as refreshing or revitalizing as Raine was, her welcome was always warm. Even in the abysmal heat of Los Angeles, anyone would want to feel such warmth.

"You're really leaving?" she asked me with a tone that already knew the answer—an impressed, reassuring tone. I remained silent and the angel said, "Well...I envy you. For my entire life I've wanted to leave this city...maybe travel east...Maybe I would keep going until I was on the opposite side of the world..." For a moment, she lost herself in the sweet, alluring fantasy. She brought her words back to reality. "Will you ever be back?"

Really, only my identity was leaving. I had to remove her mind from me if I expected to keep her from pain. I was about to pick a fight with the city's meanest bully, and I knew it would become a war. Even when her touch would have been healing, or her voice would have been musical, I couldn't keep Raine around...I couldn't...right? I had to do this.

"I will," I assured her and rubbed my thumb against the marble-like skin of Raine's cheek. "When I do," I said, "I hope things will be different. Better." As I took away my hand from her face, she followed it until she would have had to hunch over.

Her eyes opened and she smiled. "Here..." Dangling over the beginning crease of her chest, Raine pulled a necklace off of her neck.

She took my wrist and I opened my hand. Raine dropped the

most spotless, perfectly shaped glass water droplet in my palm. A silver chain—and I could only assume it was pure—made a small loop to wrap around Raine's slender neck.

"Take it." She smiled brilliantly. "I would come with you, but… my mother needs me here. I guess the child is to take care of the adult," Raine sulked, but rightfully so.

"How is she?" I asked her.

"You know…the same, I suppose. I'm just nervously waiting for the day when she goes to work and never comes back. I mean, those guys are pigs!" Her voice suddenly increased its volume. "Why does she have to do it, Alex?"

I didn't feel there was any answer to her question. I remained silent, watching her eyes turn red and irritated. She shook her head in little motions.

"I'm sorry," I softly spoke. With my index finger I lifted up her chin and leaned in close to those tender pink lips.

I pressed mine to hers, and we stood at the doorframe signing each other's lips with long, exaggerated kisses. Her skin was warm against mine, and the more we kissed, the more I wanted to let our bodies melt together.

The thought of shooting a man or throwing my fist into another was the most unpleasant fantasy I could create while kissing Raine. Whether it was a weakness or a strength she could give me, there was something about Raine, a small splinter of something that was enough to dull the sharpest claws.

She tried pulling me into the house while we kissed, but I couldn't allow myself to follow. I pulled away from her and looked into Raine's eyes. Her pupils were sometimes lost in the intensity of the turquoise, almost like a pair of blind eyes. Their color was like a silent, inanimate Siren singing for me.

Though I couldn't give in to the temptation of another kiss, I pulled Raine's body into mine and wrapped my arms around her. "Raine," I spoke into her ear.

"Yes, Alex?"

"What would you do if someone took the one person you loved away? What would you do if someone stripped everything from you?"

There was a small pause in speech, and in the still moment I felt her heart beating against my chest—perfectly synchronized thumps, pulsing one at a time over and over again.

She laughed so quietly and extended onto her toes. Back into my ear, she answered so smoothly, "I would be the better person, and rise above even the strongest temptations." She put her lips so close to mine, but never fully planted a kiss. Raine took a step away and said, "I hope I can see you again…"

"You will," I told her, still contemplating the answer she had given me, an answer I did not want to hear in such words. "I'll be around…"

Once more, Raine's cheeks wrinkled and her dimples showed. She smiled for a second before tossing me a farewell. "Goodbye Alex."

I placed the fragile glass necklace into the depth of my pocket and said back to her, sweetly, "Goodbye Raine."

Soon, night's darkness was battling away the final light of dusk just barely hanging onto the horizon. The stale shine of streetlights began to illuminate the chinked, crusty streets dressed with trash and a layer of filth.

The rats of Los Angeles were nocturnal, and as soon as the sun disappeared, all the criminals and wasted lives of the city would emerge from their deep rat holes. They gathered in the streets and, more appropriately, in the gutters.

All of them had the burning bud of a cigarette hanging from their lips or a brown glass bottle like a sword in their hands.

Everything was putrid. The people were putrid, the stench of rotting garbage was putrid, the buildings practically crumbling on their own foundation were putrid. Everything was putrid.

Big's Tower was the largest giant in the skyline. Out of all the buildings downtown, Big Rich made sure his palace was seen standing over all the others. I stood from Ed's apartment complex, glaring into the heart of this dying city. He was the reason for the crumbling buildings, the unbearable stench, the living dead people.

I took Jay's old gun from my pocket, raised it in the direction toward Big's Tower, and wanted so badly, even if it were pointless, to pull the trigger. Maybe, with a barge of luck, the bullet would strike Big Rich in his head.

Dawn would bring Big Rich's death from the palm of my hand.

THREE

THERE WAS A GATHERING AT THE FEET OF THE CITY'S GIANT. AT THE base of Big's Tower, a large, expansive ensemble of photographers, news crews, passers and all the fools beneath his spell gathered to hear Richard's words.

The tower, if it wasn't for its owner and master, its intent and purpose, would have been a valuable trademark—a sight that could have made a kind familiarity to the city's occupants. But every time I saw that tower jutting high into the hazy air, I couldn't help but picture Big Rich's blubbery face, jutting deep into my anger.

"A few weeks from now, Project Home will be more than a vision! It will be more than an ambitious dream! A few weeks from now, Project Home will be cleaning the streets of America's homeless orphans, and will be giving them a chance to grow!" Big Rich spoke more with his hands than he did with his voice.

The news was covering this special event. Cameras caught every angle of Big's chubby cheeks as he spoke. His suit, the color of midnight, and the dark sunglasses on his face, were broadcast from every news station in LA.

"Let me start by explaining this beautiful project's hopes. First," Big Rich jumped his voice, "Project Home will be opening a new set of orphanage homes for all of this city's orphans to grow up in. They will be given a home, brothers and sisters, and the right to grow that should have never been taken from them!" His voice echoed after the sudden mute of speech. The audience was silent. "And secondly," he continued, "Project Home will be constructing several of the city's largest toy stores!—Toy Palace! Every penny, every dime or dollar bill spent in that store will profit, directly, every orphanage that has been opened in the city!"

The audience shared Big Rich's enthusiasm when he lifted his meaty arms into the air, encouraging all applause.

Big Rich continued to speak, but I found my interest to be drifting in an entirely different direction. With the hood on my head, and my eyes stapled to the dark lenses on Big Rich's face, I moved through the crowd, stalking him, waiting for the prime moment. His eyes would glaze every face of every audience member, but never once did they detect me.

There were four guards at Big's protection, I counted: Two on one side far to Richard's left, and another two far to his right. And I'm sure there were more lurking like tortured spirits amongst the crowd. Even police officers stood at the ready with small handguns on their belts. It was casual to assume that immorality would take a shot at morality...not that Big Rich had any sort of morals.

"As time has moved on," Big spoke, "and as Project Home has touched the aid of thousands of people, I have had the help of true givers." Two men stood in white suits beside Big Rich in an invidious contrast.

While Big Rich buttoned up his suit, black as a panther's fur, his men—at least those worth the price of three buttons and silk ties—wore suits white like bleach.

"Mr. Ty Eval, to my left, will be facilitating all international support in aid of Project Home. Any donations of money, supplies, food or toys, will be overseen by Mr. Eval. About a week from now, Mr. Eval will be handling the largest shipment of aid and supplies Big's Incorporated has ever seen. It will be a great crutch for Project Home to lean on!" Big faced Ty and patted his back, smiling at him in approval.

Ty humbly nodded his head and held one hand up to soften the applause. Mr. Eval maintained a kind face. Cool brown hair and expressions of kind purpose.

"And to my right, Mr. Samuel Ill..."

Mr. Ill was a darker figure. His expressions were concrete and his hair was the color of charcoal. Hanging from his mouth, the last half of a cigarette burned away. He never had his lungs empty.

"He will be working with sources all across America to ensure that Project Home is spread. His business will be conducting meetings and conferences so that this entire nation knows of Project Home, and is willing to help. It is our dream to open these homes all across America so that no child has to grow up on the streets. They're our future!" Big announced! "Without them..." he leaned over his podium and lowered his volume to a whisper. "We're nothing. Thank you all for listening! I hope you will support our vision of changing this country and eventually changing this world!"

Big remained behind his podium at the feet of his tower, absorbing all the glory applauding from his audience. His smile nearly bounced the sunlight off the surface of his teeth and blinded the audience. The dimples of Big's cheeks were craters—his chub folded together when he smiled.

It was like time slowed when Big Rich raised his arms into the air a final time. I inhaled, and made a sprint toward him. I shot past the applauding fools around me, and slowly, very slowly, Big Rich got closer and closer to me.

When the distance between us was no more than a few feet, I leaped toward the fat lord. The tips of my fingers were so close to the fat pressing against his throat when I was swatted out of the air.

One of Big's guards had tackled me midair just before I reach Richard. The two of us landed at his feet, and I stretched my arm so far to reach him. I could feel the tendons and muscles in my arm stretch and tighten so much that they nearly tore, ripped and snapped apart. I pictured Jay's poor face and felt the rushing wind of my fall to death long ago. As I was being pinned to the ground by the guard, Big Rich looked at me with eyes stricken by confusion, and, without the slightest bit of intent to question, began walking away.

"Richard!" I screamed. "Richard!" Veins in my face nearly exploded from pressure. I screamed so hard and loud that my voice must have trampled over the entire audience. There was the taste of blood lingering in my mouth and throat.

I felt my own anger enter my veins like a poison or a steroid. I managed to wriggle to my back and push the guard off of me with my legs.

Before he could pin me again, I jumped to my feet and slugged the guard with a mean, hard fist. His jaw cracked to the side with his entire torso. I took one leg and kicked the man's support out from under him. As soon as he collapsed to the ground, I twisted around and charged Big Rich a second time.

Another one of his guards stepped out before my path. He threw a punch to try and detain me, but I swept under it and, while my upper body was behind him, struck the guard's stomach with my knee.

"Richard!" I shouted once more. Big Rich was just stepping into a black SUV which began to drive away before I could reach him. "Big Rich!" I stopped in the street, watching my destiny drive away.

I stood there, panting, until a guard tackled me to the asphalt. No struggle came from me—my hope was lost, my target had escaped.

"Officer!" the guard on top of me called to policeman standing nearby. He heard the guard's call for help and quickly raced over to the both of us. "Officer, detain this man!"

The officer replaced Big's guard's position over me, and held my wrists together behind my back. The metal of his handcuffs shocked the skin of my wrists and he pushed them tight.

He pulled me to my feet and walked me away from Big's Tower toward his cruiser. Every pair of eyes in the audience was watching me, watching the hooded man being escorted out like a crazy person. All the police officer needed was a white coat and the audience would have been convinced of my insanity.

"Watch your head," the officer warned as he sat me in the back of his car.

The officer drove us out from underneath the skirt of the city. We exited the concrete forest and began to maneuver through the outskirts. The buildings shrunk to little stubs like chopped trees.

Los Angeles Police Department: An amateur group of men with guns, based in an amateur brick building. There was no design to the police station. Four corners, one basement, and a single beige hallway.

The officer escorted me to one room where they dipped my thumb in ink, and rolled my fingerprint onto a sheet of paper. After my identity was placed on the paper, he tossed me into a holding cell.

Two men were already occupying the space. They sat on a single bench against the back wall.

"Wait here," the officer said, then added, "It's not like you have a choice." He removed the cuffs from my wrists and locked me in the cage.

The iron bars clicked shut and locked. Behind me, I could hear whispers snaking out of the men's mouths. I just faced the bars, daring myself not to look back. My right fist was bloody—each knuckle was split open and crusted with gore.

"So…" one of the prisoners behind me said in a taunting voice, "How old are you?" he asked, like he was trying to arrange a date. The man walked up behind me, and I remained silent. "What are you in here for? Not drinkin' all of your milk?" he mocked me right over my shoulder.

The prisoner turned back toward his friend and began laughing. As soon as he returned his mouth right to my ear, I heard him inhale, but before he could talk I shot my elbow right into his face. His head lashed back and instinct told him to bring his hands to his bleeding nose.

I faced him and chucked my fist right into the side of his head. He stumbled just a bit, but his bulky build and vicious nature kept him to his feet. I saw the second prisoner stand from the bench to aid his friend, so I grabbed the one bleeding from his nose by the shoulders, and threw him into the other.

The bleeding man was too occupied holding his nose, but the

other stood up from the ground and charged me. At the last second I hopped to the side and assisted the man's inertia in sending him into the iron bars. His face was crushed, and the man fell limply backward.

Right when the last prisoner's body hit the ground, one man in a suit came around the corner and stood outside of my cell.

Around his wrist, a golden watch conveniently told him the time of the day at any moment, which told me that he was the kind of guy never late to even the most unimportant meeting. I felt he was the kind of guy that would come out of nowhere just when you needed him.

His dark skin made the whites of his eyes pop, his lips were the same color as his skin, but his palms were pink and shoved in his pants pockets. Coffee brown was the color of his suit and matching pants and a sports jacket made of polyester or cotton. Hoarse but gentle, his voice came from a throat hugged by fat and out a mouth surrounded by heavy cheeks and thick lips.

The first thing he said was, "That was a pretty outrageous thing you did…" I said nothing. He waited for only a moment before continuing. "Can you tell me why you did it?" I said nothing. "Do you have anything against Mr. Lucifer?" When I still didn't speak, the man laughed politely and said to me, "Kid…I'm not an enemy of yours. I *can* be…but I don't think that's what either of us want." Silence of mine. His eyes fell behind me to the men on the ground—one unconscious, the other bleeding on his knees. "It seems you have a tendency for aggression…" Nothing he had said, yet, encouraged me to speak. "Okay, don't talk, but at least listen. It seems that you…whoever you are…don't even exist. You've been wiped from our system. There is no record of you ever being born…" I looked at my feet, maybe there was an answer there. "So," the man said and perked up, "would you like to tell me who you are…*ghost*?"

Before I had to answer, Ed's flimsy body came hustling around the corner like an excited puppy. He stopped just next to the man and panted for a bit. "Oh, thank God!" he exclaimed between pants.

The man in the suit looked at Ed. "What are you doing here, Mr. Reel?"

"I'm sorry sir," Ed huffed. "I just had to see him!" He turned toward me. "Hale!"

"Hale?" wondered the dark man.

"Hale, what the hell did you do?"

"He tried to attack Richard Lucifer Downtown today after a public conference," brutally summed up the man in the suit. Ed shook his head and slapped his hand to his forehead, exhaling. "Luckily Mr. Lucifer's guards stopped your friend before he actually reached Richard. A couple of my units were nearby by so one of them picked him up…" The man looked at Ed then back to me, giving me a sticky stare.

"Dear God…" Ed sighed. "Sir," he faced the man, "let him go."

Ed's boss seemed surprised that such a request was made. "*Excuse* me?"

"Let him go."

"He just tried to attack a man!" protested Ed's boss. "Who knows what would have happened if he wasn't apprehended?"

"I know what it looks like, but I assure you it won't happen again. He's gone through a hard time and was convinced that Big Rich was responsible for a certain…" Ed looked at me for the correct word. "…mishap," he finished.

"Oh…" The boss turned toward me with his eyebrows raised. "You're one of *those* people. You believe in the Drug Trade?"

"I can pay, Barrette, just let him go…" fought my friend.

All while looking right into the shadows of my eyes, Barrette considered Ed's request. Something must have happened inside Barrette's mind, because not too long after Ed's final attempt, he opened his mouth and said, "Fine." Barrette waved an officer over to unlock my cell. "Maybe *you* can teach your friend some social etiquette." He looked at me as the iron barred door was opening. "Stay out of trouble...*Hale*," he advised me with a hint of warning.

When the door was opened, I stepped out of my cage and Barrette walked away with the guard. As soon as we were alone, Ed sighed, "I can't believe you did that!" and began walking out of the holding cell room.

He pushed through a door into a single beige hallway. I followed. At the very end of the vaguest tunnel was a small elevator that Ed opened with the press of a button. He waited for me to step inside before closing the doors.

Ed fixed the hair on top of his head, fashioning a red comb over. He removed the thick framed glasses from his face and wiped their lenses with a flap of his white coat. The elevator began to lower to the station's basement.

"I got so close to him, Ed..."

"Not close enough."

"I could smell his cologne..." My friend looked at me while I spoke. "He saw me, but had no idea whom I was or what I wanted. It was like...it was like he was so used to having people hate him, that he had forgotten all the victims he touched."

"Or maybe..." I faced Ed and sealed his lips with a daring stare before he could continue. "I'm just saying, Hale, all of this is hard to...process."

I looked away.

Duh, I thought. It was so easy for Ed to tell me that this trade was a myth, and that I was wasting my time fighting air. But my best friend, my surrogate father was murdered by that man and his business. My identity was taken from me because of *him*! Of course Ed could say that the Drug Trade was a myth! *I* was being crushed by the weight of a miserable excuse!

The elevator door dinged and opened. Ed stepped through and turned back to see if I was coming as well. My eyes were focused on nothing. I stared at the air right in front of me. I could see nothing to my side—my peripheral vision was blinded by the hood I wore.

"Are you coming?" he asked me and broke my trance.

I looked up into the basement and stepped out of the elevator. Ed called it his office, but it was really just a large, dark room packed with clutter and late night hours.

Ed proceeded to immediately hunch over one of many tables and began pioneering his pencil through foothills of snowy paper. His attention was immediately transferred to the work at his table.

The entire basement was filled with several granite topped tables, and lined by granite topped counters. Only one light lit the space Ed was working at. Nothing else mattered. The darkness all around us was an impenetrable void of neglect—no attention was paid to the emptiness lurking in the shadows.

"Don't worry about Barrette," Ed said, but never lifted his eyes from his work. I began to roam throughout the basement, slapping my eyes to one box at a time.

"Who is he?"

That brought Ed's head up. He wanted to laugh at me, but never did. All he said was, "That's the commissioner. He's like the Big Rich of LA's police force," he mocked. "Though, he's not much of a leader. The police force practically dictates him...he's very insecure and very weak." Ed seemed to know a lot about the man. "Ever since the government collapsed, he's lost his role in leadership. But I know that, deep down he wishes he could make a difference. Just like you," Ed explained, but hoped it wouldn't get to my head.

Barrette sounded like a perfect alliance. A man who was scorned and whipped by the government's laziness and corruption, and a man who wanted to transcend. In that world at that time, transcending was one thing that would be sure to call you an alien.

Who would fardels bare, to grunt and sweat under a weary life? Everyone.

I formulated an entire plan in my head, and its only motive was to ask Ed, "Do you think he could help me?"

Ed snickered, "I don't know, Hale," and shook his head. "I think right now, it's you versus the world."

FOUR

VERY BLADE OF GRASS HAD SHRIVELED LIKE THE FINGER OF A CORPSE *left on the slope of a desert dune. The iron gate around Crown Cemetery became so hot beneath the sun, that any grace of rain Los Angeles got would evaporate instantly once it touched the metal. Downtown was just a small distance from the cemetery. Los Angeles was a cult of standing giants, placing their silhouettes in the path of our sun's shine.*

"Here," Jay said suddenly, bending over and grabbing something beside him. He tossed me a can of soda which landed softly in my hands, then he cracked open a beer. "To long years of friendship, companionship, and family," he toasted, raising his drink.

Together we sat on a grave, living life amongst the dead.

"To the new future of this city," I added and knocked my can into his.

We both drank. Jay made a slurping noise as he sipped the beer, and I was silent. He looked around smiling, blinking very little, breathing through his nose. Exhaling dreamily he said, "I hope one day it comes true..."

"What comes true?" I asked him.

"My dream. Our dream, now, of saving this city."

"Yeah..." I examined the thought of our dream vividly. But I was looking through a pair of inexperienced eyes. I knew he wanted me to save the city, but I couldn't wrap my hands or mind around an idea that outlandish.

Jay and I, we were the fluttering flames which would light the darkness. We were warmth that shivering people would crawl to. We were the direction in which lost wanderers would go.

I wonder if Jay knew that I would come around to the idea of killing Big Rich. I know that at that moment, the thought was still unrealistic.

Looking back on his stretched life, Jay stared at the sky and said, "I have lived a long life..." Right then I had just shaken my head at the fact that I never knew Jay's past. Maybe he said that to spark my interest, maybe not. Whatever his intention was, his past became a subject I wanted to master. "Death is a funny thing," Jay noted. "Until it touches you personally, most people let it pass by unnoticed. I used to wonder if some people found themselves invincible, like they were immune to death." Jay thought about a way to articulate his own thoughts. "I believe that man fears most what he cannot escape...and death, along with truth, is one thing inescapable. And so," he continued, "death takes its toll on everyone. It makes you realize how short and valuable life is...This is where it all ends. Right here, under this grass." He pointed down to the coffins we couldn't see. "No matter how great a person is, they will always end up here. A person can change the world, even when they know they will not always be a part of it. That's what makes a true hero. Sometimes I like to come here and think about how lucky I am not to be down there...but also, I can't help but think how my time is running out."

Why Jay spoke of death, I didn't know. For whatever reason, it got me thinking about death; mainly murder.

Growing the courage to ask this question was tough, but I 'knew' Jay well enough to take the risk. "Have you ever killed a man, Jay?" His reaction was like waiting for the most gruesome scene in a horror movie.

After taking another drink, Jay faced me to ensure complete sincerity. "Do you think I would ever ask you to kill a man, if I didn't know what it was like?" Never before then did I really think about that. "I was in the war long ago. Back when I was just a boy. When the draft came to me, I was sent to Vietnam where I served my time as a soldier. That wasn't really my thing." He rotated the can in his hands. Jay looked up and focused his eyes on airlessness, trying to recall any memories he had. "I had been a soldier for...only about a month when I was assigned to a certain project in the medical field. They knew I had a background in medicine."

"You did?" I couldn't picture Jay pulling rubber gloves over his hands and slipping into disgusting colored scrubs before surgery, or rubbing his raw eyes in the middle of the night, studying for tomorrow's test.

"Oh yeah," Jay alleged, smiling at the thought. "When I was drafted, I was in med-school. And because of that, I was sent north to work with a new science field. They were beginning something that was sure to win us the war..."

"What were they working on?"

"Well, scientists were compiling ingredients to form what they called the 'Battle Blood Formula'. But don't let that excite you; the name was more to win the war of confidence. It was really just an antidepressant, a steroid of some sort. It helped the soldiers stay involved during combat."

"What did they need you for?"

"They needed someone to regulate the limits of the formula—how much a soldier could use and how often. So I was there for research mainly, and in my research I found something in the formula that I knew would help our soldiers more than its original intent. I noticed that there was something else in the drug...so I tweaked its mechanics and made it into a new weapon, a new tool." Shaking his head, anyone would be able to tell that Jay had made a mistake. "I made it into something so much more powerful..."

"What did it do?" I found it necessary to propel the story with my questions. Jay exhaled and closed his eyes so he could narrate his story. I just sat there and listened to Jay's historic story, his life's play.

"Whenever the soldiers would take the formula, their bodies would become dependent on the drug. The formula replaced their blood supply, so, whenever they were wounded or injured, they didn't have to worry about losing blood. All they would have to do is inject more of the Battle Blood Formula. It was quite incredible. Their bodies ran off of this stuff...and soon, there was nothing else they depended on." He said that as if it were a good thing.

"So they became addicted? How would that ever help them win the war?"

"Because now, they ran on the formula. Nutrition became a minor

factor, clean air, water, none of those things mattered." That's when Jay shook his head angrily and began crushing the can. "Then the ingredients went missing, most likely stolen. When that happened, the dependency the soldiers had acquired became their reason for death. Once there was no more formula, there was nothing to supply life..." What Jay said next was typical, and I saw it coming. "Hundreds of lives ended...because of me. I was the one who moved the formula forward. I was the one who encouraged its spread...it was all my fault."

For the entire time I had known Jay, I never really knew him. Why he wanted Big Rich dead and why he was never afraid to place upon me the deed of murder. Everything I had been told, and everything I had believed, was an act of rejuvenating a community he had taken from, paying a debt he owed. The death of thousands of soldiers filled his lungs with blood, and Jay would never be able to cough enough. Someone had taken Jay's work and turned it into a man slaughtering device. Jay's intentions never stretched to harm anyone, but there he was, baring a guilt too heavy for Atlas himself to hold.

Big Rich was guilty of far more deaths, and Jay couldn't sit and watch, but in reality, that's all he could do. His frail body was nothing. And there I was...

We were both the same in different ways. Both Jay and I shared a dream that I believed every person should have gone to sleep with. But the two of us, we were lonely sleepwalkers. Idealists maybe.

An apology deemed useless, so we both sat there in the scratching moment of loud silence. There was much to be said, but nothing was spoken.

"I came here after the war, opened a shop of my own, and made the best out of the worst. I opened a pharmacy," Jay said, trying to sound happy. "It was only a matter of time before the city found out what I did and tossed me out. I was locked up for years until my case was unable to be policed. When I was released, I had so many enemies. Everyone knows what I did...so I found refuge in the orphanage home. No one there knew about my past..." Jay looked at me. I was one thing good that came out of his retreat.

"You went there to hide..." It made sense why Jay lived in a dusty attic above an equally ignored orphanage home.

"Yes. To try and run away from everything...but then I see Big Rich, *doing exactly as I did but with no intent of doing right! He knows he's killing millions, but he doesn't think twice about it. What heart is that cold? I learned that your closest friend can be your closest enemy...Big Rich's father, the man who started the Drug Trade stole my formula and..."*

Jay's watery eyes made me look away. One more sentence and Jay might as well have been balling. His lips quivered, hands shook, but his body was still. When he blinked and wiped the tears from his eyes, he shook his head and cleared his throat. Smiling, his acting didn't fool me.

I fiddled with Jay's small gun in my hand. He looked down at it and said with a drip of venom on his tongue, "Don't waste this, Hale...don't waste this..." Jay graced himself with a breath of life and said, "This is where everything ends, Hale. One way or another, it will all tie back to this. This is where it all ends...this is where it all ends..."

"They've taken another one," a gravedigger said as he dumped heavy loads of dirt from the iron of his shovel onto the wood of Jay's coffin in the ground.

A simple cloth shirt on the digger's torso was blotted with faint yellow stains of old sweat, and dark, moist spots of recent perspiration. On his neck hung his faith—a golden chain and cross. His hair had grayed and never felt the stroke of a brush. It grew long over time, as the digger refused to cut it. Skin over his throat sagged, leaving no cover-up for his ancient age.

I took my eyes from Jay's swallowed grave and looked at the man. "Excuse me?" I asked him.

"Oh," he laughed, realizing that he wasn't the only one around. "Don't mind me kid. I don't know what I'm talking about." The gravedigger was copying the words he had heard all his life.

"What did you say?" I persisted.

The digger staked his shovel into the dry, dehydrated dirt. Leaning his weight against and on top of it, he studied me. A pair of old cultured eyes descended down the length of my body.

"Okay boy," he said, then spat a blob of liquidated tobacco out of his mouth. "You want to hear an old man's senile words?"

"Humor me."

"The Drug Trade," he hissed. "Most people think it's a myth, but I know it's not. You know that fat man Richard Lucifer?—the one fellas call Big Rich. Well…he runs the entire operation. Like a king!"

I added my own spice. "Like a dictator…"

"Wait…" the digger freed his shovel and walked to the other side of the grave where I stood. He leaned in close and asked, "You actually believe me?"

"The man you're burying was murdered by Big Rich's men. He was murdered by the trade…the thing people call a *myth*…" I shook my head and, in anger, I spoke, "What sort of ignorance can believe that people are murdered by a myth. A *myth*…"

The gravedigger's reaction was surprising. He slapped one hand to his belly and laughed into the stale air. For a long time I saw the black teeth in his mouth, his cracked tongue, and the wad of tobacco eating away at the old man's bottom lip and gums.

"Kid…" he finally said as his laughing faded. "He's not special! Everyone in this God damned cemetery was murdered by that fat bastard and his business…This is Crown Cemetery! The name isn't original…"

His head turned in one direction, and I followed his line of sight. The digger was looking at an iron arc hanging above Crown Cemetery's entrance. In the bend of the arc, between the two letters of the graveyard's name, was an iron silhouette of a cracked crown.

"It's the Drug Trade's insignia," he told me. "Its identification. The infamous broken crown!" For a while he watched the crown, waiting for it to say or do something. "My entire family was murdered by it. I always found it ironic that they were buried in the cemetery they created…If you're wise, kid, anytime you see that broken crown, you'll turn around and run in the opposite direction. You don't pick a fight with *the* Richard Lucifer."

The digger sucked a ball of snot up his nose and scooped the last bit of dirt then released it into Jay's grave. He used the back of his shovel to flatten the surface, and finally erased Jay from the Earth.

"No offense, sir, but that's the only thing I want."

As I thought my words of prayer, the digger nodded his head, and made way to digging another grave.

I couldn't understand my own thoughts and logic as much as I could feel the beat of my heart, the strength in my muscles, the sweat on my forehead. I hadn't lost the sight of justice yet, but, like the most beautiful dawn rising at my side, I wanted to look at the gun in my pocket and the scabs over my knuckles.

Anger, I knew (but couldn't admit), was my excuse to hate, and to hate, was my refusal to accept.

"God damn it, Jay," I cursed to the rock in the ground, but that's all I could externally express. It was so much easier to hide myself and my *things* inside that hood.

No one could mock or strike my face if it was a shadow. No one could place blame if there was no one to place it upon. The hood, my ghostly identity, made me transparent. It allowed me to take the blow of a speeding truck, to jump without ground beneath my feet and to say *no* when the only answer was yes.

There was only one thing I was sure of, one thing I would (and did) bet my life on: Project Home would crumble, and Richard Lucifer would fall dead over his fort...his *ruin*.

As my thoughts completed themselves—Jay's only 'words' of prayer—, I left his body beneath the earth to become bones, his bones to become dust, his dust to become even more nothing than they were.

Walking through Crown Cemetery was like walking down the busiest avenue of the largest city whose people had been looked down upon by a woman with snakes. It was like passing hundreds of faceless people, but knowing each person's name. Each tombstone was a little plaque that said, *Hey! I was here once, but now I'm gone. So forget about me.*

The occasional stroller would pass a grave, read a name, but would not have the slightest, thinnest splinter of an idea who that person was and why they even existed in the first place. But there

I was, about to carve the deepest, bloodiest scar right down the face of California, and the name Richard Lucifer in its newest tombstone.

At the bottom of the hill I was descending, a man knelt at a grave. His body rocked back and forth and his lips moved to form the most sorrowful words. He bowed to the tombstone, placing both hands upon the top of it.

The closer I got, the more I could hear the man's crying and sulking blended into his mushy sentences. And the closer I got, the more I recognized his face.

He had a head of red hair and a face of acne scars. Thick framed glasses caught every salty drop that fell from his eyes. Ed sat there on his knees, crying in front of a grave. Occasionally he would switch to another—a second tombstone right next to the first.

I stepped up behind him and my shadow threw darkness all over Ed and the two graves. He quickly hopped up and avoided the shadows. Ed saw my face, and his began to form many different mixed expressions.

"What are you doing here, Ed?" I asked my friend, skipping him the duty of the first words.

"I..." Ed removed the glasses from his face and cleaned them. But he didn't wear a white coat like he usually did.

Around his neck was a pressed collar accompanied by the silkiest tie. Over them was a black suit jacket, and on his legs were perfectly ironed pants. Even the shoes on his feet allowed the sun to see its own blaring face. His hair was especially combed to the side that day.

"I...um..." My friend looked down at the graves, hoping I could answer my own question.

Paul Reel and Elly Reel were the two forgotten names engraved into each stone. Though, both of the names were eroding, and the letters were cracking with the stone itself.

"Your parents?" I asked Ed.

"Yeah," he said, layering a shaking voice. "That's them—two

God damned stones pushed into the dirt. They were killed when I was five," Ed began. "I don't remember much…They left one night; must have been going to dinner or something. I was left at my house with some babysitter. It was around midnight, I remember, when I woke up from the sound of voices. Outside my window I could see the strobes of blue and red lights circling around the neighboring houses and my own. When I went to the top of my stairs and looked down, I could see my babysitter talking to a couple of police officers. She kept her hand over her mouth the whole time…" Ed, I could tell, was digging through his memory as if it was a giant dumpster full of worthless items. He shrunk his eyes and looked at the two graves. "It turns out a couple of guys murdered them on their way back home. They were arrested the next day and found with Borm in their system and pockets…"

"Big Rich's men," I occupied the hiatus.

"Yes. Men of the Drug Trade. Men of the myth…"

"I thought you didn't believe in the trade…"

Ed looked up at me, right in my eyes. He paused for a long moment, nibbling on all parts of his lips. "I was only five when they were murdered—I don't remember anything about them, really. I'm not sad that I don't get to see them or laugh with them. I'm not sad that I never got to know my own parents or they never got to know their own son…I'm here, crying at this grave, not because any of that, but because two undeserving people died for the money in their pockets, and are now buried in the ground while the people who murdered them still have the luxury of living. And it saddens me more, to know that those murderers are wasting that luxury…" A layer of glossy tears covered the blue of Ed's irises. He sniffled quietly and continued saying, "When I told you that I don't believe in the Drug Trade, it was just because I didn't want to…but I see what you're doing, how much your compromising, just to make Jay's death worth something. And then I look at these graves, these damn rocks that don't mean shit to anyone, and I want to change that…I just don't want it to be me against the world."

"If that was the case…" I put my hand softly on Ed's shoulder. "…then I would be alone too. The Drug Trade is a tree," I told him, "and all we have to do is burn it down. If crime is merciless…justice must be too."

FIVE

I HURLED MY STRENGTH THROUGH THE FRONT DOORS OF THE POLICE department. They broke open and an obnoxious amount of hazy sunlight flooded the beige hallway. The man in my grip struggled and whimpered for me to let go.

Ed hurried in front of me, throwing up his hands and waving away officers in our path. A few men with golden badges put their hands on their guns' sheath at their side. A couple of them raised their firearms toward me as I dragged the man through the hallway.

"Put your guns down!" Ed ordered without the proper jurisdiction. "Come on guys! Put them down!" A few officers lowered their weapons. Ed walked up to a single officer and asked, aggressively, "Where's Barrette?"

The officer couldn't help but stray his eyes and attention toward me. He mumbled a few formless words. "He's...um..."

Ed forgot his patience and asked again, "Where is he?" Ed dug his claws into the man's shoulder and suddenly the officer's attention was back.

"Oh...uh...I think he's in his office, Ed." Once the answer forced its way out of his mouth, the officer jumped his eyes back to me and the man I was dragging behind.

"Let me go!" he pleaded. "Let me go!" I continued on, pulling him by the greasy length of his hair.

Ed practically marched farther down the hallway, lined with awing officers, to a wooden door against one side of the wall. He didn't even knock before crashing into Barrette's office.

The commissioner had himself sat in a leather throne over a pile of papers. His head lurched up and, for a second, he wasn't sure what to say to me and Ed standing before him. His eyes drifted down to the thrashing dealer in my grip.

Then suddenly he sprang up from his seat. "What the hell is this?" he barked.

"Barrette, please!" Ed held his hands up and approached the commissioner. "Just trust us!" he said and put both hands on Barrette's shoulders.

Barrette wiped Ed away and continued barking madly. "Trust you with what? What the hell is this?"

And then I spoke: "He works for Big Rich."

"Oh!" Barrette elevated the pitch of his voice. "So you're not a mute..."

"Just listen to what he has to say," Ed begged and stepped aside, handing me the prerogative to speak.

After pulling him to his knees, I looked down at the drug dealer and began to speak. "Tell him," I said to the dealer. "Tell him, who do you work for?" The man didn't say anything.

Again, Barrette asked, "What the hell is this?"

"Listen!" I yelped.

The dealer completely avoided eye contact with the commissioner who waited for him to say something. I reached into my hoodie's pocket and pulled Jay's pistol, then pressed it to his temple.

"Tell him!" I threateningly ordered. "Now!"

"Whoa!" Barrette threw his hands up toward me. "Put the gun away!"

"Listen!"

"You don't have to threaten me!" the drug dealer admitted, finally saying something. "He wants me to tell you. He wants you to know..."

When the dealer didn't finish his taunting sentence, Barrette stepped up to him and said, "Well?" He shook the dealer by his shoulders. "Tell me!" Now Barrette was just as eager to know as I was to ring out of the dealer.

Ed and I looked at each other, surprised by Barrette's eagerness to know. Barrette bent down toward the dealer until he spoke.

"Big Rich," he answered. The simple name coming from the dealer's mouth popped every bit of tension in Barrette's small office. "I work for Big Rich," he specified with sugar.

"Yes!" Barrette hopped up and down once. A smile was stuck to his face. "I knew it!" he jollied happily. "I knew it!" Like a small child, the fat commissioner danced around his room with his hands in the air, repeating the same I-told-you-so phrase over and over again.

Ed asked the commissioner with the most confused tone, "What are you talking about, commissioner?"

Barrette didn't turn to Ed, but me. "Hale," he said. "Hale, is that your name?" I didn't say a word. "Whatever!" Barrette was impatient...or maybe just too anxious for something. "It doesn't matter. Kid," he settled with that salute, "I'm sorry about the other day at the holding cell. The officers...they would judge me if they knew I was a believer."

"Wait," Ed leaped in. "You believe in the Drug Trade? You've believed in it this *entire time*?"

Barrette looked at him. "Doesn't everyone," he responded so casually. "Isn't it obvious? This whole Project Home and charitable giving crap...that's all it is! Crap! Big Rich isn't who he says he is... we all know it. Everything's just a cover up. There's something else going on, isn't there? He's using all the money from Project Home and those fake orphanage homes to get money for his *real* business, isn't he? Well he doesn't fool me!" Barrette proved himself. "He never has! I've always known something was up with him..."

"Then why haven't you done anything about it?" Ed asked, insulted almost.

"I told you," Barrette pouted, "the other officers would have judged me."

Ed stated bluntly, poking at Barrette's insecurity and position, "You're the commissioner!"

And then I defended my friend's attack on Barrette. "You'd rather protect your own social stature than the lives and security of innocent people?" I too was insulted by Barrette's cold heartedness.

"It's not just that! If he knew I was onto him, he would send people after me. Plus, the guy is secured tight! It would be impossible to find evidence against Big Rich...and believe me, I've tried. It won't happen!"

"What if we looked together?" I offered my opinion.

"Excuse me?" That wasn't the reaction I was expecting from Barrette. "You're just a kid! And technically, you don't even exist. You know what kind of trouble I could get in for that? What kind of mockery would come my way...?"

The drug dealer in my grip quenched attention. "Jesus Christ!" he hollered. "Will you let me go?" I stood him up just to slam his skull into Barrette's fine wood desk. The dealer's head cracked against the Maplewood, and he fell backward.

Both Ed and Barrette looked at me then the dealer lying unconscious on the ground. Then they tried to resume the original conversation.

"Commissioner," I said sincerely, "you have two people here willing to bring this guy down. We all want the same thing, Barrette." I was wrapping Barrette up in my wheedle. "And I'm not afraid to get my hands dirty..."

Barrette's distorted sense of self-righteousness spoke for him. "I can't let you break the law," he said, high and mighty.

"What are you going to do?" challenged I. "Arrest a ghost? I don't even exist...remember?"

But Barrette continued to read down his list of excuses. "I would need warrants...permission..."

"Barrette, this government is falling apart day by day. The nation is rotting right before our eyes...this is our chance to change something."

By the time I had stopped speaking, Barrette's intent suddenly transformed into something I had not yet seen, nor expected, from him. He looked at me with such focused eyes, and I could tell he was thinking something and trying to articulate it.

The sound of Barrette's voice scared me when he spoke. All this time I had the higher stand over Barrette, until he began to speak something that altered our entire conversation's motives.

In a deeper, flatter voice Barrette asked me, "What are you looking for? What do you *really* want out of bringing Lucifer down?" The question intrigued Ed, and they both looked at me, ready to wait.

"Justice," I said 'confidently'.

"Are you sure?" Barrette now challenged me. "Because every time I look at you I see this little glint of evil, just like what I see when I look at Big Rich. Now, are you sure there's nothing more to your intentions than justice?"

And I lied, "I'm sure..."

Barrette watched me for a while longer, trying to ring out anymore words with the piercing of his sight. I tried not to, but eventually I looked away, out of Barrette's rosewood eyes.

"Hm..." Barrette rubbed his chin—stubby with whiskers—and continued the conversation. "Where do we start, then?"

I was relieved that Barrette didn't continue his pressuring interrogation. Just by his few sentences, I could understand why Barrette was commissioner. When the government was actually effective, I could picture Barrette in a gray-bricked room circling some guilty innocent person, slowly pulling the truth out of the criminal.

But in the nation's current state, truth was irrelevant.

"At Big Rich's conference," I began, "I heard him say something about one of the largest shipments of supplies and aid...by that he really means the largest shipment of Borm."

Barrette: "Why would he be bringing so much of it in? Why now?"

I told the commissioner, "He needs money to complete Project

Home. Once the Borm arrives, he'll be selling it all throughout California so he can raise enough money to support the project's needs."

Then Barrette had to ask a question that pertained to the very core of our entire plot. "What is the purpose of Project Home? What is it going to achieve—opening all these orphanage homes and toy stores…? I don't understand…"

"Everything is a part of his trade," I answered the necessary, unanswerable question. "The orphanage homes, the toy stores… everything. They're all pieces to this puzzle…"

"How?" Ed asked. "How are the orphanage homes a part of it?"

I could smell the bubbling denial in his breath. To accept that his childhood and home was a part of the trade had to be gut-wrenching. I remember when the truth came to me—it felt like a hole was burning through my stomach. Everything I knew was just a simulation, a projection of Big Rich's scam.

I began to tell Ed and Barrette the story, the origin of my hate toward Big Rich and his miserable business. "They came to me a year before I was legally allowed to be released from the orphanage. It was my seventeenth birthday, not too long ago. They offered me a job, a position in the trade. It was my strength, my potential that was attractive, they told me. The orphanage homes…they're recruiting centers for the Drug Trade."

"Mr. Alexander Hale," a voice confirmed my name from behind me. It belonged to the orphanage owner—Mr. O—who had his face buried in a peach colored document. "Seventeen years old," he congratulated. "Excited to leave this place?" Mr. O was plenty aware of the reputation that was molding on my tongue. He chose to 'treat' it with sarcasm.

His voice seemed like it was blown or smacked straight out of a baritone instrument; a tuba or bass drum. When he spoke the fat on his throat jiggled with the motion of his jaw. I assumed he had lost his razor, because around his mouth and under his chin was a forest of whiskers. The man expressed his lack of self-maintenance through both his looks and personality. A bush of coarse hair grew like a black weed on his head, and slowly spread its domain across his face.

"Sir..." I was hesitant on saluting him with such a title. "I'm only seventeen. I thought I had to be eighteen..." For some reason, I protested the bendable rules and the fire-torch jurisdiction of the orphanage and Mr. O.

His voice told me, without the assistance of words, that he was trying to get somewhere. Just the haste of his every sentence flying off of his tongue like bullets from a gun told me so. "The rules are different now; you have permission to leave early. But before you go anywhere," As if I were going to pack my bag immediately, "how 'bout you come with me so we can...fill out some papers." He tipped his head and a vague shadow fell like a drape down his face.

It wasn't an offer, because after he spoke he threw his arm across my shoulders and began moving me toward a metal door in the cafeteria of the orphanage—a portal to oblivion, an infamous entrance to an exit. His body odor raced up his arms and through my nostrils. I tried to pull away, but his force was too strong.

At the metal office door we stopped and Mr. O knocked twice. It opened, and we walked through.

Worse than a prison cell, worse than a void full of nothingness, the office, through the portal of Hell, was a concrete cage of vacant, window-less walls and gray bricks. There was a single desk, desolate from any other furniture or any purpose. One light hung from a tenuous wire, dripping the slightest amount of florescent into the room. Behind the desk, there were no file cabinets (organization was lost) or pictures of Mr. O's family (he was a man of crime, not family), but instead two guards in pressed collars and white suits. They stood there like concrete elephants, elephants in the room. The owner released me and made his way behind the desk.

"I'm guessing you're aware of a man named Richard Lucifer...am I right?" Mr. O asked immediately.

I had known the man by a different name—"Big Rich?" I asked in return.

"Sure, if that's what you would like to call him," Mr. O cooperated and continued: "He is the owner and creator of this place." He held his arms

out with his palms toward the ceiling and looked around. As if 'this place' was worth even the weakest sort of praise. Then Mr. O lowered himself into a tarry pool, changing the subject not only with the meanings of his words, but the tone of his voice. "And I'm sure you know of his other business." He placed the weight of his torso on the desk, holding himself up with straight arms, looking at me peculiarly.

"I…" I considered telling him that I knew, but tried to play dumb instead. "I don't what you're talking about…"Admitting my knowledge would lend Mr. O leverage, I felt.

The weight of my words snapped Mr. O like a twig. He slammed his meaty paws on the desk and yelled at me, "Don't play dumb! I know you know, Hale! You're not the kind of person who would let something so big sneak past you. You're not blind, are you?" I didn't answer. "Are you?" he shouted and demanded to know.

"No," I said shyly.

"Then tell me! Tell me you know!"

"I…"

"Come on, Hale! We both know you'd fight as hard as you can to find the truth…you're not one of those people who live in blissful ignorance. So tell me…"

"The Drug Trade," I said simply.

He slammed his hands on the desk and stood straight again. "Precisely!" he yelled, pointing at me. "This one's a wise one," he said, flicking his index finger. Turning, Mr. O must have expected there to be a window, because he stared at the wall, absent of any such thing. "I've been watching you, Hale. I've been watching your anger…the aggression you choose to hide. I've been watching you grow for fourteen years! Fourteen years of watching you clench your teeth and tighten your fists! And fourteen years of watching you figure this place out…" I didn't say a word, and he laughed through his nose at the silence. He leaned in again, asking expectantly, "So, you have figured this place out, haven't you?"

"Figured what out?" I asked, providing no cooperation.

He bellowed loudly, echoic like a troll's voice. "Are you sure you don't want to use that brain of yours? Or do you want to pretend you're really

this stupid? Come on, Hale...I know you've figured this place out." I shook
my head.

"Why don't you just say it," I proposed, "since you're so anxious to
have me know?" The owner thought about my suggestion and began talking.

"This place," he said after accepting my offer, "is a place for people
with no families, no other lives, no one to go to other than us. You are all
nobodies. You are all abandoned souls living for no particular purpose; only
to take up room in this rotted building. People like you have nothing to lose,
and if any of you were to disappear, no one would notice a difference."

"What are you trying to say?"

Mr. O bitterly said, "What I'm trying to say, Hale, is that people like
you are perfect for a place like the Drug Trade. People, who can defy morals
and not feel any source of grief, people who can suddenly vanish off this
Earth with no questions being asked! This orphanage is a breeding ground
for Richard's trade. A recruiting center for people like you! People like you
who will leave this place and become a part of the most powerful thing in
this city. Protected by, and a part of, the Drug Trade..."

"Why are you telling me this?"

"I can see your anger...I can see your lack of mercy. Someone like
you would be a great addition to the trade. You would be a benefit to the
business!"

"And you're offering me a job?" I asked, offended.

"All you have to do is nod your head..." Mr. O waited for my movement, but it never took action.

"No," I told him, my answer like lead feathers.

He pulled back with a surprised look on his face. "What?" His inter-
view wasn't going as he expected.

"No," I repeated.

"What do you mean no? You have no idea what you're passing up.
This offer will lead you to either great wealth," he then looked at the two
men who each pulled out a small pistol, "or, if you deny, to great pain."

"This offer is offensive. To think that you believe I would ever accept
such a request is offensive. I hate people like you, and when it comes to pain,
my hate makes me numb. I will tell you again—no."

"You can't be serious," he convinced himself. "You hate people like us? You, Hale, are just like us! You're no different! You would kill a man just because you felt it necessary…you're cold blooded, even if you want to believe your veins are full of fire!"

"I said, no. You can try and manipulate me, but it won't work."

"You're going to end up dead if you don't accept this offer, kid. It would be a waste on both of our parts…" I remained silent, but Mr. O took one more shot at coaxing me. "You don't want to die, Hale. There is no such thing as ghosts. When you're dead, you're dead!"

"We'll find out when I come back to haunt you."

He smirked, then shook his head. "What a shame…" He cued a guard over to me.

The ape raised his rifle, and drove it my face.

I woke up many hours later after being tossed around in some stuffy trunk of a car. It seemed as though the guards were driving through a forest off any road.

When the car stopped, the trunk opened and broken light began to bleed through a black bag over my head. One of the guards took me by my arm and hauled me out of the trunk.

I fell to my stomach, unable to catch myself—both my wrists and ankles were tied. As they began dragging me, I felt loose dirt ruffling beneath my feet. The sound of crashing waves and racing wind surrounded my ears. The howling wind was like Mother Nature's desperate singing, and the crashing of the waves were like cymbals in an orchestra.

I was still blind, and it became when no sunlight soaked through the bag and into my eyes. When the apes removed the sac from head, my pupils didn't shrink to small black dots against the blueness of my irises, but instead grew larger at the sight of darkened clouds which climbed over the orange sky like an oil tidal wave. Below me, beyond the sheer edge of the cliff, even more violent waves tried to climb up the rocky wall. The ocean was colored evil lavender beneath the storming sky threatening the rarest downpour of hail and rain.

They took me by the joints of my elbows and gave me a hot ultimatum.

There was no escape to what they said. As I stood on the edge of an endless cliff, one of the suited men said to me, "Jump, or we'll shoot you."

My toes hung off the natural skyscraper, and after turning around, looking into the eyes of their guns' barrels, I had decided.

If I were to stand there, they would shoot me in my back and I would fall anyway. Though my hands and wrists were tied, I had more obvious hope in jumping without holes through my body. And it wasn't my pride that made me jump. It was the idea, the epiphany, that if I was going to die, I would die free of cruelty's grasp. And though its grasp was ineluctable during such a certain circumstance, jumping and giving myself the tiniest chance of survival was good enough.

So I jumped, hoping luck could catch me.

Not much of a life flashed before my eyes as I hurled toward the water. Breaking its surface was like breaking the surface of a concrete pool, just barely soft enough to swallow an anchor. Unimaginable force was taken for me to sink beneath the waves. When I did, undulate bubbles came rising from below and stuck to my figure. Above, the sun and cliff and storm were disfigured by the constantly moving water current.

Even though no one would have ever been suspected to survive the fall, I waited under the water to assure the men above of my death, slowly... slowly...sinking...

I had to squirm endlessly like a worm to keep from sinking. Floating in between the surface and the rock bottom, I fit my legs between my arms so my hands were in front of my body.

Coming to the surface after the most torturous swim, with a gulp of longed air, I looked to the rocks against the cliff wall. The waves played with me—nature's doll. It was hard to keep my head above water. Every now and then I would sink below and swallow the ocean's water. The current, though, began forcing me to the shore until the water depth was shallower. When I finally was able to stand, I took time to catch my breath and clear my head.

My spine clattered with fear and my body shivered from the chills of the dead from what I had seen. Mangled deep between the jagged rocks, the corpse of a kid, my age, was rotting. It had been there for days. The flesh was peeling like wallpaper in the orphanage, and held a moldy green color to it. The kid's face was buried in the rocks, so I didn't know if I knew him or not. But he was from the orphanage, and he had experienced what I had just gone through.

I peered up to the far top of the cliff. There were no white-suited guards. They had already given up their faith in my survival. Then it began to rain—a heavy drop of water released from the mouths of clouds. When I kept my head still, I could feel every single raindrop splatter on my face.

I had just been murdered, but reborn amongst those rocks.

"After that, I didn't know what to do...eventually I made my way back and came to your apartment, Ed." I looked at my friend who was intently listening. "I just walked until my feet hurt so bad that I couldn't anymore...I don't know how long I walked, all I remember is killing that man...strangling him to death."

"Oh my God," Barrette exhaled. "That man is monstrous. I can only imagine how much you want him dead..."

"I'm going to kill him," I sent the fact to Barrette. He looked at me, wanting to protest, but unable to find courage in his sympathy.

"Okay," Barrette said, "let's take that son-of-a-bitch down."

SIX

ᵈᴰ WAS A CYCLOPS. WHILE HE SQUEEZED ONE SHUT, HE PRIED HIS other eye wide open as it twitched around, hovering over the barrel of a microscope. I could tell that these highly intellectual, highly mathematical gears were rotating in Ed's head, grinding together to move one large logical thought.

On one sheet of glass below the eye of the microscope was a sample of Borm, the subject which Ed studied ferociously. But to the more common, inexperienced person, the sample was a blue blob of gel sitting lifelessly before Ed's study. There were tiny air bubbles inside the Borm, and I couldn't imagine what kind of crap was also in it.

I stood there for a long time in the silence and concentration of Ed's focus. He had been studying the Borm all night, and found it impossible to break away from the drug's intrigue.

The rest of the basement was dark, and the only light in our area was light from the microscope which shined from below, and through, Ed's Borm on the glass sheet. It was barely enough illumination for us to be able to see each other's faces.

"Barrette gave me some Borm he found on that dealer of yours to analyze before they took him in," Ed said as he pulled up from the microscope. He blinked heavily a few times, flicking away the unbreakable focus crusted on his eyelids.

I asked him, "Did you find anything?"

"Well..." Ed returned his single eye to the microscope. "It has the same characteristics as many antidepressants and steroids, except this is to a whole 'nother degree..."

"How so?" I wondered out loud. But I knew Ed was eager to explain.

"I don't know how it works, exactly," Ed said, "but it's absorbed into the blood and travels to the brain instantly. Blood is ultra-vulnerable to the Borm, it seems. It's like putting a sponge into water...the Borm just absorbs nearly all of the red and white cells. And it doesn't take much...it looks like only a few ounces of this stuff can supply its host for hours."

I brought myself in close to look at the Borm, although I didn't see it in magnified detail like Ed. "What's it made out of?" I asked the scientist Ed Reel.

But my question wasn't near quizzical to him. "I've identified a few ingredients like Ginger Root extract, caffeine...basic things that can be found in practically anything. That explains how Big Rich has been able to get his Borm into the country..."

"You mean aside from our careless government," I threw in my own commentary.

Ed shook his head and ignored my inserted biasness. "Big Rich doesn't smuggle any illegal items into the country," explained Ed. "The Borm must be made somewhere inside American borders... probably somewhere in Los Angeles or California."

"You believe the Borm is factory made?"

"It would take days to create Borm by hand. It would only make sense if it was factory made, but what would Big Rich's excuse be for owning an entire factory? Or factories...?" he asked and expected more than hoped for me to have an answer.

I thought about it for a moment: How one man could run an entire operation (and not to mention one of the most expansive and wealthiest operations) under his sleeve? How could he fool the public and cover up an entire business with a simple excuse? Wouldn't he have to grow a scab just as large and expansive as the Drug Trade itself?

But he did have a scab...Project Home. Project Home was one big cover up—one big, bloody scab that covered the raw flesh beneath it. I knew the orphanage homes were recruiting centers... but what about the toy stores? Toy Palace had to have a bigger part in the operation.

Then my own gears turned and grinded against each other until they armed an idea that had to be right.

"The toys!" I suddenly devised and shared with a screaming voice injected with the greatest, sweetest, bitterest, sourest, the most savory, excited, dreadful, wildest conclusion.

Ed wrinkled his eyebrows. "The toys?" He couldn't follow, and for a genius, my hypothesis was nothing above average.

"Toy Palace—if anyone were to question him about any factory or factories, Big Rich could blame it on the toys! That's why he's constructing all those stores!"

Ed understood. "There's only one way to find out," mischievously, he said to me. "Looks like you're gonna need to have a word with that dealer of yours..."

"I'll see you later," I told Ed and exited our conversation and the congestion of the basement as soon as my objective was assigned.

Up the beige, unending, and yet so short, hallway, I opened the door to Barrette's office without knocking. For the commissioner of police, Barrette seemed to invest the majority of his time into papers. Papers filled with useless sentences and words that would never solve a crime or stop a mugging.

"Can I help you?" the commissioner asked without even looking up to see who had entered his office.

"I need your help."

Luckily I wasn't a man holding a gun to his head, or else Barrette would have never known the difference. His vigilance wasn't suspicious. I pressed a fist to my face and coughed. Barrette looked up, and his composure suddenly changed. He nearly jumped out of his seat, and his flinging hands knocked several papers from his desk.

As he gathered himself and the scattered papers, Barrette

stuttered his words, blushing slightly. "Oh! Kid! What..." He cleared his throat. "...what are you doing here?"

Before I continued to my own business, I asked Barrette, "Are you okay, commissioner?"

"I'm fine," he swore. "It's just...you shouldn't be here..."

I swatted away his attempt at avoiding confrontation and said, again, "I need your help."

"*My* help?" surprised, Barrette asked.

"I need to get in a room alone with that dealer I brought to you..."

"For what reason?"

"Ed has isolated some of the ingredients in Borm, and we have reasonable suspicion to believe that the drug is made inside American borders..."

Barrette thought then articulated his opinion. "I thought Richard's sources were global..."

"Only for the Borm's ingredients. After they're shipped into the country, they're formulated into the drug itself," I began to explain as Barrette listened intently.

"Wouldn't Rich need a lab or factory to make the Borm in?" he added his input which I had preconceived.

"That's exactly why I need to see the dealer. I need to see if he knows where the ingredients come from and where the Borm is made," I said.

"Right..." Barrette finished sorting his papers aimlessly. He completed his organizing and directed me. "He's in the holding cell for now. I'm sure you're familiar with the place..." He tipped his head and shot me a slow glare from below his eyebrows.

I turned to exit his office. Across the hall was a door that reeked of secrecy. I looked back at Barrette behind his desk and asked, "What's in there?"

He looked at the door in my background then smiled. A slight laugh defended his words when he bluntly told me, "I don't trust you enough yet to let you go in *there*..."

No argue spilled out of my mouth. I accepted his honesty and headed farther up the hallway until it branched off into a second beige tunnel—one lined with individual cages, both large and small.

The dealer sat in the back left corner of the cell farthest into the holding cell hallway. Slowly, I stepped in front of the iron bars. He heard the clack of my footsteps and slowly, easily looked up at me.

As soon as his memory recognized the face beneath my hood, the thug's eyes widened and he practically crawled up the wall on his back.

"Remember me?" I asked him with a stinger in my voice. His breathing turned into panting, and his heart beat was like a rock band's drums. "I need you to tell me something. If you don't, I'll make sure I get in that cage with you."

He didn't fuss or foolishly protest. "What do you want to know?" he wondered immediately, wisely.

"I know the Borm is composed somewhere inside the country, and I'm assuming inside California. *Where?* Where is the Borm made?" I jumped right into the aggressive questions I had to ask. The dealer kept his mouth closed. And I thought he wasn't a fool. I looked to my left down the hall at an officer. "Officer," I called his attention. "Open this door."

The officer moved from his stand and began walking over, unclasping a heavy amount of keys looped to his belt. The thug inside his cage noticed the approaching officer and panicked. "No, no! Gray Moss! Gray Moss! We make it in Gray Moss! It's a small neighborhood far east of here...I swear...Gray Moss..." Like confessing was an exhausting chore, the man slumped on the bench and exhaled heavily.

"Are you involved in the process?" I continued.

The man rolled up the sleeve of his shirt and showed me his tattoo of the broken crown—his permanent identity in the Drug Trade. "Yeah..." he answered lazily. "I'm a Deliverer. My station is in the city, but I go to the coast now and then for *special* deliveries. I've seen where they make it...that beautiful drug. The *Borm...*"

The dealer said that like it was a precious treasure given to him by the gods rather than a fat man with a pretty smile.

"And where do the ingredients to the Borm come from?"

"All over the world," he assured me with no fight. "But don't ask me any of the specifics…no one knows exactly what goes into the Borm, or where those ingredients come from. No one but the boss…"

I hadn't yet let up on the persistence. This particular thug was soft and easy to claw my way through. "Where are the ingredients dropped off before they go to Gray Moss? Where do shipments arrive?"

An opposing snicker rattled from the man's mouth. He grinned evilly and stabbed me with the meanest glare. "You think I'll just answer every single one of your questions, kid? You're interrogation is worth the safety of this final shipment. I know what you'll do if I tell you…"

"Really?" I asked and stepped as close to the bars as I could. "And do you know what I'll do if you don't?"

He was brave enough to laugh at me a second time. The man folded his arms casually in front of his chest, and let his body fall into a relaxed position like a slumped, brainless piece of meat.

"I've seen worse," he promised me.

"Are you sure?" I gave the man one last chance to test the limits of my persistence, my need to know. My fists curled into a tight ball and the knuckles on my hands jutted out like the tips of worn daggers.

He raised his eyebrows to fail the final test of my patience. I returned my look to the officer and he completed his steps over to the cell. As he began fiddling with the keys on his chain, I eyed the thug to spot any weakness.

The dealer assumed we were bluffing. He took the threat and made it a joke, but as the officer put the correct key into the lock of his jail cell, the thug began questioning himself. And then the officer pulled the iron barred door open, and I stood in the doorway. My shadow lay over the man like a body bag.

He began to scramble in my silhouetted darkness, darting back and forth between the two side walls of his cage. I took one step in, and my shadow grew. I took another, and his body bag began filling the entire back wall of the jail cell, breaking open a depthless void of shadow behind the 'man'.

He was a buzzing fly, but I caught him by his shirt and yanked him close to me. "Where do the shipments arrive?" I shook him. "Tell me or I'll throw you out of this life…"

I know he considered it, but never actually answered my question. Instead, the imprisoned Borm dealer cracked his head into mine. His skull hit my nose and shot a sharp pain right into my eyes. My vision fell blurry with the amount of building tears provoked by his heavy hit.

The dealer was just a smeared figure. I saw one of his limbs jolt out and I tried to block it, but his punch arrived at the side of my head quicker than I had thought. The hit staggered me to the side.

The dealer shouted out in victory then began to throw up his leg for a kick. I caught the attack by his upper thigh and threw him across the cage to the officer's feet. He unsheathed his baton and hit the dealer once over the head.

While I wiped the tears from my eyes and tried to ignore the pain in my face, the officer began to speak. "That guy's not gonna get up anytime soon," he said. "Listen…don't tell the other officers I helped you, but I think I know where those shipments you were talking about might be arriving." I looked up at him with bloodshot eyes. My acknowledgement, though silent, was a pass for him to proceed with the information. "One of my partners was patrolling far out east by the coast. He reported a large vessel anchored out at sea, and another small one docking at a port that has been out of business for years."

"What port?" I asked him.

"Port Lybric," he quickly responded then provided further detail: "It's the only port out at the harbor directly east of Downtown."

"And you think it could be Big Rich's men?"

"Well...I don't know why any regular vessel would dock at an abandon port in the middle of the night..."

It made sense. I thanked the officer and returned to Barrette while he scooped up the thug and tossed him back in his cage.

Every prisoner who existed claimed that they were treated like animals, and that such apathetic care wasn't deserved. And, continuously, they proved every external pair of eyes and ears wrong. They were given the chance to be civil like a human being, but, as the Born dealer had just expressed, they chose to be untamed like a terminally ill animal, choking on the rabies foaming about their lips.

The door was already opened, but I knocked my knuckles against it before entering Barrette's office.

"What'd you learn?" Barrette hurried to the point.

"An officer...I mean, the *dealer* told me that Big Rich's shipments have been arriving at Port Lybric down at the harbor east of Downtown LA," I reported to the commissioner.

"Port Lybric?" he asked, stunned with the knowledge but plenty aware of the location. "That place has been abandon for years...though, I suppose that's why Big Rich chose it." Barrette laughed at the irony he caught buzzing around us. "People say that Richard's own son destroyed the port..."

I wrinkled my eyebrows at Barrette's tale. "Big Rich has a son?"

"*Had*," Barrette corrected. "At least, that's what people say."

"Why would his son burn the port down?"

Where to begin? Barrette reclined with a finger against his lips. He finally said after piling the story together, "Apparently he wasn't like Lucifer. He stood for what was right while his father stood for things much less just. So, back when the port was still being used by the public, it was Big Rich's prime spot for bringing in his shipments. He had been working with a guy who owned the port—splitting half of his royalties with him just so he would keep his mouth shut. One day," Barrette advanced, "his son crept into the port under the cover of night and burned the whole harbor to ashes."

"What happened to him?—Richard's son...?"

"He disappeared that night...some say that his own father buried him alive, some say he threw him into the ocean with an anchor strapped to his chest. But those who are firm believers or skeptics of the story say that the son burned alive in the fire he started..."

"What do you believe?"

Barrette abruptly broke out of his narrative voice and fell back into his fat leather seat. "Well it makes the most sense for the son to have died in the fire...you should see the place—it's just one big ash pile. But that's just what people say. Who knows if the kid ever existed? Either way," he continued on, "Big's Incorporated hasn't used that place since it was destroyed. At least, that's what I thought..."

By nature, by creed and curiosity, I traveled east of the city where land met water, where both sides won, where both sides lost.

Either Barrette's tale he told was true, or coincidence was rolling dice across the board game of the harbor. With every step, ash and fine-grained debris was kicked up beneath my feet. It wasn't hard to imagine what the harbor was like before charred ruins became of it. Most of the port's black skeleton remained standing, a crumbling reminder of the blazon.

There were a few buildings on the very edge of land that jutted higher than three stories. But the buildings were hollow—every lifted level had been burned and collapsed to crumbs on their foundations.

The harbor was a town of itself, or at least the burnt corpse of one. It was a small patch of buildings that was planted just at the ocean's reach. Now, though, it was a single scar, a graveyard for the business and traffic that had once occupied these ruins.

Some walls of several buildings had bent over and nearly collapsed inward, leaving jagged structures standing in the dry black snow. What should have been sand was ash, the ashes of an attempt to shine light upon the darkness.

Maybe crime, maybe Big Rich and Project Home was fireproof. There I was, standing at the top of a hill overlooking an empire withered to a weightless dust, and all that brought its demise was a drum of gasoline and the flame of a match. But it was only a limb of this empire that had deteriorated. The rest stood amongst the skyscrapers and blindness of Los Angeles.

They called it the City of Angels, when it should have been called the City of the Angel, because I seemed to be the only one who cared about the rapid descent of the city's sanity and morality.

Every time I passed by a wooden telephone pole or an empty window, I imagined a MISSING poster with the picture of an angel on it. I wanted to believe that maybe somewhere, someone was searching for the same thing I had been fighting for. I had hope—though rapidly demising hope—that someone out there hadn't given in to the easiness of crime.

It would have been so easy to forget everything I had been told and to crush my motives and my purpose like aluminum cans. But then what hope would the city have? I was its savior, not Big Rich. I could open the eyes of the city enough for its people to see the truth.

After bringing the city's king to his knees, the people and wasted lives of Los Angeles would taste the freedom they could have and the morality that could clean their filth.

Couldn't they?

Or maybe those people who lost all sight of justice and its form should be burned to ashes. Maybe those people under Big Rich's wing should die when he would be killed. To kill one man would be to kill a thousand more.

SEVEN

HE DIDN'T WALK ACROSS THE WORLD, RATHER THE EARTH SLID beneath her feet. Her walk was so seamless and laced with grace that Raine's head never bobbed the slightest bit. The golden tails of her head playfully swayed behind her back with the motion of each graceful step she took.

From across the street, I could smell her sweet aroma: The scent of clean cotton basking below an amber sun while being brushed by the hand of a breeze that had rolled across an ever-stretching wheat field.

Both of her eyes were the forms of windows to her soul to the greatest extent. Neither of the two forgot any of Raine's brilliance, nor the lambency of her own self. They were lagoons of glowing, turquoise water that would taste sweeter than any sugar and more refreshing than the water from a desert oasis.

Her skin was so soft, like the surface of a marble or the color of a pearl. Like the cheek of a newborn, when, more appropriately, Raine was just as virtuous.

Raine trotted down the steps from her home and boarded the sidewalk. She walked with both thumbs in her pockets and her eyes stuck straight ahead. Though, if a situation was to call it, she could quickly look to the side or over both shoulders.

A streak of light followed her and every distance she covered. I followed Raine from across the street, having to focus on not smiling rather than smiling. Raine's vibes melted off of her. I couldn't help but feel warm and comforted in her presence, even if I was so far away.

Our neighborhood was its own existence on the outskirts of Richard Lucifer's domain. His territory was the dark forest of sky-scrapers and rapids of traffic filled streets.

The less fortunate, and those proven innocent of Big Rich's business, watched their lives pass on the porches of their single story houses, or on their dirt lawns, or in the chinked streets.

Every white picket fence had lost its paint and shriveled into rotted planks of wood sticking up from the ground. Green blades of grass baked and sheathed their beauty into little roasted strands that shed from their dirt. The shingles on roofs broke away one at a time like leaves on an autumn tree, dandruff on a dry scalp.

There were bones to pick meat off of, puddles to drink from. But in the city, in the shade of Big Rich's giant gut, a peasant could live like a king. Nothing is free, though. In return you would sign away your purity and option of calling yourself innocent.

You sign away your soul to the foul business. You hand your body to the mercilessness of Borm, and slowly you die. You walk around like a zombie, and suddenly you're not the king—you realize that Big Rich is the only one wearing a crown. You're nothing, not even a peasant anymore. You don't have the right, the privilege, the law to call yourself human. You have seen things, felt things, and stood by while things happened. You had the chance to stop it, but you didn't. And then maybe one day you realize that this *thing* you've become will be nothing more than a pile of bones beneath the earth. You will have given nothing, you will have never tasted life, and you will have never touched the happiness that comes with 'innocence'. But then one day you realize, you're no different than anyone else.

Raine kept walking down the streets and toward the trunks of the architectural giants far in the distance. I don't know why she was entering the forest, but I could tell by the motivation in her eyes that she had a mission. And for some misconceived reason, Raine believed that she could handle it alone.

I equaled my pace to her's and, the entire time, walked parallel from Raine across the street. There was no face beneath the hood on my head. No eyes to *really* be watching. But inside the hood I could see only directly ahead. So I faced Raine, pasting my eyes to her walk and her delicate expressions that formed on her face.

Her shoulders lightly rocked each step she took, and naturally there was—if even the slightest way—a smile in the bend of Raine's lips. She passed by an alleyway that was no darker, nor more particular, than the countless amount of alleyways before.

But as she passed, the shadows reached out at her, and snatched Raine into the darkness. There was no sound, no evidence that Raine had ever been there, and if so, no clues suggesting that she was taken. I was glued to the ground by the occurrence. For a while I focused on the darkness, slapping myself to see if my eyes were fools.

It was only when I heard Raine's scream bouncing around the walls of the alleyway that I bulleted across the street and stopped just outside. Light from the sidewalks stretched into the alley for a few feet before being swallowed and digested by impenetrable darkness.

Raine's screaming was intensified. She was already pinned to the concrete with a man between her legs and four others around them. They all encouraged their buddy with barbaric chants and whistles and sentences most provocative.

Raine's body nearly disappeared beneath the man who lay on top of her. He held both of her glass-like-wrists with one giant widespread paw and used the other to undo his pants. His arms were covered with blubbery layers of meat (fat) and gnarly tattoos that slithered and flew and wrapped around his entire body. The man wore a jean vest with raggedly torn arm sockets so he could brag to society about his flabby meat swinging with gooey motions.

Soon, his pants were lowered to his ankles, and I saw the man touch Raine between her own legs. She burled a shriek and tried even harder to escape the man's perverted indecency. He almost had her jeans removed completely from her legs when I charged him.

Without any regret or superstitions about what could have happened, I threw myself into the alleyway and its engulfing darkness. As soon as I reached him, I grabbed the barbarian by the back of his jean vest and ripped him away from Raine. I threw him like a doll behind me and his weight collided with the unyielding concrete brutally. He rolled for bit before lying still and unconscious.

His pals were taken by surprise. They whipped their sight toward me and, once realizing what had happened, charged at the hooded man disrupting their precious moment.

To my left, the closest attacker was already cutting a punch through the air in my direction. I managed to throw up my left arm, defend myself from his punch, and slung a right-handed-fist into the man's cheek. After just my first attack, a strange, unexplainable surge of adrenalin and rage began pumping through my veins. Their moves fell slow, and I suddenly grasped the ability to move fast and strike powerfully.

I looked quickly to my right, but a fist had already reached my face. My head snapped backward from the attack, and my already-injured-nose took the concentrated force of the punch. Another attack struck me in my stomach—the man to my right had summoned a kick. I hunched over a bit, but from that perspective I saw his last and final strike heading toward me.

Without warning I sprang up from my hunch and blocked the man's left hook. He threw one with his right arm, but I blocked that too. And, relentlessly, he began to charge his left fist toward me a second time. Just as each one of his hits before, I blocked the left hook with my right arm and cracked a left fist of my own into the man's stomach. His posture collapsed and his head lowered. To his bottom jaw, I wielded an uppercut with my other clubbed fist and forced the man off his feet.

Right behind him as the man fell, was my third opponent. I was preparing an offensive attack, but when I lunged at the man,

I was grabbed from behind by the fourth. He prevented me from whirling any attacks at the thug.

I threw my legs around, hoping to free my arms from the anaconda grip that constricted my entire body. The man in front of me removed a gleaming object from his pocket, and soon I realized that the reflection of the street lights was bouncing off of a knife's silver blade.

He grinned, but it was more of a teeth-flaring. As he snarled and growled, the man with the knife tossed it back and forth between his two hands, and slowly approached me. He got close, and I could see the sharpened tip of the blade that was sure to pierce my skin and let me bleed out in the alleyway, just like I could only imagine what Jay had done...

Around his fingers, the man twirled the blade to hold it like any classic horror character would. He was an arm's length away from me when he raised the knife above his head and braced for a deep penetration. His mouth was foaming and his eyes had orange flames dancing around their irises.

He inhaled once, and forcefully dropped the knife toward me. Before it could pierce my own body, I used all of my strength to whirl the man who held me to where I was standing. His own friend stabbed him the back, and the man's grip loosened as he fell to the ground.

I was free.

The man had lost his weapon in the back of his gurgling friend who lay at our feet. I twisted around and, without any prior experience, I bent my right leg and shot a kick into the man's gut. He was chucked backward into the opposite alleyway. The sidekick knocked a rush of air out of his lungs, and he crumpled to his knees, gripping his stomach.

I left him no time for rehabilitation before I marched to where he knelt, brought him to his feet, and held him to the brick wall behind. I pressed my forearm to his throat, making his speech choppy and broken.

"What the fuck do you want?" the man found it acceptable to ask *me* that question.

I pressed harder, "What do you want with *her*?" Raine was lying motionless on the concrete below us. "What do you want with the girl?" My voice was hoarse and discomforting, even to myself.

"He wanted us to kill her," the man managed to say, despite the tight choke I had on him.

"Who wanted you to kill her?"

"Our *boss*..." the man replied.

With my free hand I ripped a piece of his sleeve from the man's arm and looked at the skin beneath. A broken crown—permanently drawn into his skin. "Big Rich?" I asked him, even when I knew the answer.

Truth was much sweeter coming from the mouth of a liar.

He hesitated a bit, contemplating if he should affirm the identity of his boss. But the man, wisely, finally confirmed saying, "Yes. Big Rich..."

"Why does he want the girl dead?"

"Because..." I thought his answer would slide right out of his mouth, but the thug stopped, catching his tongue.

"Why?" I yelled and demanded to know. Only to split his skin with my knuckles, I released his choke and socked him in his eye. Immediately after, I returned my forearm to nearly crushing his esophagus.

"Because..."

"I assure you, I'm a lot worse than Big Rich. If I were you, I would worry about running into me rather than the fat man..."

"You don't know my boss!" he snipped. "You don't know what he's capable of..."

"Why does he want the girl dead? Tell me!"

"He knows you're after him!" the thug finally released. His words were practically exhaled from his mouth lifelessly and without motivation. "He knows you want him dead..."

"What does that have to do with Raine?" I continued muti-lating the man's confidentiality.

"Oh," the man lifted both of his eyebrows. He felt the advan-tage he was gaining over me. "So you *do* know her? Think about it," he told me, "why would my boss...Big Rich, want your little girlfriend dead? Huh?" I thought about it, but the thug beat me to his conclusion. "He wants to *weaken* you. He wants her out of the picture so you have nothing to fall back on!"

"I don't even know her," I lied, and the man caught my bluff.

"Oh," he snickered, "it's too late for that. We all know...her name is already out. Raine Waltzer is as good as dead!"

I tightened my grip on his shirt and pressed hard against his throat. The veins of his forehead began to pop out. His face turned cherry red and his eyes, I could tell, were being tormented by the pressure. I screamed loud and threw him down to the side.

"She's dead, kid! Accept it! Sooner or later, she'll be plucked from your life like a pretty little flower!" He was totally amused by the words snaking through his teeth. I brought back a foot and slammed it into the man's side. He groaned and curled his entire body in. "She's dead!" he persisted, and I kicked him again. "*Dead!*"

I felt my teeth grow into fangs and my nails sharpen into claws. I turned toward the man with the knife in his back, and yanked the blade from his body. Turning back toward the other, my shadow molested his entire figure.

"If crime is merciless," I began to chant darkly, "justice must be too!" I raised the knife over my head and forced it down into the man.

I pierced his side and the mushy flesh between each rib. Then his neck—I began butchering his entire body with the blade. I ripped apart the tendons and vessels in his throat and neck, slit open his stomach and gutted him like a fish—not that he was any more important.

His intestines spilled out like a soggy meal. A horrible stench lifted off the opened carcass and burned my nostrils. But I inhaled deeply anyway, so deeply that I was breathing in the man's life. I began crushing his head, impaling his skull over and over again with the dulling blade.

Not long after I mangled the thug's entire body, it became unrecognizable. A mound of mushy guts and soupy blood half spread across the alleyway. My panting was wolf-like. Beast-like. Me-like.

I held my arms away from my sides, terrified to make contact with my own self. My mind had cleared (I wish), but I still shook. I stood there for a timeless moment looking at the mount of lasagna. And then from behind I heard a high-pitched moan.

I turned around and saw Raine waking up. Quickly, I dropped the knife and raced over to her. Blood had turned my hands all red, so I wiped them on my hoodie's front and bent down to where Raine was tossing slowly.

"Raine?" I called to her. She didn't answer. "Raine?"

She was completely incoherent for now, and when I looked behind me at the butcher house around us, I figured it was best her eyes stayed closed. I slipped my arms beneath her limp body and picked her up.

I would say it was like carrying her out from a wedding, but the background behind us was smeared with blood and splashed with endless gore. The stench began to get to me—it reeked like week old carcasses and began oozing out into the street.

As soon as I had Raine in my arms, I left the butcher house.

We had walked several blocks away from her house, and by the time I got back, my arms were burning from carrying Raine the entire way. Her arms and legs and head flopped around, completely loose and limp. She must have fainted from the anxiety of the scene rushing before her.

It took no effort to push in the decaying front door of her home. I used my foot and a blast of unpleasant scent raced across my face. I flinched from the stench radiating from inside Raine's house.

The house was not the home of an angel. A horrible aroma of

nicotine and alcohol just loomed in the small living room of the place. There was hardly any light inside, but I could see the dump Raine was living in. Beer bottles sat empty on every countertop, ash trays overflowing with the gray remains of cigarettes loitered on the tables. Every cushion on the single couch was torn open and emptied of white fluff. The blinds on each window were barely hanging on. Burn marks freckled the carpet throughout the house. There were only two doors, and when I caught a whiff of sweet aroma, I knew which room was Raine's.

The atmosphere completely changed when I entered her bedroom. It was like another world on the complete opposite end of the spectrum in comparison to her mother's environment. Her walls were painted a smooth, artic blue, and all across them were different forms of art. There were stretched canvases with beautiful days painted upon them—cotton clouds churning in a bath of brilliant blue, green hills gently rising and falling like the chest of an infant.

Her bed was neatly made, and a small desk was pushed into the back corner. Stacks of novels and books full of poems compromised any workspace. Her wardrobe was sparse, but tasteful. In her small closet hung only a couple different shirts, all of brisk colors.

There were no candles, but the small, four-walled room maintained a scent the same as Raine's. It reminded me of a mountain lake so clear that the rock bottom could be seen from its rippling surface. It reminded me of a lavender field that ran all the way off the horizon like a purple dressed woman running, with her arms spread, until she reached the endless edge of her life's horizon. A horizon pure and flawless. Even when there were no birds, choruses rang in the air.

Carefully, I set Raine down in the soft sink of her bed. Her breaths were light and hardly noticeable. I knew she dreamt. Maybe of spreading out in green grass, maybe holding hands with a ring on her finger. Or maybe her dreams were abstract scenes narrated by her unconscious mind. Maybe she stood in a white void with random items and colors floating by. Maybe there was a tree with all of its roots hanging in the empty space below it.

Whatever the dream was, I knew the world behind closed lids was better than the world I stood in.

Her jeans were ripped and stained with dirt in places from the mugging. Her shirt was ripped at her chest with nothing but skin and the underwear she wore beneath. I took one hand, shaking, and made a silent trip to her chest. I set my palm down on her warm skin and felt it rise and fall with Raine's breathing.

Her lips were perfect. Their color was a warm pink. Across her nose and cheeks, a shy constellation of freckles spread out. And I just knew that behind her closed eyelids were blasts of turquoise—beautiful, fantastical turquoise.

"I'm going to change this city, Raine," I said to her, but really only to myself. "I'm going to kill Big Rich and destroy his trade... and everything will be better. I know it will...right? I know it...the world is better without Big Rich. He tried to kill you...he killed Jay...Oh, Jay...an old man just...just walking, and they killed him coldhearted. Why is crime so merciless? How can a heart be so cold and stone, that nothing can thaw or move it? But I have a solution, Raine. If crime is merciless, justice must be too...If crime is merciless..." My thoughts drifted away from Raine's imperfectly perfect body, and dropped into a bleak and dark alleyway, much like the one I had just escaped.

I saw Jay walking alone. The ground was moist from a recent rain, and the air was soggy. He watched his feet as he walked. There were only a few feet left before Jay could have exited the alleyway, but just before he did, a man stepped out from around the corner.

Jay looked up, startled a bit. He tried to move around the thug, but couldn't. After teasing Jay for a bit, the thug pushed the old man back into the depth. Jay wanted no confrontation, so he turned his body around to try and leave the other way.

But another man stood behind him. He shoved Jay into the grasp of the second, while he dangled a fine blade in front of Jay's eyes. Without hesitation, the man in front drove the knife in Jay's belly. Jay wanted to scream, but it hurt too much. The man stabbed him again and again. Over and over until Jay was dying on the concrete, and still, the thug stabbed him.

Suddenly, people began to pass through the alleyway. Regular people—some wore suits, some carried briefcases, and others dressed themselves casually. The alleyway became a highway for foot traffic.

Big Rich's men continued to stab at Jay. Eventually he hadn't even the energy to struggle the slightest bit. People continued to pass, the thugs continued to murder the old man. They carved their names slowly into Jay's skin, but no one stopped to do anything.

I tried to run toward him. I tried to reach the men so I could break their necks and hold Jay in my arms. The heavy foot traffic prevented me from ever reaching Jay. I saw him look at me. The old man extended an arm and reached for my help. I reached too, but never actually touched his fingertips.

The flowing crowd of people vomited me out of the alley, and suddenly I was back in Raine's bedroom. My breaths shook, trembling from the fear and rage inside me. "If crime is merciless, justice must be too," I recited to myself again. "Justice must be too…"

Raine was still asleep. The sound of her breathing was soothing, but not soothing enough. I pulled Jay's pistol from my pocket, and visualized myself shooting Big Rich right in his heart. Then, he would bow to *me*. Then, the city would be saved. I would be a hero. I would leave my mark.

I left Raine's house, leaving her the option to decide if that night was real or not. Maybe it was a dream…

Either the moon was invisible, or nowhere to be seen. The blanket of pollution in the sky stripped every person in Los Angeles the luxury of star gazing. Even if I wanted to take the time and appreciate nature's beauty, I couldn't. Looking up would just remind me of mankind's arrogance, his selfishness and naivety. The missing stars and absent angels were just another one of mankind's proclivities—his habit to make all good things temporary.

He says all good things must come to an end. He says that life isn't fair, but the only reason he can say so, is because he made it that way.

Stepping outside was the same as stepping into a layer of fat, and running a mile across the dunes of the Sahara. I was heading to Ed's place for the night. I took a long stroll to avoid the butcher house alley. As I stopped at Ed's door to open it, I felt a pair of eyes burning through the back of my coal colored hood. I peeked just barely over my shoulder and saw a man standing across the street.

His apparel was dark like mine. A long black coat hung off of his body, and a shadow dropped over his face from the brim of a hat. I turned fully around to look directly at the mysterious man. He just stood there, and I could tell he was looking at me.

Before our contest of staring grew old, the man pivoted to his left, and slowly sauntered down the street.

EIGHT

"**W**HY ARE WE HERE, JAY?"

"I want to show you something..." Jay, with his graying hair, told me with such an empty conclusion. As I had been asking the same question over and over again, Jay answered it with words identical to his last.

We were trapped in the afternoon and its traffic both on the sidewalks and in the streets. It seemed we were moving against the current, pushing through tough layers of people one at a time—biting through the city's meat, looking for its heart.

There in the obvious center of LA—the heart of our rotting corpse—was a building, a tower blanketing all the other buildings in its shadow. There, in the obvious center of Los Angeles was the palace of our king. There, was Big's Tower.

Unoriginally named, but sure to clarify ownership. The tower-like building resembled Big Rich himself: Gaunt, barbaric in height, tough in stature and on constant display to every pair of eyes whether they liked it or not. Its walls were round, and at the tower's very top, a series of spotlights lit a single helicopter pad atop the world.

Big Rich had to ensure that his domain was large enough to conquer every block of the city. It was a complete monopoly in territory. All it needed was a silk black tie to ring around its rooftop and all of Los Angeles would be fooled.

One form of life was actually living outside of Big's Tower. At the tower's feet, just out of reach from the first step, the roots of a tree nuzzled *happily in a round spot of soil, a trunk grew perfectly straight, and a lush, full canopy exploded into a green fire of leaves.*

Jay stopped me from walking on, and turned to face the tree. He stood there just feet from it, leaning his head on all sides of his neck, making sure to capture every perspective of the tree. I was more distracted by Jay looking at the tree, so it took a long time before I even noticed it.

The old man looked down at me with smoky eyes, then looked back up. "Imagine that the Drug Trade is a tree," Jay asked my imagination. I stood beside him and far below his height. "Of course, there are several parts that make up that tree, just as there are many parts that make up the Drug Trade. Now imagine this…" He held out his hands, moving them around in the air like he was caressing the entire tree. "The canopy is the centerpiece. Without it, the tree would only be a nasty skeleton. It gives the tree shade and shelter from the sun. It gives it life, something for people to look at." I slanted my head to try and see the tree just as Jay did. "The Officials are the highest branch in the trade. Three men in suits who oversee the entire operation."

I stepped in. "Big Rich is one of them?" My ten-year-old-brain was following along pretty nicely.

"He's the greenest leaf. Big Rich is the king while all the other Officials are merely royal servants…they're substance that adds a little more to the business. The Officials are the image, the faces of the Drug Trade. They're always in the public eye—they're the only real view the public gets of the trade."

"Like distractions?" I queried.

Jay considered then confirmed my question. "Yes," he said. "Without its canopy, the tree would be pure ugliness. No one would want it around. People would chop it down. It wouldn't be allowed!" Then Jay lowered his hands from the air. "But the canopy cannot exist without the trunk…"

"Who is the trunk?" My questions were hasty and impatient. Jay was taking a slower route when my focus wanted to speed.

But Jay understood and answered kindly, "There is a group of people called the Traders. They regulate every transaction, purchase and sale made within the Drug Trade. Traders carry all the nutrition from the roots to the canopy. They give the trade support, just as the trunk does to the tree. Without them, the Officials would fall to the floor."

I began to understand then took Jay's analogy from him. "But the roots...nothing can exist without them."

"Correct..." Jay's silence made room for my words to fill everything in.

"But they're never seen...they're under the dirt. So who are the roots?" I asked the old man, handing him permission to continue.

The old man was happy to continue. "The Deliverers," he told me simply, nearing the end of his analogy. It was an answer of necessity, but Jay elaborated: "A scattered part of the trade, really. They support the entire tree, but isolate them from the trade and all they need is a little tug to pull them out of the soil."

With eyes nearing a fog, Jay looked down at me by his side. I was caught massaging my eyes all over the soil and trunk and lush green canopy. The tree in front of Big's Tower was the perfect touch.

Nothing else held such color. The tree was tall and lush with a perfectly bent trunk and rich, dark soil at its base to feed the roots. When sun hit it, its light would be filtered through the leaves and pour out beneath the canopy as golden blades. I looked up at the blue sky then back down to the tree. Too bad it stood for something much less cheerful.

"So...the Drug Trade is a tree," I repeated, in a summarized fashion, to myself.

Jay nodded. "Yes," he answered, "and all you have to do is burn it down."

"The Drug Trade is a tree. It is made up of several parts and pieces, and each one is as important as the other. We cannot collapse the Drug Trade without destroying its every mechanism." I paused, to assure Barrette understood the analogy. He sat behind his desk with his fingers to his lips, nodding and listening. "The Officials," I continued, "oversee the entire project. They give the public something to look at, something to distract them from reality. The Traders... they're the trunk, the main support beneath the Officials. They regulate all of the Drug Trade's transactions. Without them, there would be no business." I was nearing the end of my explanation. "Everything starts with the Deliverers, though. Once they have delivered the ingredients or packages, the Traders distribute them to Richard's sources. But the entire Drug Trade depends solely on the Deliverers—they're the roots of the tree," I said. "That's where we need to strike first."

Barrette was surprised, hit with immediate concern and recall. "How do you suppose we do that? Doesn't Big Rich have more security than the White House?" he asked, so sure Big was completely untouchable.

"His operation is sleek...they won't go down without a fight, but Big Rich can't afford to have an entire army of security if he expects to remain unknown," I told him. "The trade depends more on anonymity than brute force."

He threw is upper body atop the desk separating us. "So what do we do? Run in there with our guns drawn like we're breaking up a fight?" Barrette asked very sarcastically. He doubted anything would be able to penetrate the operation. But as I said, the Drug Trade was a runner, a silent assassin, not a tank.

"The trade is systematical—it's planned, it's detailed. Big Rich has given it a strict schedule. Every delivery and shipment occurs in equal intervals, which means we know when and where, exactly, to strike. But our operation must be as planned and intentional as the trade," I revised any theories Barrette had of attacking, adding even more rules to the advancement.

"Hm..." He felt the stumps of whiskers all over his cheeks and chin. For a moment he thought, knowing that a specific, systematical plan must arise. "Do you have a plan?" The commissioner sure wasn't going to lay out a blueprint on his own, so I had to do it for him. Luckily, I already did.

"Yes..." I began to jump right into the prologue that would set up my attack perfectly. "The Deliverers arrive every month under the cover of night. Several separate sources from all around the globe deliver the Borm's ingredients to a single location." Barrette was following. "From there, the compilation is transported to the coast where it is delivered."

"I see…" Barrette stood, ready for action. "When exactly is this shipment going to be made?"

"Soon," I answered without much detail.

"How soon?" the commissioner dug a little deeper.

"I don't know," I honestly admitted. "But we don't have much time, I'm sure. If Big Rich expects to finish Project Home, he's going to need the money from this shipment. I'm guessing we have a few days…"

"Can you figure out when the shipment is occurring exactly?"

"There's nothing a little intimidation can't do…"

"Good!" Barrette was delighted. "If we can finally find some solid evidence against this guy, we can expose him to the public!"

I sighed. "I'm afraid a majority of the public is in on the scheme with him…"

Barrette lowered his dignity and sat back in his seat. "Dear God…is it just us against the world?"

"Isn't that enough?"

"A little backup wouldn't hurt." He grunted, and blew air through his circular shaped lips. In habit and under the tension of the future, he rubbed his temples, massaging them with the callused tips of his fingers.

"Speaking of backup…" I moved directly in front of Barrette's desk and crouched so his pouting head could see me. "We're going to need the entire police force if we expect to win this shipment over. I have a plan, but I won't be able to execute it alone…"

Barrette leaned in. "In case you haven't noticed, kid, the police aren't really fond of you. I mean, I'm taking a risk just by talking to you…let alone helping you! And then to ask *them* for help…I don't know…" The stress was getting to Barrette. His cropped coarse hair was a bit grayer since the last time I saw him.

"Maybe something will change their minds"

"I don't believe in miracles, kid," Barrette expressed his practicality.

The personification of surprise: Ed barreled into the

commissioner's office looking like he had been running down the steepest hill all the way there. Ed's glasses sat crooked on his face, but he never bothered to fix them.

"Hale! Hale I need you!"

"What's wrong, Ed?"

"Just come on!" Then Ed left, bolting right out of the office.

I stood and followed him outside into the hallway. When I expected him to head left toward the elevator to his basement, I looked right and he was entering the room with the holding cells in it.

"Ed!" I called, hoping to slow his pace with my voice. "Ed!"

I entered the holding cell hall and saw Ed at the very end of the stretch, staring into the last cell. It looked as if his hope was crushed, as if he expected one thing, and it ended up being something entirely different. Ed just stood there, aimlessly staring in that cell.

I got half way to him and slowed my pace; I was careful not to disrupt anything. "Ed?" I asked, nervously. "Ed, are you alright?"

"I don't understand…" my friend mumbled without opening his mouth. "How could it be…?"

I asked, "How could what be?" and stood next to him. He looked at me with glassy eyes behind his truly glassy glasses. Ed said nothing, but I knew he wanted me to look into the cell. And at that point, I wasn't sure I wanted to turn to my left.

I did, and inside the cell, just where I left him, was the drug dealer on the far back bench of the wall. And then the same sight that brought Ed's stomach to his legs, hit me just as hard.

The dealer sat still, leaning his upper body against the wall in the corner of his cell. The color of the moon's face wasn't as pale as his skin. His cheeks were sunken in—I could practically count the number of teeth in his mouth. Around his eyes were purple rings that bruised the dealer's eye sockets. But there were no eyes behind his lids, I knew. They had shriveled like raisins.

There was no external bleeding on the man, no sign of an attack or murder. I turned to Ed who was baffled by the occult death. Several times Ed parted his lips to speak. Nothing ever came out.

The two of us stood there, looking at the man's corpse. All of the man's fat had disappeared...I could see every bone in his hand, the cartilage in his nose, and heavy dips where his temples were.

I took the burden of speaking first. "What the hell happened? How's he dead?" Ed tried to speak, but nothing was audible. "Was it poison? A suicide capsule?"

"No..." Ed finally murmured. "I know what killed him, but I need something to make sure." He turned to me, ready to fire a favor. "I need a subject..."

"A subject? Like a rat or something?"

"No, Hale. A person...I need a live person that I can run a few tests on." Ed's favor wasn't the friendliest. Though, with all the dirt under my nails I figured nothing could stain my purity more.

"Okay," I obliged. "I'll get you your subject. But what the hell happened to him?" I pointed in the dead man's direction.

"I..." I knew Ed was keeping it back from me. We had been friends since our first moments in the orphanage, so I knew whatever it was that Ed kept from me, was for my own good. "Just get me that subject...and then I might be able to tell you." After he spoke, Ed whipped around and hurried out of the hall.

I looked close at the dead drug dealer before a rush of chills spread across my body. I too turned and left the room with the holding cells. Barrette was standing outside his office in the beige hallway.

"Is everything alright?" the commissioner asked me after seeing Ed blow right past him. "What happened?"

"That dealer I brought in here the other day..."

"What about him?"

"He's dead," I stated, heavy like a war-hammer.

Barrette's eyes widened. "What? *How?*"

"I don't know...Ed does, but he won't tell me. He wants me to get him a live sample..."

That also took Barrette back. "What the hell has gotten into him?"

I shrugged. "I don't know, but it looks like he has something big. So I'm guessing we should just do as he says…"

Barrette cocked his head over to the elevator doors that had just shut Ed inside. "Poor kid…" he said. "Well," Barrette walked back into his office. "In the meantime, take a look at this." Across his desk, Barrette slid a colored photograph of some building. He waited for me to understand, but the only thing my perspective saw it as was a random building. "That's Toy Palace…"

"What?" I asked so abruptly.

"Yep," Barrette shrugged.

"What do you mean?" Fear was slowly starting to creep into my sentences. "It's done?"

"His men just finished it yesterday. Big Rich is going to be celebrating its grand opening next week…"

"That means Big Rich is going to have another factory to make his Borm in. Once Project Home is complete, he'll be producing Borm twice as much as usual." My hope sunk with my head.

"But isn't that the point of Project Home?" asked Barrette, building to something grander. "To spread it across the entire nation and encapsulate America in his business…?"

I nodded. "I'm afraid so. If that happens," I oppressively released all the air in my lungs. Before I continued, I gathered my breath back. "If that happens I don't see any chance of us stopping the trade. Project Home is Richard's way of immortalizing the business…"

Barrette tightened his entire face in concentration. He bit his thick bottom lip and scratched his hand with the stubble on his chin. "Maybe I should send a squad over to Toy Palace for investigation. If we can bring it down before its grand opening, then Big Rich won't have a chance of producing Borm on that scale."

I asked, "Won't you need a warrant to investigate?"

"Oh…" Barrette's idea was discouraged. "That is true…the God damned system. I would need reasonable evidence if I wanted to storm that place...suspicion isn't enough. Plus," Barrette began saying, "I don't want him to know the police are already on his case."

"Maybe I can help," I suggested. "I'll go take a look and see if I can find anything. If I do, I'll make sure to bring the evidence back to you."

"You find evidence," the commissioner spoke hopefully, then threateningly, "and we'll swarm that place like it's a God damned fort!"

For a split second, I could see this thirst, this glint of desire flaring in Barrette's rosewood eyes. It was temporary, but as he spoke of bringing Big Rich to his knees, there was something propelling his voice.

Barrette was the one person who stood out. Like me, like Ed. When all influence told him to look the other way, Barrette refused. He made sure that they were the blind ones, not him. The commissioner knew what had to be done, and he knew that the deed of necessity was the only one due.

Our plan was set for collapsing Toy Palace. Finding evidence would be as simple as stepping into that God forsaken place. I would take the drugs right from that fraud shop, bring it to Barrette, and together we would cripple Project Home.

Before I left, I said to Barrette, "I have to go get someone for Ed to analyze..."

The commissioner caught my innuendo for a kidnapping. He eyed me with one raised eyebrow. I could tell a struggle took place within him for Barrette not to oppose me. He was sponsoring a crime of his own perception. "Do you have any idea whom you'll snatch?" he defiantly asked.

I had an idea, terrifying and close to unconquerable at first. Mr. O maintained control over the orphanage—he recruited members for the trade and dealt with a majority of Project Home.

That's all the orphanage was—a place to grow people with no family or loved ones. Then they're picked them from their roots and used in the trade. Mr. O and all the authority at the orphanage churned the soil we were planted in, fed us what we thought was love and care. It was when we were picked and thrown in the dirt, under the sun to wrinkle up and die, that we realized everything we had thought to be true was deceit.

Mr. O was a good person to gather information from. The only thing stopping me was the nightmare of going back to that place, but the look on his face when he would see me back from the dead kept my motivation awake.

"I'm going back home," I spoke. Barrette looked at me, asking a question with his eyes. But I said nothing more before I had exited his office, and left the police department.

I headed south down the street lining LA's outskirts. Up north four or five blocks were the rolling stone hills of Crown Cemetery. Directly in front of me (directly west) was the skyline of Los Angeles and the height of Big's Tower.

Out front of the orphanage was a concrete lawn, two windowless stories, and one door; it was not an attractive building. Nausea built up in my stomach and soon in my throat, but a deep breath later I was inside the orphanage. Abandon by any life, the orphanage home was different than when I had left.

Undoubtedly there would be kids in the wake of us graduated orphans. Apathetic toward any expectation, there was nobody. The home was emptied. No Mr. O, no kids, no mediocre chefs. And I couldn't help but wonder what happened to them. Undoubtedly, they were surrendered as slaves for Project Home.

To my right was the large, heavy metal door that hid away all the secrets of the orphanage. I walked up to it and listened for any sound of life inside…

There didn't seem to be anyone. I held my breath, and I could at last hear the tiny sounds of rustling papers behind the door. With a knock on the metal door, Mr. O's voice leaped out at me.

"Who is it?" he asked through the door, loud and aggressively.

I deepened my voice and called back, "I have a delivery…" I

heard Mr. O's heavy steps walk to the door, and, after unlocking several locks, he opened it.

From the quick glimpse I caught at first, the office hadn't changed. Still, the walls were a vacant gray, and a single desk accompanied the room.

There was only one time I was in there, and that was the day I died.

Mr. O did not yet realize the ghost standing in front of him. The shadow on my face was all that held back his recognition. I walked into the office and shoved him inside with a bump of my chest. Mr. O was alarmed by the sudden violence and took refuge behind his desk.

"Hello..." I said, chillingly, to him.

"Who are you?" Since the last time I encountered the almighty Mr. O, he had lost his high standing. Now he seemed like a baby hiding from the monster beneath his bed.

Picking up the side of the desk and tossing it like it was nothing, probably didn't slow his heart rate any. Upside down with its legs stiff in the air, the desk fumbled to the ground, clearing all obstacles between me and Mr. O.

To him, I must have been a mugger looking for a few bucks or something, because when I marched close to him he put up his hands and assured me he wasn't a threat. Even with a loaded gun in his hand, he wouldn't have been a threat to me.

Not sticking my fists right through his chest was a challenge. When I grabbed him by his polo shirt and heaved him against the door behind us, he couldn't help but blink at me, aghast. For those moments, I was unrecognized, but when I removed the hood and revealed my face, his seemed like it wanted to play a game of never-ending hide and seek.

"Hale!" he exclaimed with a missing breath. "I...uh...I thought you were..." Mr. O began a bargain, trying to recreate his innocence he had only at birth.

"Dead? I am...but just like I said, I'm back to haunt you..."

"It's you, isn't it? You're the one who's trying to fuck up all of Big Rich's plans. I...uh...I always knew you were capable of such great things. That's why I chose you in the first place." His charm was defective.

"You chose me so you could use me."

"No. I would never do that...I would never try to use you. You're too handsome and strong to use...it would be a waste," Mr. O swore. "I wanted you to take a stand next to me, that's all!"

"Shut up! Or I'll staple your lips together!" I pushed him against the door harder, shaking him when I yelled.

"What the hell do you want, Hale?" Coincidentally his charm shifted to manipulation. "You're not going to do anything to me. You don't have the guts and we both know that."

"Maybe when I cut you open, you won't have the guts either." I tensed up, maybe from the poison in my veins. I didn't care though; I let it take me over. "I need to know some information, and you're going to help me."

"Oh, *really*? And why should I?"

I slammed my elbow into his collarbone, snapping it like a dried twig. He bellowed and clinched his entire face tight. "Tell me about Toy Palace!"

Even amongst the shock and pain he was experiencing, Mr. O said nothing. I broke his other collarbone. He bellowed once more, and his eyes rolled back into his skull. I shook my head and lugged Mr. O over my shoulder like a sack of blubber.

Now he was a lab rat. I was taking him to Ed to run tests like he had asked. Unfortunately, I couldn't kill Mr. O if I expected him to be of any use to Ed.

Stumped, and not sure how to react, when the police officers saw me dragging Mr. O behind with his feet and wrists tied, they stopped to gawk. He blurted offenses about how much he hated police, and now, how much he hated me. Quick hits to the head shut him up, like flicks to a dog's nose.

"This is your test subject," I said to Ed as I entered the basement and Mr. O stood to his feet.

"Great, you're in on this too?" Mr. O grieved, feeling teamed-up-on.

Ed helped me bind him to a chair to enforce good behavior. He stuck a needle into Mr. O's arm to draw blood, but as it began flowing through the clear tube leading into a small bag, it wasn't a blood red like expected. It had been completely won-over by blue color derived from his addiction to Borm.

"The Borm," both Ed and I thought out loud.

"So Mr. O," Ed started as I tightened the last knot around Mr. O's wrist, "do you use Borm quite frequently?" His answer was spitting in Ed's face. While Ed wiped it away, I hit Mr. O some more. "Do you?" Ed asked again.

"Yes, every day." Finally some cooperation. "Why? Do you want some? We could make a deal!" Ed looked at me to possibly find the humor in Mr. O's comment. Every other thug before Mr. O wished they could buy their way out of trouble. It worked for the government, for the corrupt system, but not for me.

"Stop playing around," I said, taking out my pistol, ready to fire it at his head.

Ed noted his answer and continued surveying. "Where do you get your Borm from? Who's your source?"

"You two really think I'm a fool, don't you. I ain't giving away my source..."

"Fair enough," I said, and cocked the pistol.

"Wait! Wait just a second! I'll tell you." This was a surprise to both of us. "If you untie me." There was the catch.

A single kick pushed the chair over and landed Mr. O on his back. He grunted with a bit of pain and struggled against his bindings.

"Who is your source?" My voice made him flinch.

"Big Rich...it's Big Rich!"

"I know that!" I yelled. "Where do you get your Borm, Mr. O? I know you don't get it directly from Lucifer."

"If I tell you, you have to promise that you didn't hear it from me... okay?" Ed and I agreed that was fair. "Okay, it's Toy Palace...the toys! We smuggle the Borm through the toys and into the store. When it's open, people can come and buy Borm right out of Toy Palace!'"

"I knew it," I said quietly. Mr. O was quick to dampen my note.

"It's funny isn't it; how deceiving we are. How blind *you* are. Toy Palace is merely a factory. We'll be making the Borm there once it's open to the public, and selling twice as much as we ever have! The whole place, it's gonna be one big transaction. No one knows the complete ingredients for Borm, or how to make it. Big Rich is the only one. So, we collect shipments from sources around the globe and take them to the factories where machines take care of the rest. From there, we pack 'em and sell 'em!" Such bragging brought satisfaction to Mr. O. He laughed, and I could see every gold plate of every tooth in his mouth. His caramel colored hair was darkened by grease, thinning with age. "But don't think about stopping it," Mr. O said. "The one down the street from the home, that's just the beginning. We'll be pulling in money, *and* Borm, by the tons." Pleased with himself, he laughed at my uselessness. "You won't stand a chance. We're pulling in a shipment at midnight tomorrow—you're hopeless! You've got nothing! *Nothing!*"

"You don't have to worry about that!" I raised my voice because I knew he might be right.

"You might want to reconsider your...plan."

"Why should I?"

"Killing Big Rich, that won't solve anything. You'll just cause this city even more pain than it deserves." Mr. O closed his eyes like he was relaxed and ready to sleep. "And if those words are coming from me, you know it's true."

"*He's* the one causing this city more pain than it deserves. Him, and people like you."

"I'm just warning you, kid. If you knew more, I know you would reconsider..."

"What do you mean?" I asked him.

"Just let your friend do the tests," Mr. O cut me off from my question.

After that, I never got Mr. O to speak. It was like he was hiding Armageddon in his back pocket. His knowledge was fearfully powerful, even though I didn't know what he knew. Just by the way he spoke, the hints in his tone, the threat in his teeth.

"I'll run the tests when you leave. They should be ready to analyze in a couple of days. Come back then," Ed informed me to do so.

Mr. O's horrible truth took my feet step-by-step to Toy Palace, just down the street from the orphanage home. The giant store wasn't open for business, but the doors were unlocked.

Toy Palace was indeed a palace of a building. Bright red brick compiled every wall of the store, and on the roof, stumps stuck up like a medieval castle. Two smokestacks in the back of the store were dressed, disguised, as two castle towers. Every now and then the smokestacks would burb toxic fumes into the atmosphere.

In a large arc over the entrance, the words TOY and PALACE were strung across, with a giant teddy bear, dressed identical to Big Rich, bursting out of the wall between them, holding its arms open for a friendly hug. Two sliding glass doors opened automatically when any potential customer approached. I walked right up to them, and they gave me prerogative to enter.

Two employees made sure their eyes never left me when I entered the store, considering the many options as to why I might be there. One was approaching me to ask about my unwelcomed presence, but all I did was draw Jay's pistol and hushed him with a threat.

He wisely backed off. "Sir," he said timidly, "you're not allowed to be here."

"Shut up! If you make a move or say a word, I'll fucking kill you." I continued to look around the toy store. "You too!" I threatened the only other employee who was rubbing a wet mop to the hardwood floors.

The inside of Toy Palace was cavernous. The ceilings were as high as the sky and supported, in the corners, by giant wooden squinches. Two sets of stairs curled around a pair of doors and climbed to an entire different second story. All the walls were comprised of wooden shelves, and every wooden shelf was heavily populated with toys.

Could Mr. O have lied? Nothing looked out of place. Ordinary toys and harmless puzzles were all that filled the place. No factory, no Borm, just toys. The beady eyes of the stuffed animals seemed to watch me when I walked, and I tried my best to ignore the toys.

These are just stuffed animals, I thought, approaching a line of turquoise colored bears. *Harmless stuffed animals.*

It was when I noticed the neck of a stuffed animal snapped to the side that Mr. O's words seemed hurtfully honest. If I were in the business of stuffed animal serial killing, I would have assumed this one was murdered. The neck alone didn't stand out to me, but a tube stuffed inside its white cotton. Even the tube wasn't an attention grabber without the blue, gel-like substance inside.

Slowly, I took paranoid steps until I was staring right at the broken toy. I looked behind me at the employees who pretended to be innocent. I took the bear in my grasp and made sure not to remove the glass tube of Borm.

Contraband had been taking place inside of the toys. They were the Borm's ultimate disguise. The Deliverers would take a package of these animals to the orphanage, and no one would look at them twice because they thought nothing more of it. No wonder why Big Rich was a respected, know-to-be charitable figure of LA. Every one of his donations and contributions were all just disguises for his trade.

Knots tied in my stomach when I looked around at all the other toys. To me, their disguises cast by the wicked spells of blindness had all vanished. The cabooses and carts of the trains that ran along the rim of the ceiling all held ounces, and even pounds, of Borm. Not puzzles or building blocks, but Borm cuddled inside of packages that were made for toys. Bouncy balls didn't bounce because they were packed with even more drugs. And when I saw through a bare opening into the back room, I caught the metal arms of machines and conveyer belts all working to produce more and more Borm.

The cashiers swallowed deeply when I looked at them both, suspecting them of their true crime.

"You're all pigs!" I yelled. "Soon, I'll burn this place to the ground, and I hope you burn with it!" Walking out with the crippled toy, I turned my head barely over my shoulder and said, "Make sure your boss knows I'm coming for him. Send my regards, tell him he's dead."

NINE

ARRETTE STOOD ABOVE ALL OF HIS OFFICERS, FASTENING HIS SUIT while the men in uniforms loaded their guns. The commissioner looked nervous, as if he felt all of the officers' judgment melting into his skin.

"Okay," Barrette cleared his throat. "We need to make this quick and clean. Evidence has been found against Mr. Lucifer suggesting that Toy Palace is being used as a lab for drugs. All we need to do is apprehend any employees inside, and seize every bit of Borm we find. If they put up a fight, we'll fight back and prove them guilty. We don't know if there are any weapons in the building, or if Big Rich even knows we're coming. Which is why we need to make this quick! We need to get in and out. Six patrol cars, twelve officers. Three units will post outside of the building and watch for any backup that might be called on us. The other three will follow us," Barrette meant him and me, "into the store. Apprehend anyone in there and seize all manifest."

And then an officer's voice burped from the small crowd listening to Barrette. "He's going with us? The kid isn't even an officer! He doesn't even exist!" The man wailed his fist in the air. "He shouldn't be allowed!"

I stood next to Barrette with my head tipped so none of the golden badges could see my face. Barrette raised his arms to settle the uplifting crowd.

"I'm aware of the circumstance," he told them. "I am plenty aware…" Barrette made eye contact with every pair of searing eyes beaming at him. He pulled his collar away from the hot, clammy skin underneath. Perspiration began to glitter his forehead.

"Send him back to school!" one spat his words at me.

"He's a criminal, not an officer! This is our job!" another yelled. "Not his!"

"Wait 'til he's gone through puberty!"

"We all worked to become officers, he hasn't done shit!"

"Arrest him!"

"Throw him out!"

Barrette was stuck in the onslaught of verbal bullets slamming into him. He looked frantically at the crowd before him. The officers were beginning to unsettle like popping kernels.

He looked at me and I looked at him. We both knew that it was a time to choose a side. I know his reputation wanted Barrette to nod his head toward the officers. I know his social stature advised him to agree with the badges.

But a silent assassin spoke inside of him. He looked at the officers once more, and silenced their childish ranting.

"Shut up!" the commissioner shouted, then fixed his coffee colored suit. "Shut up! All of you! We have a lead, but not because any of you sons-of-bitches discovered it. It was this, *kid*! You're not police officers so you can get paid for sitting around on your asses! There's a criminal inside the walls of this city, and he is going to tear it down if we don't do anything about it! Who cares that he's a kid, who cares that his records are lost? We don't need prejudice molding under our nails right now! We need justice! And justice in any form," clarified the commissioner. "This kid has brought us the most significant case we've had in years, and all you shitheads can do is mock him?"

"He's asking us to attack something that may not even exist," an officer said to Barrette. "The Drug Trade could be a myth..."

"We can choose to disregard it," Barrette spoke softly. Naturally his crowd had to lower their volume to hear the commissioner speak. "We could choose not to believe it..." Barrette was laying

out options in front of the officers so they could see them for themselves. "Or we could transcend, we could rise above the common
person of Los Angeles. Look where they have gotten us! Look how
far this City of Angels has fallen. Now, what are we left with? This
kid has found the heart of this rotting city. Whether or not the
Drug Trade exists, this is our only sliver of justice we can hope
to attain. Do you realize that?" The commissioner looked into
his audience. Every officer looked away. "What do you want?" he
asked them. No answer. "Do you want to stand by and watch your
home shrivel up like it never meant anything? Ever since one, fat
bastard took LA by the neck, we have been afraid to call it our
home. This is our city!" Barrette shouted desperately. "The City of
Angels! It doesn't belong to the crime that has infested its streets!
So whether or not you leave your ignorance behind, you're going to
fight with me because we're all at fault here! We're all guilty. And
if we dare try to bring justice with our own guilt, we had better be
bringing our *own* justice…"

In the last moments of Barrette's speech, he stood before the
officers with tears blurring his vision—little salt water droplets
wadding up in the corner of his eyes. But Barrette suddenly left
the small room.

I followed him out into the department's main hallway. He had
his head in the wall, rubbing the back of his neck with his hands.
At his feet was a small, shallow puddle of tears. I heard him snif-
fling and breathing with trembling motions.

"Oh God…" he said either to himself or to me. "What has
happened? Where has justice gone? The city's own officers can't
manage to find it…Now who's left to decide when, where, and who
justice is brought to?"

"Barrette…" My voice was spongy. "You don't have to do this…
this, this crazy thing…it's my deal. Not yours…and, whether it is
justified or not, I'm going to kill Big Rich. I'm going to stop Project
Home…but I can't expect anyone else to understand that. My best
friend, a man who I looked up to like a father, was murdered under

Richard's hand. *I* was killed by Big Rich...I was killed by the Drug Trade."

Barrette said nothing for a while, but eventually he stood and looked over at me standing beside him in the beige, color swallowing hallway. His eyes were irritated red, and glossy with tears.

He opened his mouth and asked me, so forwardly, "Who the hell are you?" Barrette wanted an answer—a true, raw answer.

Now I was caught under the weight of his question and words. Like I was deaf and mute, I stood lifelessly. But inside there was a rush of thought. Who was I? What did I want? I figured as my life's own narrator I would already have those answers in stock.

With one last ounce of consideration, I reached my hand up and pulled off the hood on my head. It was the first time Barrette had seen my face: My blue eyes and pitch hair lying with sharp points on my head, my pale skin and kind yet rigid face. It was the best answer I could have given Barrette, but I added more spice.

Lifting my hand for a shake, I introduced myself. "Alexander Hale," I said to the commissioner. "My name is Alexander Hale."

"Conner," the commissioner told me. "Commissioner Conner Barrette."

Our handshake was interrupted by the voice of an officer. "Commissioner," the man said. Barrette looked over to the officer standing in the doorway of the conference room. Behind him stood several more layers of golden badges, waiting. "We're ready."

Before anyone else could absorb the personable features of my face, I returned the hood and shadow to my head. Immediately, my persona had changed.

Grateful, Barrette nodded his head and wiped away the last of his tears. "Okay!" he shouted, fully back in command. "Load up! Six squad cars, twelve officers! Travel in pairs and be careful...we don't know what's waiting for us."

At the ending lift of Barrette's words, the officers scrambled and exited the police department. We had left the beige abyss of the station, but outside was no less of a nightmare.

The sun had been an oversized, moldy tangerine vomiting its heat and must upon every square-inch of Los Angeles. And the sky had been a fool to lose its brilliance against such a melted opponent. Everything, all the buildings and neighborhoods, every street and person about those streets had been suffocated in the haze's thick, rusty color—a desert fog which filled the lungs of its walkers with grains and dust so tiny, but so obviously there to choke on.

Only thirty minutes east was God's biggest gulp of water, and still, my lips were chapped, my tongue was cracked and split just as the pavement of the road was. Sometimes on the 'hottest' days, I would believe that the heat was beneath my skin, slithering through my veins; a molten serpent.

Just as the commissioner had ordered, the officers spread themselves into six cruisers with Sirens on top and LAPD stenciled onto the side. I took a seat next to Barrette in a car that wasn't as uniformed.

Barrette put his hands on a steering wheel that belonged to a vehicle just as beige as the department's hallway. He spoke through a transmitter hooked to his car and wired to all the others.

"Toy Palace is south of Downtown LA. We need to post around the corner until we're all together." Before he could put it down Barrette had to clarify, "Don't let anyone know we're coming. Remember, quick and clean. Over." He released the button of the transmitter and started his car.

As we pulled away, my eyes hooked to the man in the dark coat and hat. He stood on the side of the road, watching me, standing still like he had been waiting for all of us to exit the police station. Even under the light of day, I couldn't see his eyes or face. Just empty sockets it seemed. The man watched me as Barrette drove off. And until he was gone beneath the horizon, the mysterious man pinned his eyes right to my face.

We had been driving for a few minutes when the silence between us grew louder and louder. I had to deceive my classic demeanor and speak. "Do you have a family, Barrette?"

I was hoping I didn't just start a conversation that would lead to a tragic story and then to the reason why Barrette had devoted his life to criminal justice.

Barrette kept his eyes on the road but said, easily, to me, "No. Not anymore. My mother died long ago when I was a child. Illness," he specified, "not murder or anything like that. She was sick...so I guess you *could* say Cancer murdered her." The commissioner paused to rummage through the useless and plentiful parts to his past memories. "My father was a police officer. A good one, too. He's the one who inspired me to become an officer...I never would have guessed it would come to this. I don't think I would have taken the job if I knew it would be this way..." I looked away and studied the bland dashboard right above my legs. "He died a long time ago too. When I was just a kid."

"Illness?" I asked.

"Oh, no," he responded politely. "*He* was murdered. It was an ordinary day on the job. In a way, I feel guilty knowing that it was his last time getting out of bed that morning. He kissed me and my mom goodbye, and told us that he would be home for dinner..."

"He was *murdered*?"

"Yes," Barrette answered without the slightest bit of rage in his voice.

I could tell that Barrette wasn't the one to hold a grudge over anyone's head. He was the kind of guy who held all optimism to mankind. To me, that was a foolish perspective. After seeing what man was content on doing, after seeing that a heart so stone exists, it was impossible for me to be optimistic. I'm not even sure I was hopeful. But I knew I wasn't alone. The only explanation for a city this bad was hopelessness.

"What did you do?" I asked the commissioner who was becoming more and more human to me.

"Well, I was ten," he said back. "There wasn't much I could do. My mother hadn't died yet, so I still had her...but as soon as she figured out that she had Cancer, the story changed. I remember her screaming at nothing, just the wall in front of her. Even as a kid, I knew she had lost hope. I swear I could taste her bitterness..." Ashamed at his own mother and maybe at the people who provoked her change, Barrette shook his head and tightened his jaw. "And I remember the day when I walked into her bedroom and saw her hanging from the ceiling..."

The phrase caught me off-guard. I leaned away from Barrette instinctively. "I thought you said Cancer killed her..."

"Not *real* Cancer, Alex. It was my mother's anger; it grew like a tumor inside of her, and eventually...it killed her."

I was angered by someone else's story. "Those sons-of-bitches!" I snarled meanly. "Not only did those punks kill your father, but they killed your mother!" I punched the dash board and cratered a large dent in it.

Barrette began to laugh like I had just told a joke. He looked at me, and laughed harder. I swear that tears began to build in his eyelids. He continued laughing for a long while until my heavy breathing weakened.

"Oh, kid," he said, trying not to laugh...failing. "You see, that's what I thought at first too! I wanted to punch holes in the wall! I wanted to scream at the top of my lungs!" He laughed quietly, softly, soundly. "But then I saw my mother hanging there by her neck. Her eyes were open and I looked into them. I could see the flames in her pupils that continued burning even after she had been extinguished. Then I realized, the same anger I was feeling, was the same anger that killed my mother. It was the only reason she was hanging there from the ceiling..."

The commissioner left room for me to talk. He wanted me to either listen to, or ignore what he had just said. I said nothing back. His story was different than mine...Jay was murdered by Big Rich, *I* was murdered by Big Rich!

"It's just like Lucifer's son..." Barrette spoke again.

"What do you mean?" I didn't understand the relation.

"He was so angered by his father's business and choices...he was

probably neglected and made to feel like the trade was more important to Big Rich than his own son." Barrette paused. He wanted me
to understand the rest. He turned to see if I was following, but had
to finish. Barrette decided to sum it up and said, directly to me,
"You *burn* in your own fire." The commissioner stared at me for a
while, looking for that little glint of evil in my eyes.

We had tunneled through the mangled roots of the city and
broke through to the other side. A few blocks on the outskirts was
Toy Palace, just down the street from the orphanage home I grew
up in, and a few miles from Ed's and Raine's place.

Barrette returned his voice to the transmitter. "Okay, boys," he
said like he was a general in a war, "here' s what we're going to do.
Squad cars A B and C, cover the entrance. Form a three-point-block
outside of Toy Palace. The rest of you will enter the store with me
and…" Barrette turned to me, trying to collect a name, "…Phoenix,"
he finalized. I slapped him with the most querulous look. "Have your
firearms ready and your finger on the trigger. If you see anyone with a
weapon, you have permission to engage the suspect. Squads A B and
C, have your rifles drawn to the entrance in case anything gets out of
hand. Open fire at any attackers coming from the outside."

We could see all the officers in the squad cars ahead of us nodding their heads. One by one they confirmed their order over the
radio, and we were ready to proceed.

"Toy Palace is a block ahead of this. Quick and clean, boys!
Quick and clean! Let's go!"

Like impatient bulls waiting in their stalls, the gates opened and
the squad cars wheeled out of park. All six of them raced toward
Toy Palace, with me and the commissioner keeping up behind.

"You ready for this, Phoenix?" Barrette screamed over the
excitement, uncontrollably laughing from the adrenalin in his
veins. "You ready?"

We were just a few doors down from Toy Palace (the cruisers
ahead of us were already screeching to a halt, forming their positions) when an explosion ignited right in front of our car.

All I saw was a ball of orange and black erupting from the concrete. The commissioner's car drove over the explosion, but its raging force lifted the two ton vehicle off the street and tossed it to the side.

We were barreling through the air and whipping around inside the cruiser as it flipped several times along its side. The windshield cracked and the side windows broke out all over my face and into my eyes. The ceiling crumpled inward toward us, leaving no room for Barrette or me to move our heads.

It was like the car would never stop moving. I heard the shattering of more glass, and when the car finally came to a violent stop I saw the interior of a shop neighboring Toy Palace.

I heard Barrette wincing painfully next to me. Blood from my face began dripping on the ceiling of his car—we were upside down, hanging in our seats. Another explosion erupted on the street outside. Then another. Giant booms belching fire.

"Barrette! Barrette are you okay?" I tried to turn and look, but my head was stuck and the crumpled ceiling broke our sight from each other. Barrette didn't answer. "Commissioner Barrette! Are you alright? Can you hear me?"

I struggled to unbuckle my seatbelt, but couldn't get enough leverage or find enough space to move my arms. Blood continued to drip onto the ceiling, and soon there was a pool of blood growing deeper and deeper right at the tips of my hair.

"God damn it! Barrette!" I finally manage to unbuckle my seatbelt. When I did, I fell right into my own pond of warm, red blood.

My spine was curled, my body was crushed into a little ball and I brought my feet down to the same level as my head. Like a crab, I formlessly crawled feet first through the shattered window of my seat.

I exited the vehicle and dropped to my back. When I lifted my head up, looked down the rest of my body and saw the violence out on the street, I was finally able to process what had happened.

The commissioner's car had tumbled through a wide window into a small wedding dress shop.

Mannequins were knocked to their sides and dirtied with char or grease from the car. Glass powder overtook the carpet and the metal frames of the shop's window were mangled and deformed. I didn't take much time to look out on the street before I turned around to the car.

Its belly was facing the ceiling, and the entire rest of the vehicle was crushed and damaged far beyond repair. Oil and grease and all other kinds of the cruiser's fluids were dripping out onto the carpet.

I looked back into my window to see if I could spot Barrette. I called for his name once more, and still, no response. "Hold on, Barrette!" I called in case he could hear me.

Like navigating through a junkyard in the middle of a battlefield, I crawled around the car to the driver's side. Explosions lit the wall of the small shop every time they boomed out on the street. I could hear endless rounds of gunshots popping, and the voices of officers crying.

I was on my hands and knees looking into the driver's side window when I saw Barrette hanging motionlessly just as I was. "Barrette..." I called a little bit softer now that I was right in his ear. "Barrette wake up...come on, commissioner, wake up..." Careful not to reinjure any broken bones or marks on Barrette, I shook his shoulder lightly.

His eyes popped open and their whites were the only clean part on his body. Frantically he looked around inside the wreckage. His instincts told him to struggle, but I told him to remain still.

"No, no, no! Stay there, commissioner. Don't move..." I peeked over the car to the war out front.

"What...what happened?" he asked me, trying to stay calm.

"We..." I couldn't even answer the question, but when I saw more outside, I began to understand.

Officers were ducking behind their cars, firing their rifles at men on roofs across from Toy Palace. Others battled thugs with guns in the street. It was obvious that Big Rich knew we were coming, and didn't want us to see inside Toy Palace. But how did he know?

"We were ambushed." I was finally able to articulate. "We were ambushed my Big Rich's men! Are you okay?"

He looked around at himself and concluded, "I'm fine, I'm fine. Go help my officers!"

"But, sir..."

"Just go! I'll get myself down from here, okay?" I looked at Barrette—his face, too, was covered in drips of blood slowly streaking down his skin. "Go!" he ordered. "I'll be out in a second!"

I didn't argue. As fast as I could I climbed over the wrecked vehicle and out into the street. Black rings expanded on the asphalt from where some explosions detonated. A few other police cars rested on the sidewalks with burning trunks or engines.

On the roof of a building directly across from Toy Palace, a man lugged a large, cylinder shaped weapon over his shoulder. A rocket launcher, I could tell from watching any war movie or action flick. He had jammed one more missile into its loading chamber and aimed it at a stationed cruiser providing cover for three officers.

I looked at them...and the rocket launcher...them...and the rocket launcher.

I saw the thug with the missile close one eye and steady an aim over the cruiser, then I picked up my speed toward the three officers who had no idea about how close their deaths were.

"Move!" I screamed and cried and shouted as loud as I could. "Move!" They looked over to me, sprinting toward them, waving them away with my hands screaming, "Move!"

But just when the officers noticed the man on the rooftop, he had launched the rocket. It traveled so fast, with a white, smoky tail streaming behind it. The cruiser was gone, and now a fiery demon lifted into the air from where it once was.

The force of the explosion threw me far back. I skidded along the asphalt and rolled around for a while before fully stopping. Debris from the cruiser landed all around me and the street like metal hail or comets. A terrible ringing screamed inside my ears, and no matter how hard I willed it, the buzzing wouldn't subside.

My orientation was completely thrown off. I thought that up was down and left was right. I rolled onto my back and faced the orange sky. Then I saw the dark silhouette of a thug, and next the bottom of his foot.

The force of his stomp would have crushed my skull like an egg if I hadn't caught his foot with both of my hands. He continued to fight me and push down against my arms' strength.

I tightened my grip on his ankle and rolled him to the side. He hit the concrete and I saw a small handgun clatter away from him. I jumped to my feet quicker than he could, lifted my foot above his head, and stomped on his skull.

Just as I had thought, it broke just like an egg. His skull was a thick shell, and his oatmeal brain was now a yolk.

I bent down and took his gun. When I came back up, there was already another thug racing toward me with his fists drawn. I raised the gun in his direction and pulled back on the trigger. It jumped in my hand and nearly threw my entire arm back. I thought I missed, but when I redirected my sight from a flinch I saw the thug fall to his knees, then his face.

Behind me, though, was another eager punk looking to win in a brawl. I turned and looked right into his punch. My reflexes had grown keener, so I was able to block it on the first try. His arm stopped midflight, and I rammed the metal gun right into his face. Every bone broke inward.

In a jagged, uneven circle around me were approaching thugs. I was now the biggest opponent. They were all taking it slow, trying to savor my meat. Noticeably, the circle around me began to shrink.

My experience in shooting a gun was amateur, but I knew I didn't need a polished badge or specialized training to point and shoot. As long as the thugs weren't immune to the bullets of my gun, the hope of me actually hitting them was enough.

So I began.

I swiveled to my right and steadied the gun over my first victim's chest, and pulled the trigger. To my left, I shot at another man's head. Behind me, another got a bullet in his leg. I felt like I was on a rotating platform shooting a pellet gun at targets in a carnival.

The gun made me flinch hard each time it fired. It threw my arm around like a strong man winning an arm wrestle against me. Its power scared and thrilled me at the same time.

A guilty pleasure, a satisfied craving, a quenched thirst.

As I shot them, I watched the men die all around me, but they didn't fall easily unless a bullet pierced their skulls. It was like the pain of every shot fired was useless. It was like none of the men felt the burning bullets penetrating their bodies. And each time I shot them, little squirts of blue would burst from their wounds.

Soon, though, with the help of every other officer, I stood in the middle of a corpse gathering, soaking my feet in blood. I looked down and saw myself in the blue violet reflection.

My face was gone. Only a shadow was there to either greet or intimidate those who I approached. I saw the glint of evil Barrette watched for…but it was satisfying. I enjoyed the fear I could bring over people, and seeing it in myself was most pleasant.

Then I noticed the silence filling in around me just as the blood at my feet had.

I looked up at the street infested with bodies and mangled metal, marked with scars and burns. The remaining officers had finished the last of the thugs. I saw their bodies lying in the gutters and in the middle of the street.

They all looked at me standing in the middle of the bloody body pile. Each officer calculated the amount of lives they collected, and measured them to the amount I had at my own two feet. Then I think they saw it; they saw the evil burning like a kindle in my eyes.

I looked back down at myself in the reflection and looked into my own eyes. There wasn't much color anymore. The electrical blue in my irises had faded, dimmed into a color nearing black.

My face was scratched all over—my eyebrow was split open, same with my lips. And inside my mouth, both rows of teeth were stained red from the blood I was swallowing. Lines of blood had dried on my face from when I was hanging upside down in the car.

Barrette! I remembered and thought to myself. I turned over to the small shop our car had rolled into. There Barrette stood, staring just like every other officer was. His face was battered and bloody too, but nothing like mine.

His eyes rolled around the death bed of all the thugs and fallen officers, the burning vehicles and the holes in nearly every building around. His head dropped and shook, hanging. Barrette turned around, and walked in the other direction, building distance between him and the warzone.

TEN

I WATCHED ED EXAMINING SPECIMENS UNDER HIS MICROSCOPE AND shuffling papers over and over again like they were never in place. Cursing and stressing at himself, Ed finally passed out over the table, or at least wished he did.

With his mouth pressed against the top of the table, he spoke, but I couldn't understand what he was saying. Just mumbling noises drooling from the corners of his mouth.

When I didn't respond at all, he lifted his head—eyes bloodshot and skin loose with patterns of the table pressed into his cheek—and despised, "This is impossible…"

"What is?" I asked him.

"I'm trying to break the formula of Borm down to its essential elements. But every time I get close, I run out of samples. If I expect to get *anywhere* with this, I'm going to need a lot more Borm…" Ed looked at me, and I could see the favor fizzing in his eyes. He would soon ask me to go fetch more Borm for him.

Regardless of my lazy attitude toward it, I asked Ed, "How much do you need?"

His eyes sorted through the mess on his table, scanning what he had, didn't have, and needed. After he tossed a few guesses around in his head, then mixed them with a bit of logic, Ed turned to me and replied with a number, "Just one pound. I don't need much, but I can't proceed without it. I know Barrette has been having his men keep an eye on a few places around the city—dispensaries for Borm. But you would never be able to pick one out from many other building. Big Rich keeps them pretty far beneath the radar. All Barrette had to do was talk around." As I stood there with both hands in the pockets of my hoodie, Ed removed a slip of paper from beneath a stack of others. He handed it to me and explained, "It's a bar a few blocks away from Big's Tower called the Broken Diadem. There's a Borm dispensary in the back of the building, but I'm guessing they're not just going to let you saunter in there..."

"I'll get it for you," I complied. "Once you've created Borm yourself, what are you going to do with it?"

Ed seemed startled by the question. Quickly, he straightened his back to a rigid stiffness and cocked his head toward me with a single jerky motion. "What?" he asked, even when he heard me. "Um...nothing," Ed told me. "This is just to figure out how it's made...nothing else..."

I waited to see if silence could ring any more words out of Ed, but he never spoke again. "Okay," I said, and turned around to exit the basement. "I'll be back soon with the Borm." Ed nodded his head and returned to his work, finally letting loose his rigid posture. "Oh, yeah," I said before entering the opening elevator, "where is Mr. O?" I asked.

"He's upstairs in a holding cell. Barrette's detaining him here until I'm done running my tests. The quicker you bring me those samples, the quicker we can send him to county," Ed hinted at my speedy return. I nodded my head, and stepped inside the elevator.

Along with the outstretched yard of Crown Cemetery and the decaying stubs of houses that molded along the outskirts of Downtown LA, was the police department—an isolated building full of isolated ideals. At its front doors, I could see the peak of Big's Tower rising above the flattened tops of the city's every other building. I stood there looking at the tower, wondering what kind of view one would have of the city from so high above. Would a scarred, filthy labyrinth of empty buildings and broken windows, bare lawns and sidewalks of garbage and blue blood, suddenly become a beautiful landscape of refined architecture, elegant spills of green parks and a glittery puddle completing the western horizon and filling the depths of Earth.

The sun was directly above me, sitting at noon. Though the ball of fire wasn't well pronounced against the rusted sky, I could tell, by a bright glare through the haze, where it was. The hood on my head shaded my eyes from the glare, but the hoodie hugging my arms and chest intensified the heat. I felt that my skin was a wax, and slowly, I was melting away. Soon, I imagined, I would be a puddle dressed in dark apparel and a pair of jeans.

As I walked my way into the city's labyrinth of blocks and streets, I fastened the leather gloves to my hands and prepared the rage inside me to spark a brawl. The Broken Diadem, as Ed said, was not a building to draw any attention out of the ordinary. It was squashed beneath a skyscraper of apartments and lofts.

A yellow neon sign sketched the outline of a crown, scarred down the middle by a nasty crack. Any knowledge educated about the Drug Trade would spot the insignia from blocks away. I stood on the sidewalk opposite of the bar, fumbling any sort of plan. All I had to do was get the Borm, and get back to Ed.

But when I crossed the street and pushed through the windowless doors of the bar, any sort of slyness I wished to attain was immediately lost. As the doors shut behind me, every pair of dilated eyes slowly crawled over to my direction. Every drinker at the bar, gamer at the pool tables and diner at the round tables stuck a scowl to me. Whether or not they were aware of my specific persona, every member in that bar could sense my misplacement in the Broken Diadem.

No natural light was let into the bar. To the left was the wooden topped counter of a bar capable of seating about ten drinkers on highly elevated stools. Beyond the counter and behind the bar tender were shelves designated completely for the numerous bottles of liquor and syrups. A series of round tables occupied the right side of the bar. In the corner of the dining section hung the boxiest television which was barely capable of producing a single image.

And in the deepest section of the bar pushed into the far back, was a bare collection of pool tables, and an even poorer collection of drunks with cues in their floppy hands.

No one, not even me, said a word. I stood there for only a while longer before slowly walking to an open seat at the bar. I sat myself between two thick drunks who reeked of nothing but whiskey and alcohol. I looked to my right: A man with two chins, bubbly cheeks and the attempt of a mustache turning his skin into fuzzy sandpaper.

He brought a tiny glass of colorless liquor to his mouth, drinking away the nothingness in his pockets. Now he dips below zero, finding a way to empty himself even more.

And to my left was a man who pursed his lips to the round mouth of a bottle dyed brown. He burped after every gulp, then took another immediately after. I looked over at him, and he looked back at me with eyes enameled by a noticeable layer of drunkenness. He returned his eyes forward and his mouth to the bottle.

The bar tender clanked a bottle at my hands crossed over each other on the counter. I looked up at him through the shadow of my hood. "It's on the house," he said to me, and proceeded to cracking open the lids of even more bottles. In front of my hands, as well as the brown bottle, was an ash tray, filled with half smoked Borm wraps and their ashes.

I took the bottle into the leather palm of my hands, but never brought it to my mouth. Instead, I looked back to my right at the man sipping at his whiskey. Far behind him in the distant background was a small rectangular frame pushed into the wall. Beyond that was the Borm dispensary Ed told me about. The whiskey sipper took a glance at me, and I brought my head up so the dimmed light spread a ray across my eyes. He could see the rage within them, the craving that he knew I was about to settle.

The man made a defense motion, a reach for his pocket. Quicker, though, I pulled back my arm with the bottle in hand and slapped it across his face so hard that it cracked over his cheek, and a scatter of broken glass carved his skin. He surged backward out of his stool, crashing to his back on the floor.

With the glass dagger in my hand, I lashed my arm to the left, splitting the skin of the man's throat. As the wound broke open, a rush of blue blood burst out his body and hit me in the face. His hands shot up toward his throat to hold the cut together. I stood, gripped the legs of the empty stool to my right, and spun back around, smashing it across the bleeding man's back. He jerked forward, breaking his skull against the counter's surface.

Behind me (as I saw when I turned around) was a layer of customers building an unbreakable line, preventing a clean escape. I simply said to them, to all of them, "I'm looking for some Borm. Tell me where it is and I'll leave without hurting anymore of you…"

None of them trusted my aggression. Many of them laughed to each other—little hisses of chuckles snaked through the crowd surrounding me. Still, no one answered. I saw a quick motion ignite to my left, and as I looked, a fist was burrowing its way into my cheek. The punch threw me to the side, but I caught myself on the bar counter then slowly returned to full stand above six feet. A small man was standing before me, readying himself to throw a second punch. He flared his teeth, just as all of my other opponents had before him. After a quick cry, the man fired a second punch at me.

This time, though, I caught the attack by the man's forearm, and watched for a moment as an instant surprise settled on his face. With my left hand, I wrung him by his neck, lifted him a foot from the ground, and, like a lead filled doll, hurled him into the layer of drunks. They all yowled, and some were taken to the floor by the thrown man.

Another attacker was already charging me, breaking through the layers of men. The skin over my knuckles nearly split when I barreled my fist into his face. But I couldn't yet find rest—to my right was still a fourth opponent with an ego swollen and mistaken enough to think that he could beat me. He ducked under my first swing, but as he hurried himself closer to my reach, I felt for a glass or bottle of any sort sitting on the counter to my side. I smashed a cup of clear liquor across one side of his face. Behind me, I filched a Borm wrap from an ash tray, and ignited a personal blazon on the man's face as I touched it to him. He shrieked loudly with a high pitch, and hurled himself around, trying to extinguish the flame spreading across his head. Just as he had pushed his way through the wall of men, he forced his way back out.

I heard the rushing air of an approaching, attacking man behind me. Blindly, I shot my leg outward—flattening the bottom of my boot to his diaphragm, collapsing it inward, disabling his balance. He was blown off his feet by the gust of my kick. His grunt was cut short, and just like the man I had previously thrown, he tumbled through the crowd.

There was hardly any time to react when I returned forward, and a man's foot was rushing into my stomach. Again, I was thrown into the bar counter, but before he could raise a fist, I charged forward, grasping the cloth of his shirt, carrying him along with my unstoppable sprint. I screamed loud, exhorting as much fury as I could.

The line of people in front of me and my train-like dash parted, making room for me to continue forcing the man in my hands forward. His spine bent backward over the edge of a pool table. A horrible crack snapped from his spine and popped in the air. Every person in the bar heard it, and as his back broke, they each winced loudly. I pulled back my right fist, and wrecked it into the bone of his face.

From behind, a pair of burly arms (covered in tattoos and wiry hair) wrapped themselves around me. The grip began to tighten, and as my lungs were unable to intake air, I thrust my head backward, colliding with my capture's nose and brow bones. But the single strike didn't loosen his arms. I, again, thrust my head backward, then, with the sharp heel of my boot, stomped on the man's right foot. Beneath the strength of my every attack, his bones broke, both on his face and foot. I spread my arms, prying apart his metal hug. Several pool balls sat still on the table, and while whipping my body around to face him, I snatched one. And upon arrival to facing my new attacker, I swung the ball to make impact with his left temple.

There was a quick flash beside me, and I saw the stick of a pool cue swinging toward me like an anorexic baseball bat. I leaned backward, dodging the attack. As the cue swung past my face, I heard and felt the air warp around me from the speed of the strike.

The tip of the cue made impact with the pool table. I chopped my forearm across the middle of the stick, and as it snapped in half, I took the top end like the handle of an elongated blade. It was easy to penetrate the man's soft belly with the wooden point of the broken cue. His eyes widened to large circles as the cue stick stabbed him, and a gurgle of blood later, the man was dropping to the floor.

I held the broken cue in my hand, and fended off the other men who threatened to leap forward. Back and forth, I swung the wooden spear like I was fending off a pack of coyotes with a torch made from nothing but a tree branch, animal fat, and an unrealistic spark ignited from two rocks. And unrealistic was the most realistic word I can use to describe the brawl. Still, there were more than ten of them, and only one of me.

Each of their mouths were made foamy by the white saliva puffing around their lips. They all craved my blood, I could tell. But the future I saw didn't consist of that bar smeared over by my crimson colored blood, but the blue, Borm ridden blood of each and every one of them.

Although I didn't show it, and although I never backed down like they had hoped, I was horrified by the combination of Borm addicts and drunks. Those with more Borm than alcohol in their system felt invincible, and were numb to any great pain I could bring to them. But those who were piloted by the deliriousness of booze had no logic, no common sense, thus no limits to what they could do.

I was one kid with a stick in my hands. There was a weight sagging in my pocket, and I knew exactly what it was. Before the men had a chance to take advantage of the disproportionately sided feud, I ripped Jay's gun from the depth of my pocket, and the mere sight of it flashing before their eyes cleared room around me.

I said once again with a hollow voice of omnipotent boom, "I'm looking for some Borm—tell me where I can find it!"

"Put the gun down kid," began the coax of a man who stood closest to me, showing me the palms of his hands. "Put the gun down..."

I marched up to him and grabbed the man by the collar of his shirt, yanking him close to my face then digging the barrel of the pistol into the soft flesh beneath his chin. His head was pushed up and back, and he looked at me from the tops of his bottom lids.

"I'll blow your God damned brains out. Tell me where the Borm is," I promptly ordered again. He could smell, feel and see the patience fading within me.

He simply extended an arm tipped with a slim finger, pointing toward the back room I had previously seen. "Back there!" he cried. "Back there!" I ejected him out of my grasp, sending him into the arms of men who still persisted on threatening more of a fight.

I walked backward toward the room, clearing my way with the aim of my gun. Occasionally, I jutted my head over my shoulder to see if any sly opponent was creeping up behind me. Soon, though, I had backed myself into a small room painted white and lit with LED tubes lining the longer walls of its rectangular shape.

There was a door hanging open, and as I fully entered the small storage space, I swung it shut, and listened to the click of the locks as they sealed me inside. When I turned, two faces were baffled, staring at me with ghostly eyes that could not comprehend anything. And then I saw what had possessed them—the two keepers each held half empty bottles of pure Vodka, and between them both, two used Borm sticks and a box of matches. They weren't a threat at all. The two just watched as I pillaged my eyes through the shelves of Borm.

The Borm was contained in glass tubes. Their color was truly electrical and vivid without ever being exposed to air. Plus, the LED lighting intensified their stun.

I took two bottles from one rack, and shoved the pound of Borm into my pocket. The two men were still flossing their eyes around me, unable to truly process the situation. I walked up to them, and neither of the men flinched or leaned away.

Like stealing candy from a baby, I took the two bottles from their hands, picked up the matchbox from between them, retreated Jay's gun back into my pocket, and readied myself to reenter the bar full of awaiting drunks and addicts. I knew that they were ready to rip me apart, ready to slaughter the adolescent stealing their treasure.

So (as ready as I would ever be), I pulled open the door, and once again I was standing before a stirred mob of slanted eyes and lips that refused to hideaway the sharp teeth behind them. With one bottle in each hand, I spread my arms outward at my hip, revealing my useless arsenal of weapons. Some of them smiled after realizing the pleasure they would bask in while killing me.

I rolled one of the clear bottles across the floor in front of me, out of the small room and through the parting crowd of men. They watched as the bottle rolled by, spilling Vodka out across the floor, tracing its path with the liquid.

When they returned their sight to me, I had the second bottle above my head, ready to chuck it. And, as expected, I threw the last bottle from my hand, and it precisely landed where the rolling bottle had stopped. It shattered, and soaked most of the area with alcohol, including some of the men's feet. None of them had yet understood my tactic, but when I pulled a single match from the scavenged box, and scraped it across the rough textured sheet along the box's side, their imaginations began to speak and run wild.

The flame ignited on the end of the small matchstick, and very slowly, lowering all suspense and drama with me, I bent down, and touched the flame to the small trail of Vodka. Precisely following immediate contact, a spine of flames rose and raced toward the puddle where it was allowed to expand into a dancing bon fire of orange and yellow and blue flames.

All of the men around the puddle jumped backward, avoiding as much as a scolding as they could. While their distraction was most prominent, I made a foolish, yet desperate dash across the trail of flames, through the fiery gathering, and out the other side.

I broke through the strength of two men standing behind the residing fire. They fell backward, but I preserved the speed and force of my inertia until flying through the Broken Diadem's front doors, and hasting myself onto the sidewalk.

The drunks and addicts quickly escaped the bar, skipping their eyes from one pacing face to another, hoping that they could find me. But there were too many people flowing past the bar, and eventually, they accepted the damage done and the stolen Borm.

I was out of breath, leaning my back against the brick wall of an alley. I retrieved the two stolen tubes of Borm from my pocket, and looked at the gel inside. Like I was treating it to the fullest inspection, I rotated the tube around in my hand, but eventually released a swell of breath, closed my eyes, and thanked my own self for escaping alive.

When I returned to Ed, I slapped the two bottles to the granite surface of his table and spoke with an uneasy tone, "Those better be worth the trouble I went through to get them."

Ed scurried his eyes across the table to the tubes, and his hands quickly followed. "Thank you!" he jollied. "And don't worry, I'll make it worth it. This is going to help immensely." He uncapped one bottle, and looked at me for a moment until he was done saying, again, "Thank you."

I nodded my head, but gave him no verbal acknowledgement of his graciousness. I asked him, anyway, "What are you using them for, exactly?"

He answered with the most elastic words, and without making eye contact. "I'm just doing a bit of research. You know," continued Ed, "it's interesting."

"Come on, Ed. Why won't you tell me?"

"It's nothing," he swore without even parting his lips. "I promise…"

Nothing in his voice sounded stronger than a termite. "Ed…" I knelt down to match the level of the table, and morphed the tone of my voice as if I were talking to a toddler. "What's going on?" I asked the same question with different words.

"Nothing," Ed answered with louder, more abrupt speech. "At least, I don't know if it's anything…"

I asked, "What does that mean?"

"I think I found something in the drug that could be very important, very influential in your decision to kill Big Rich." He squeezed a drop of the Borm sample onto a glass slate, and slid it beneath his microscope. "I can't be sure right now, but hopefully, after I'm done doing some more tests, I can be certain."

"What else do you think is in the drug?" Without the hope of a direct answer, I asked Ed anyway.

"Like I said," he began to explain, "I can't be certain right now, so I think it's best that my suspicions are *only* my suspicions. Besides, you have enough to worry about. Look at this, though…" He took a drop of blood from a bag that had been refrigerated. As soon as he let the droplet fall into the tiny amount of Borm, it was completely absorbed. The Borm lost its pure blue color just a bit and held a tint of violet. "The Borm is like a dry sponge to blood. It doesn't take much for a user to replace their entire blood supply with this stuff…"

"Wouldn't that kill them?"

"No," Ed answered, amazed. "It seems that the Borm is capable of completely substituting for a human's blood. The drug provides its user with nutrients, and the advantages, as well as disadvantages, that are most commonly found in steroids."

"Then what's so bad about it? What are you trying to keep from me?"

"Trust me," Ed requested kindly, "just wait until I have a solid conclusion."

I trusted Ed's protection, and decided not to pursue a permanent answer anymore. Truth, it seemed, was much more brutal and bullying than one would ever hope it to be. At least that's the way I saw it. I knew that the truth was bitter and out of control, and I knew that it was merciless.

In a way, beyond my preference for truth never to fully enter my life, I found myself as its own personification. The criminals of LA, the criminals of the world cannot be petted and nurtured bysociety's tolerance. Much too often does it take advantage of tolerance, then shreds it apart like a little girl's doll. Justice, if it ever expected to be the victor in life's trapping arena, had to be merciless, just as crime was.

Otherwise, fighting crime with tolerance molding over my knuckles would be like fencing with a stick against a double-edged sword. And though morality would never be fully perceived through society's eyes, I couldn't allow myself to become a suspect in its demise.

Most of LA's occupants lived in bliss—some by choice, and others by a lack of experience. I was only seventeen when I knew my life would end as I put a bullet through Big Rich's eyes, yet, I saw through a pair of aged eyes, a lens of perception brutally stripped raw by crime's mercilessness. Of course a charter school boy born beneath the rain of old money, pampered by the delicacies of gold, rotted by ungratefulness of life could never find justice in murder, violence or rage. But if I took the luxury and illusive blissfulness from his life, then maybe justice wouldn't take the form of a winged baby. Maybe justice wouldn't always wear a halo. Instead, maybe it would wear a hood.

A flash of gold wiped past my eyes, then a whip of blond hair. I saw the two turquoise pools of her gaze. Suddenly, I was in a boxy room with walls of shadow. Everything was black, everything was colorless and perfectly in tune with the image of evil. Everything but a corner, lit by a single lamp buttering the shadows with as much illumination as it could.

From where I stood, the lamp in the corner of the abysmal room was distant. Details in its shade and post were scarce, and none of my body stood in the most faded light radiating from the bulb. But I desperately wanted to immerse myself in it.

I took one step toward it, but my foot my taken back by the gluey arms of the shadows, reaching for my ankle. I ripped my foot free, and took a full step toward the corner. It was like walking through a swamp of tar, quickly solidifying around my knees. But I forced myself to pull closer to the lamp. I would not allow the shadows to drown me in their darkness.

The muscles in my arm nearly tore apart and ripped as I stretched a reach toward the light. The tips of my fingers were just inches away from the light's edge when, suddenly, the lamp's only bulb exploded. It shattered, and as soon as the murky air touched its flame, the light was extinguished.

My dream (or whatever it was) had been shattered like a tube of Borm that rolled off the surface of Ed's table. He too was startled, and his head hopped up from the microscope.

"Damn it," he cursed, then looked at me. "I'm so sorry," he said. "I..." Ed searched for a deeper apology, but, after I had been caught in a temporary trance, I held up my hand, hushing his voice.

"It's okay." I looked down at my feet, at the blue, jelly-like puddle oozing around my shoes. "It's okay," I repeated. "Don't worry about it. Just keep looking for whatever it is you're looking for. If you find something, tell me."

Ed shook his head, even though he didn't want to agree to such a proposal. Whatever it was Ed desperately needed to find had to be something terrible. He told me that it was enough to alter my decision of killing Big Rich, and he knew better than anyone else that no rock, stone or marble was as concrete as my motives.

The thought, silent to Ed, opened my mouth once more, "He deserves to die." Ed had heard that many times before, and every time those words rustled outside the caves of his ear, he simply nodded them away. "He murdered Jay, he murdered your family, Barrette's family..." I waited, hoping that maybe Ed's personal encounter with Richard's touch would bring agreeable words to his mouth. He sat silent. "Big Rich created me," I said to my friend like it was a confession, an admission of guilt. To *me* it was, but to the people (even Ed) who thought they knew me, it was not. "He created me, and I'm well aware that I'm not any sort of angel or peace maker. But I also understand that the resonance of his actions spawn such retribution. And if he continues to exist...not only will families continue to be butchered, but more people like me will come about..."

"Isn't that what you want?" asked Ed, then looked at me through the corners of his eyes.

No, I wanted to answer so firmly. But I had to creep around my concussive sureness. "I'm not doing this because I have seen justice or because I have been enlightened to act outside of myself. I'm doing this because I was murdered, because my best friend was murdered, because everything I thought to be true and honest was all a part of Richard's God damned plan! If more people like me existed," I continued onward with a voice once again soft, "then that means more people will have seen what I have seen. And if killing Big Rich is not my life's most altruistic act, then ensuring that no one sees what I have will be."

ELEVEN

O N THE TOP STEPS OF THE LOS ANGELES PUBLIC LIBRARY, RAINE flipped her pages, jumping her eyes from line to romantic line. Every once and a while, her eyes would stray from the pages and look at the orange, dirty textured sky. Then she would squint from the brightness and heat of the sun, and return to her book.

I felt that maybe she was trying to pull her fantasy plots out from the pages of her book and set them right over the filth of the city. She wanted to kiss in front of a sunset with no worries that the next day may be the final end to mankind's last bit of morality. Raine was so hopeful, but so full of doubt. I could tell that, day by day, that little crack of light in her horizon sunk lower and lower.

I watched Raine from across the street, through the spaces of passing people. I was the only one who stood there.

Every once and a while I thought that Raine noticed me. I thought that maybe, just maybe she made eye contact through the shadow of my hood. I could've walked over there and sat next to her on those sandstone colored steps. I could have removed the hood from my head and felt the 'sunlight' on my face.

Even with the blaring sun, there was no sunlight to hold. In the backdrop of the public library was Big's palace, his tower climbing with endless height into the sky. Its shadow fell off the side of its round walls and landed on top of the library.

It was the portal to Hell aside the Golden Gates of Heaven. And there sat an angel.

Her eyes were milky, not energized by an electric flow, not glowing blue like a fantastical ocean. Leaps fell short from word to fictitious word, and they fell down the page until soon they were climbing back up, trying to make the jump again. She sat there flipping the books' pages for a long time, and I stood across the street, admiring her beauty and basking in the vibes that radiated from her body in the form of a warm, but oddly refreshing, current; an aura of herself, the single cone of a spotlight shining beyond the clouds of dirt and grime.

Daylight was leaning at a sharp angle. In the east, darkness was rising and battling away the light in the west. Raine looked up at the sky and realized the amount of time she had spent reading her romance novels.

Raine slapped shut the books and packed them into a small bag she carried at her side. She stood, and glided down the stairs of the library.

Once she was on the sidewalk, Raine looked back up at the dimming sky and chose a fast pace. Her legs wiped past each other in frequent strides. Even still, her head never bobbed. I was confident that the Earth was just moving out from under her. All she had to do was lift her feet.

She crossed the street to the side I was on, and I nearly walked in her shadow. Raine had a feeling someone was following her, but never bothered to look. She took a left down the stretch of a littered street exiting Downtown LA.

Before I made the turn, I turned over my shoulder and looked at Big's Tower. I looked back at Raine and back at the tower.

I have to tell her what I'm doing, said the sappy voice of my 'heart'. I didn't know I had one.

Then my monster spoke. *No! Forget about her—she'll get over you.*

You need her, Hale…you know you do. She's the only good thing in your life! protested my heart.

My monster shook its slimy head. *She's a weakness. That's all you need to know. If crime is merciless, justice must be too. Big Rich must die! Raine can't get in the way! She'll make you tender, she'll make you weak!*

Grace isn't a weakness, counterattacked my heart. *You're numb, Hale! Not only can you not feel your own pain, but you're numb to others' pain. Your apathy will kill you...*

No, without pain you're invincible! Big Rich doesn't have a chance. Turn around, climb to the top of that tower and put a bullet through Big Rich's eyes!

In both hands I weighed Jay's rusted pistol and Raine's spotless raindrop necklace. I considered both, and would answer to both. I faced toward Raine's direction, and returned Jay's pistol to my pocket. My monster retreated into its cave.

Raine had traveled one block ahead of me. She was a slim figure in the distance. Our neighborhood was several exaggerated miles from Big's territory. I continued to follow Raine as she passed one block at a time.

A long ways from downtown, Raine stopped at the curb outside of a building that didn't seem too specific itself. It held no personality, and the building's inanimate expression was completely blank. There was one pair of windowless doors, and above them, the simple shape of a silver triangle hanging like an emblem.

Raine looked up at the sign and considered entering. Eventually, after a long-lasting sigh, she walked toward the doors. A round man held out his arm and prevented little Raine from entering. She spoke a few pressing sentences to the man. At first he seemed unrelenting, but eventually, at the end of Raine's sentence, he lowered his arm and let her through.

She disappeared into the brick cave. The bouncer layered his hands on top of one another and faced the street before him.

He saw me as I approached, and just by my shrouded figure he suspected me of intentions other than a late night full of dollar-bills and strippers. I was five feet from him, and the bouncer was already shooting questions at me.

He was a thick, gaunt man with freakish height, dark skin, and fat lips. "What do you want?" he demanded the question with a thundering voice.

"Let me in."

He laughed at me. "Come back when you graduate from middle school." That's all he said before he crossed his hands and faced forward again.

I repeated, a little bit more violent this time, "Let me in, or I'll break your God damned neck!"

The threat twisted his head toward me. He stabbed me with a tight glare and frozen eyes that should have turned me to stone. "Get the fuck out of here!" he began shooing me away. "Now, before I break *your* neck." The bouncer stepped close to me and his giant gut touched my chest. I had to look up at him and over his stomach.

I knew the troll wouldn't let me in. Rotating my body away, I pretended like I had given up, like I was leaving. But before the bouncer's confidence swelled too much, I twisted back toward him and thrust my foot into the cap of his knee.

His bones broke inward, and the Bouncer collapsed, screaming at me. I lifted my foot over his head, and crushed it like a melon. After looking around at the street to spot any witnesses, I entered the club.

Pink fog filled the entire club—there was more sex and money than air. Breathing was a struggle, and maneuvering through the dancers and mostly nude women was even more challenging. Silver poles speared out of the ground around every bar and table. A dance floor was pushed into the far back of the club.

Two men in gray suits stood on both sides of the door behind me. I could feel their eyes burning a hole in the back of my neck. At the corners of bars, around the stripping poles and dotting the rest of the club, more guards kept their hands crossed in front of their waists and their eyes sharp.

I looked for Raine, but my eyes never hooked to her. I would have thought that such a misplaced person would be easy to spot. No matter how hard I tried, I couldn't spot Raine.

A woman dressed in nothing but lingerie suddenly stepped in front of me. She was quite immediate in the business she was offering. "You wanna have some fun with me, baby?"

Before I answered her, I scanned my eyes across the crowd once more for Raine, but she was still out of sight. Deepest into the cave was a series of back rooms. I looked at the woman who was luring me in. I knew that if I accepted her implied proposal she would escort back me to those rooms.

I looked at the slimly dressed stripper and accepted her scripted hospitality.

"Right this way, baby," she said, turned toward the rooms, and walked away, wagging her butt at me. We dug through the mounded people and strippers, bars and tequila cluttered tables, until we entered a small, faintly lit room.

Inside, there was one chair and a circular platform before it. Beads hung in replace of a door, and the walls were covered in mirrors, not wallpaper. My escort flipped herself around and hung off of me with her arms around the back of my neck.

"What are you in the mood for?" she asked in such an impure tone. The lady put one leg up on the platform, opening her body and menu just a little bit more. But my appetite wasn't hungry for anything she could offer me except information.

"Where's your boss?" I jumped to my thesis and asked her.

My sudden shift in business surprised and confused her. The woman couldn't gather enough words to build a sentence in the time it took for me to ask again. "He's in the back room," she answered without much effort. "But...you won't be allowed to see him. Now come on," she moved her half naked body closer, "have a taste." She grinned and pulled off what little clothes she wore. I knew it was a body a hundred other men had seen before me.

"Put your clothes back on," I insisted. "Where's the back room? Take me there."

"I'm…I'm not allowed…"

"Take me!"

With the embarrassment and threat I had brought into the room, she redressed herself and led me to a closed door along the very back wall. Another bouncer refused to let the employee in. "He's got company," he told her.

"Please," begged the whore, "this man wants to speak with him."

The bouncer looked over the woman's insignificant height to where I stood. He smirked directly at me. "Who the hell are you?"

Me: "I need to speak with your boss—the owner of this club."

"He's busy," the man rephrased his early comment. "And why the hell should I care if *you* need to see him? Who the hell are you? I've never seen you 'round here before…" The man pulled down a pair of dark, expensive looking shades from over his eyes.

Quicker than any of his reflexes could move, I drew Jay's pistol and jabbed it into his gut. The whore saw the firearm, looked around innocently and walked off. "I'm a ghost," I told the man, "and I'm here to haunt your boss. Now let me in or I'll shoot you and walk right through the walls…"

He didn't play chicken with a loaded gun pressed against his stomach. The bouncer rotated himself fully around and opened the door to his boss's office. When he returned to his original facing, I forced forward and pushed him into the room with me.

"See you in Hell," I quickly said to the man, and drove the butt of my gun to the top of his head. His body fell limp like a sack of Borm.

Then I faced the boss behind his desk, with Raine nearly pulled into his lap. She looked at me with the boss, and he quickly stood, pouring Raine off of him. Raine snapped her eyes toward me, though she didn't know who I was. I tipped my head farther down to ensure my identity's secrecy.

His fury spoke. "Who the hell are you?" I whipped the aim of Jay's pistol over his head and suddenly I held all dominance. In a more civil, calmer tone, the boss in his gray silk suit asked, "What do you want?"

"What are you doing with this girl?"

"She came in here on her own!" The man hugged Raine's waist and strung her back into him. Raine's expression alone told me that the boss wasn't lying, but her desire was not the only thing bringing her into that room. I marched a step closer to him.

"Tell me what's going on, or I'll shoot you dead in your own club!"

"Okay, okay!" the boss raised his arms. "You tell him," he said to Raine who didn't speak one word.

"*You* tell me!"

The man shook his head in frustration and irritation then answered my question. "She's looking for her mother..." He faced Raine and said with a horrible tone of voice, "Unfortunately she's not coming home."

Raine's hope fell to her feet. "What...?"

"I'm sorry sweet cheeks," he apathetically apologized to Raine who was beginning to cry. "*My* boss came by and picked up some of my ladies. Your mother...as fine and gorgeous as she is...was one of the first to go. And unless you want to walk your ass all the way to Miami, you can't see her again."

"You sold her?" Raine asked.

"Don't take it personally," suggested the boss, "it was only business."

Then I stepped back in with my own ruthless opinion. "You sold a woman like God damn candy? You sold this girl's mother for a few bucks?"

"It's business!" he, again, explained.

Before I fully proclaimed my feelings, I turned Raine's way and shouted, for her own good, "Go! Go straight home!" With salty tears falling behind her, Raine ran out of the office.

I walked around the desk to the boss sitting in some fancy leather seat. He didn't enjoy the confrontation, and held up his hands to arrange some sort of agreement. "Come on, pal...we can settle this. Just give me a number! Go on, give me a number!"

"You sold a woman like she was a piece of property! She was that girl's mother!"

"Why do you give a rat's ass? Huh? What's in it for you?"

I pulled the hood off my head so he could see my face before he died. "The only reason I'm alive is so I can kill the criminals like you. You were born a piece of shit, and you'll die a piece of shit." I covered the man in my dominance and my broad figure's shoulders.

The whole time I reached for his neck, he was spitting plea after plea, begging for his life. "Have mercy, man! Have mercy!"

"Mercy?" I asked in a cry. "*Mercy* is the only reason I'm here pointing this gun in your damn face. Mercy is what has made your life such a waste to this world. No," I said, "I will not have mercy. If crime is merciless...justice must be too..." My finger was trembling not with fear, but with the craving that I was readying myself to settle.

"What are you, some kind of damn vigilante?" the boss showed a slight sliver of sophistication.

Just before I shot him dead, the bouncer whom I presumed to be unconscious grabbed me by the shoulders and yanked me away from his boss. The man threw me across the office and my back flattened against a wall.

But I immediately stood and charged the man. My head rocketed into his stomach, and I forced him into a pin against the wall and struck him again and again with sharp knuckles. The man's boss tried to squeeze in an attack from the side, but I kicked the little man back into his little throne.

The bouncer carried a handgun at his hip in a holster. I socked him with one more furious blow, then pulled the weapon from its dusty sac. I shot him once in the chest, then turned toward the boss in his leather seat. He only wished he was holding a clean white flag to prove his surrender.

"There's no room for mercy," I said to him, and took his life at the pull of a trigger.

Even over the music that rocked the club, the gunshot exploded out of the small office. When I exited, approaching bouncers had their hands at their hips. I flung my newly acquired gun up to aim, and began pulling back its trigger over and over again. Each time, my arm would shake and rock back, a bouncer would fall to the floor. The bouncers who had not yet been stricken by my bullets stretched their arms to reach the guns at their sides.

I sprinted to find cover where there was none to be sought. A few shots were fired, and I could feel the heat of bullets buzz by the back of my neck like blazing fireflies. I dove over a bar counter topped with a metallic, reflective surface. Once I had scooted my back against the inside of the bar's counter, I searched for any sort of weapon.

Leaning against the bar's backside was a shotgun waiting to be fetched if someone like me were to enter the club...or if someone like me where to enter the club, and happened to need it. I took the shotgun into my hands, and pulled down on the fore-end, ejecting one empty shell from its barrel. The metal tube clattered to the floor with a chilling sound, and all other noise but the beat of my heart and the panicking of my breaths fell silent, hushed completely.

When I heard a brief, impermanent pause of gunfire from the other side of the bar, I hauled myself to my feet and twisted around. Aiming at the first bouncer I saw, I pulled the trigger, cocked the gun, and continued to the next. The bullets of the shotgun blew out the barrel like lead mist.

I made a dash around the bar, and while bullets were striking the walls right next to me, I never bothered to look back. I exited the club with the shotgun in my hands, and turned toward the door where I slipped it through the handles.

A moment later, the bouncers and guests inside the club were trying to open the doors, but the metal barrel of the gun would never allow them. On the ground, the (dead) original bouncer was bleeding out of his impaled skull, and would cook beneath the sun the next morning.

Raine was far down the street by the time I clawed my way out of the club. She was sprinting for home, burning away all the sticky emotions in her eyes and mind. "Raine!" I called after her, but the distance between us was too great.

So I picked up a sprint and chased Raine. I was shrinking the distance that separated us, calling her name and praying to nothing that she would stop to take a breath. But it seemed she was breathless. No fatigue slowed her down; no amount of pain stopped her legs from moving faster than her heartbeat.

I could hear her panting, crying, sobbing with all her might. "Raine!" I called again and several times more. "Raine!"

Raine was about to cross the slim, concrete river of a street when a van hurled itself around the corner and put a block in Raine's path. She forced herself to a stop before crashing into the side of the vehicle.

A side door opened and several men stepped out. She knew immediately what was going to happen if she didn't fight...

The men grabbed Raine by the arms and legs, and threw her into the back of their vehicle. I heard her shrieking and saw her struggling inside the van, but their force was too great.

"Hey!" I bloodied my throat to scream so loud. "Wait! Wait!" I increased speed and ran as fast as my body would allow me...and then even faster. But I was on the other block when the men shut the door to their van, and it drove off down the street. "Raine!" I cried, literally cried. "Raine!"

I felt totally helpless and guilty watching them take her. The weight of culpability began pushing on my chest. A common breath wasn't enough—I had to gulp as much air as I could possibly fit in my lungs at one time. My heart was suddenly untamed and wild. I wanted to chase the car or somehow follow it to their destination. I wanted to draw Jay's pistol from my pocket and fire a perfect shot at the van's driver.

"Raine!"

I fell to my knees, and it felt as if the impact shattered them.

The veins all around my body (in my hands, wrapping around my arms, popping off my forehead) were glowing orange. For a long while I looked at them, wondering what was happening. And then I could feel a heat growing hotter and hotter inside of me. I began slapping my arms and chest, trying to dampen the flames that were flowing through my veins. But there was nothing I could do. Soon, the fire began to claw its way out of my skin. All over my body, fiery demons began to break free and hop around. I screamed, but only a stream of fire bellowed from my mouth. The heat traveled to the very middle of my chest where it expanded and erupted out of me.

TWELVE

ED WAS ALREADY IN BARRETTE'S OFFICE, HUNCHED OVER HIS DESK engaging in an intense discussion. I had never seen Ed so distraught. His glasses were missing, the comb over on his hair was trashed, and heavy, dark sags drooped beneath his eyes.

The commissioner didn't look too well either. His forehead was bruised and cut open from the past accident outside of Toy Palace. Small little stitches covered his entire face, and he wore a cast around his wrist. Barrette's hair was even grayer, the grayest I had seen it. Through their entire conversation, Barrette rubbed the inside corners of his eyes while Ed threw rambling sentences at him.

Neither of the two noticed me standing in the shapeless doorframe. I listened to what Ed was saying, but I heard no good news.

"We can't let him kill Big Rich, sir...I mean," Ed struggled to find the correct wording, "do you realize the amount of...of harm he would put the entire city in?" Every one of his sentences was racing and hard to understand clearly. "It would be insane, Barrette! Completely outrageous! I mean this...this isn't good, commissioner. We can't let Project Home spread the trade across the nation, but if Big Rich dies then...then..."

"Then what?" I, uninvited, plopped my voice right into the middle of their discussion. And silence fell over us.

Barrette opened his eyes and Ed turned around to face me. Neither of the two had anything to say, or at least the pretended not to. Just by the words I had heard of their conversation, and enduring the pain of Raine's abduction, I was burning in the acid of a foul mood. It seemed they were waiting for me to speak first...or maybe they didn't want to hear my voice at all. Ed obviously wasn't going to answer my question with such notice. They refused to look at me, refused to inform me with the information I deserved to hear.

"What the hell is going on? I deserve to know!" I broke out. "So fucking tell me!" Even I was surprised at my sudden increase in hostility and volume just as Barrette and Ed were. "That man took everything from me! *Everything*! I deserve to know anything regarding my choice to slaughter him."

"Hale..." Ed began to speak bravely. "This isn't about—"

"No!" I blurted. "No! I'll tell you what this is about! This is about you," I pointed at Ed, "and you," I pointed at Barrette, "losing sight of what's right! Losing sight of what needs to be done if justice is meant to be found! We can't sit back and tolerate what's going on...that's what brought LA to its knees! We bow to that fat bastard because we're too weak and laughable to stand against him!" Ed was leaning away after smelling the animosity burning. "Lucifer is one man who has made a mockery out of our tolerance! Out of our mercy! He has made a mockery out of an entire God forsaken city!"

"Hale..." again, Ed tried to extinguish my flame.

"Shut up, Ed!" I snapped at him. He broke backward; I had never held such hate between us. "If we ever expect...if *I* ever expect to find justice, we can't be merciful! If crime is merciless..."

Ed armored his boldness and outgrew my dominance. "Hale!" he screamed louder than any volume I had been peaking. "This isn't about you anymore! This is about the entire city, the entire nation!" I wrinkled my eyebrows inward, querying silently. "Mr. O is dead!" my friend handed me another innuendo.

"*How*?" I asked plainly.

Before he could answer, Ed took a glance at Barrette who sat behind him. It was like he needed permission from his boss before proceeding. When Ed turned back around, his eyes didn't meet mine. They fell to the floor and Ed failed to respond.

"How?" I asked again. "How did he die?"

Ed who was still studying the dusty ground, began his answer with, "There were no signs of injury on him. No signs of sudden or past illnesses...nothing..."

"Then how? How did he die?" My patience was shrinking—I had to pry the answer from Ed's stubborn, much too cautious, much too common mouth.

Barrette stood. "Kid..." I could tell he was trying to avoid the conversation.

"Don't, Barrette! I want to know! Ed," he looked up at me, "how did Mr. O die? Tell me..."

Ed's answer was as concise as they came. He spoke only a few words. "It was the Borm," he answered at last.

"What? The *Borm*? What do you mean?"

The commissioner chimed in again. "Kid...it doesn't matter right now."

"Yes it does!" I yelped back at Barrette.

"Hale..." Ed came close. "What I'm about to tell you changes everything...everything you thought you knew, everything you wanted to believe..."

I swallowed, and, while I truly held no confidence, I told Ed, "I can handle it!—*tell me*."

Once again my friend slipped his sight back at Barrette who only turned and looked away. Ed came a little bit closer. "Mr. O died, because he didn't have any Borm in his system."

I didn't understand how that could be. "How does that make any sense?" I asked Ed, the brilliant scientist.

"You see, Borm is an all-in-one drug...it contains a little bit of everything. It gives its user energy, strength, awareness...the Borm actually nourishes its host, sort of like a symbiote. Much like blood does!" Ed described. "Remember those samples you gave to me?" I nodded. "And remember how the Borm just absorbed the blood?" I nodded again. "Well, for heavy users such as Mr. O and half the population of Los Angeles, the body builds a dependency on Borm.

The drug replaces your body's blood, and all of its nutrients. It's incredible! So, when people like Mr. O consume so much Borm each day, their entire blood cycle is absorbed by the drug and then, it's not blood that nurtures the brain…"

"It's the Borm…" I finished.

"Exactly," Ed affirmed. "Mr. O couldn't take any Borm for the two days he was detained…eventually, after the Borm in his system ran out, his body had nothing to dwell off of."

"I don't understand," I began explaining to Ed. "How does that change anything?"

"Well…" Now Ed was treading in threatening water. He widened his stance and braced himself from the rage he was expecting to come out of me. "Remember how that drug dealer who you brought in a while back told us that the Borm was made in a factory, and that Big Rich was the only one who knew the ingredients to it…"

"Yeah…I know…"

"Well…if you kill Big Rich, and no one is around to coordinate the shipment and make the Borm…" Ed waited for me to finish the rest, but I was too scared to say it. "Everyone who uses Borm will die with Big Rich."

Ed hustled backward and out of my reach. I didn't lunge at him or raise a fist. I was left frozen in my own fiery body, staring at my feet and the blood I imagined filling in around them.

To kill one man was to kill a thousand more.

"But, you know…that doesn't matter, right? I mean…maybe someone else will figure it out…right? Maybe someone else knows the ingredients…" Ed was trying hard to make the situation better. He practically massaged everything in the room to calm the tension he felt was tightening.

All I said was, "No," and continued staring at the floor and my feet. "They deserve to die…"

That sentence brought both Ed's and Barrette's attention right to me. Barrette turned around and Ed perked up. "What?" Ed asked, hoping he had heard something different.

"All those fuckers," I clarified and looked up, scowling. "If anyone was dumb enough to have ever bowed to Big Rich, they deserve to die just as much as Lucifer does."

"Kid," Barrette started, "you're talking about an entire city! An entire population! One of the biggest this nation has to offer…"

"Then won't that open people's eyes? When an entire city falls dead, people will look…people will see what this God forsaken world has come to."

"Thousands of people will die…"

"Just as they deserve to. They made their choices," I said. "They chose to take from this society and never give!"

"And you think that killing them will give something back to our society?" Barrette continued to fight.

The question stumped me a bit. My flow of words was drained, but I quickly recuperated. "No," I admitted, "but it'll stop them from taking. Just like you said, commissioner, this is our last chance to attain justice. I'm not going to let it slip by…"

"But, you see…" Barrette came around his desk holding his index finger like a ruler toward me, "I don't think you're in this to save our city…I think you're in it for something else…"

"Don't you dare," I rattled my tail.

"Why not?" Barrette challenged me. "Why not? You think you're the only one who has been hurt? This isn't about you, kid! It never should have been! This is about the City of Angels! This is about our entire nation!"

"I'm trying to save the city, Barrette!"

"Are you?" he asked me.

"Yes!"

Barrette stopped his lecture and studied me. His eyes crawled all around my body from my feet, to my head, into my own eyes. I knew he was looking for it, the flames in my eyes. But I had to look away, break our eye contact.

Before walking back around his desk, all Barrette left me with was, "You burn in your own fire, kid. Remember that when your leg gets caught."

An awkward void of speechlessness filled the small office. Ed began feeling uncomfortable while Barrette sorted through papers and I just stood there considering the commissioner's words. He eventually stepped in and began speaking.

Ed said, "Mr. O told us that the shipment is arriving tonight at midnight. So, we can either stay here and bicker like school girls, or we can go and actually help save this city." Ed hopped two wide eyes between Barrette and me.

The commissioner kept his eyes busy in his papers but I said, "I have a plan, but I'm going to need as much help as I can get…"

Barrette threw down his papers. "Do you think we're in the position to help you?" He raised his arms—palms to the ceiling—and gestured for me to look around. All of the sudden, the little Barrette had was not enough to make a difference. "I lost several of my men yesterday. Now their wives and children don't get to have a husband or father around anymore." There was acridity in his voice, such bitterness he had been avoiding his entire life. "You've cost us so much…*ghost*! And to come back here to the place you destroyed and ask help from people *you* hurt, it's repulsive! No," Barrette began to deliver me his answer, "I won't help you. *We* won't help you…"

I tried to coax him, but he cut me off before I could even get started. "Barrette…"

"I said no, kid! Get the hell out of here!" He waved me off and sat back down in his leather throne, then threw his head in his hands.

When I looked at Ed, he looked away. Not even my friend, the one who had been nothing but loyal my entire life, had any words to say to me. I looked back at Barrette, but it was clear no one in that building wanted anything to do with me.

So I left Barrette's office, stomped through the decomposing building and crashed out onto the street, completely scrambled and staggered by what had just occurred. All my plans, my hopes and ambitions were dependent upon Barrette and the officers. Now, I had *nothing* but myself. I could hear Barrette's words creeping into my head, mocking me if I dared to call myself human.

It was the first time in a while I truly felt like it was me versus the world. Not even my ginger friend was there to pat me on the back. I looked up, and couldn't help but stare at the height of Big's Tower.

My fists tightened so much that their knuckles nearly split the skin over them open. I wanted to punch the street and watch my own blood drip down my wrists. I wanted to hold my face in a puddle of blue blood and drown.

Jay was dead, Raine was gone, and both Barrette and Ed had taken enough of my abuse. Raine was the most torturous to think about.

Was she dead or alive? Was she crying or had she run out of tears? I kept picturing her chained to a wall, waiting for me to break in there and save her...how hopeless she must have been thinking that I had left the state and no one was there to free her.

There was only one place that could handle my flood of tie-dye emotions.

I passed beneath the black iron arch of Crown Cemetery and crawled up the easy sloping hill of graves. The cemetery was end-less—layer upon layers of hills rolled all out across the land, each filled with nothing but headstones.

I found Jay's sticking up from the dehydrated dirt he was buried under. The three letters of his name engraved into the rock had already begun to fade, and the stone itself was eroding away. I collapsed right on top of it, crying as soon as I hit the ground.

My tears began to soak the stone and moisten the dirt below me. I cried and cried, but no one was there to hear me. "What's hap-pening?" I asked anyone, crying still. "What the hell am I doing? I know that man deserves to die...but why is it only *me* trying to bring justice? I'm completely alone, Jay...there's no one else. I ran off Barrette...Ed doesn't want anything to do with me...I've lost the help of the police. Now all I have is this poisonous rage and your God damned gun! But what, in any dimension, is a gun going to solve? And why...*why* do *I* have to hold it?" There wasn't anyone to talk to, but I continued to let my words erupt like lava from the mouth of a volcano. "I'm gonna be down there with you," I said. "I'm going to die, and no one is going to miss me. I wanted to leave my mark, to make a difference! But it seems that one person's bitterness spreads like a mold until you're too consumed by it." From my pocket I took Jay's old, rusty pistol and rotated it in my hands as I spoke. "I'm killing him for you, Jay...I don't care about this city anymore. Everyone in it, they're all evil...they deserve to die. I'm gonna kill Big Rich, and watch everyone else rot alive..."

A pair of feet landed right in front of me and a partially familiar voice spoke. "I'm sure you've been told that what you're doing is wrong," assumed the gravedigger with his dusty voice. I looked up at his silhouette blocking the sun from blinding me. "Well, I'm not here to tell you why you shouldn't kill that man. In fact, he deserves to die."

"Why...why are you telling me this?"

The gravedigger chuckled. "I'm closest friends with the dead. Every day I bury two or three or four poor souls beneath this dirt. The only reason I'm here to bury those bodies is because of Lucifer. He's the reason for all of this..."

"If I kill Big Rich, then all of Los Angeles will die..."

"It's the deed of necessity, boy. If that's what needs to happen, then it must be done," said, sweetly, the digger.

I began to stand. I rose to my knees and stopped, then continued later to my feet. "If I kill Lucifer, then I'm responsible for the deaths of thousands of people."

"And if you don't," he began, "and Lucifer spreads the Drug Trade across America, we'll all be responsible for the death of an entire nation. Billions of people," he added.

"Why me?" I asked him. "Why do I have to kill Big Rich?"

He smiled two rows of black teeth and spat out a wad of tobacco. "The only reason Big Rich has been allowed to take control of LA is because everyone asks that question. You can't expect from others what you don't expect from yourself, boy. Take that rage of yours and use it, don't let it use you. You and I, we've both seen the raw truth of our society." He chuckled, introducing his next sentence. "Me, I'm an old man, but you've been given a chance to use a great strength and change the world with it! You're just a boy, and you already know what must be done. You have your whole life ahead of you," he told me, wishing that his skin wasn't wrinkly or his hair wasn't graying.

"People will hate me...I'll be criminalized, I won't be a hero," I assured the gravedigger who just smiled at me, leaning on his staked shovel, fiddling with his gold necklace.

"People will hate you because man fears most what he cannot overcome," prophesized the digger. I suppose Jay's word were not only kept to him. The digger pointed at the face of Jay's grave where the quote was carved. "It seems like he knew what had to be done as well. The truth, well...that's one thing inescapable. They will hate you," he agreed, "but those people worthy of your saving will open their eyes a little bit wider. We can't expect to be pretty in an ugly world. When Big Rich dies and Los Angeles falls, someone or something will rise out of the ashes."

Then Barrette's words crept back to me, like a fiend into my mind and across my tongue. "Your burn in your own fire," I said to the digger. He knew those weren't my words.

The digger pulled his shovel from the dirt, turned, and began walking away from me. Over his shoulder he called back, "Use it— don't let *it* use *you*!"

My eyes traveled back down to the gun in my hand, the omen in my palms. "If crime is merciless, justice must be too...justice, must be too..."

THIRTEEN

Port Lybric was tucked into a cove along the coast. While out west, was an unending watery prairie, the dirt hills of California tumbled in the east, hiding a far view of LA and its decaying masterpiece. Its character was no different than the city's. It had been neglected, nearly forgotten, and used for occasions far beyond its original purpose.

I wished there were stars to look up at, but there was nothing. Only a dusty sky—one more sign of mankind's arrogance lifted into the air after being brushed off his shoulder.

I was standing alone on the shore, wishing that Barrette would be there to help me. The harbor was completely and utterly desolate. Its only company was itself and the zombie monster on its ashy beach.

There was a large barge out at sea, and I knew that, soon, smaller vessels would be zipping toward land for the Deliverers to drop their packages. I waited for a long time before anything happened. The moon lifted higher into the sky and its dry gleam barely made it through the congested haze.

At first, the ship was the bare existence of a light on the edge of the ocean before it dropped off around the world. As time ticked closer to midnight, and as the moon was known to rise higher into the sky, our light grew closer.

Someone spoke behind me, popping the bubble of silence around my ears. "Jesus Christ..." Barrette swore to himself, watching the distant barge from the shore just as I was. "Are you ready to do this?" he asked me.

I turned around quickly, spooked by his voice. There stood Barrette and a whole barrage of officers loading their weapons or polishing them. Barrette raised his brows, waiting for me to speak.

"I...I thought you weren't going to come..."

"I wasn't," he said. "But...I had to come—for the city, not for you. So," he said happily, "let's get you suited up and we'll do this thing."

An officer behind Barrette threw me many choices of weapons: Two rifles, two sharpened blades, a pouch of grenades and an armored vest. I loaded the weapons onto myself.

Barrette was shaking his head the entire time. "Man...maybe I should've stayed back at the station, kid. Are we really going to do this?"

We were walking toward a building burnt to a near cinder. Its roof had collapsed, its foundation was a pile of dust, and the air within it was the home for floating dust and microscopic debris.

As I pulled the silver zipper of my hoodie all the way up, I looked at Barrette—though he could not see my eyes—and said, with no absence of confidence, no lack of positivity, and no room for any other answer, "Yes."

The building we deemed base was one of many ruins piling up in the harbor. Every floor above us had collapsed, so Barrette, an unfamiliar officer with a rifle, and I planted our feet amongst rubble and concrete debris. We peeped through the square from what used to be window.

The officer with his rifle adjusted a scope mounted on its body, and looked into it with one eye open, one eye closed. A few muffled words spoke from both Barrette's and the officer's transmitter on their chests.

"Alright," Barrette said, "everyone is in position...now it's just up to you. Are you sure you got this?"

"I'm sure."

Barrette exhaled before he continued to speak, and even when he spoke, the commissioner fit all his stress between every word. "Okay, kid. It's time to go." He brought the radio close to his mouth and said into it, "The ghost is heading out. Be ready."

"See you on the other side," I told him and exited base.

The closer I walked to the start of the dock, the faster my heart thrashed in its cage. First I could hear the hissing and lapping of the Pacific, then I could feel every movement of each wave that crashed into the beams of the wooden dock.

It was a bright circle now, and the ship was beginning to make an image behind all the light's glare. There were several men on the deck of a small vessel lugging many heavy crates onboard. Each Deliverer was armed with sleek rifles and smooth hope.

When I squinted my eyes and looked behind the boat and its bright light, I could see the enormous, lazy body of a barge floating far away on the horizon's surface of the Pacific.

And then I saw what was really in front of me...

My stomach sank as if it had fallen right into the water, and I could only imagine Barrette slapping his palm to his forehead, watching from the window back at base. When the ship was close enough, the single bright light broke into two, then three, and eventually four, and it became chillingly clear that not just one vessel was approaching Port Lybric, but four.

I wanted to curse myself, but knew it would add only more pain to the blow. I patted myself down to ensure I was still carrying my new toys.

When the vessels were just moments away from docking, I took hold of two guns slung around my back, and prepared to unleash their beast. The weight of the rifles was heavy, but I knew it wasn't compensation: both guns were as deadly as the Reaper himself.

I turned my head over my shoulder and walked my eyes all the way down the dock to base, where I could see Barrette, waiting, hoping, praying to nothing but the killer inside me.

My fingers itched.

The first vessel was close to stopping, and I turned the remaining few feet of the dock before me into an entire speedway to sprint down and leap off of. I lifted right off the edge of the dock, hurled myself over the water, and, guns drawn, took aim midair.

A simple, square shaped cabin sat right in front of me where the captain of the ship took control. I shot both of my rifles and fired through the glass of the cabin. Both panes shattered, and inside I could see the captain thrust backward off his feet with little bloody holes all over his body.

The vessel's entire head rocked when I landed on its tip. My legs kept moving, and I leaped through the window where the captain laid dead.

Outside on the deck, Deliverers transferred dialogue like a game of hot potato. I could hear them, just beyond the door of the cabin I was in.

"What the hell was that?" one queried hurriedly. They all shifted their positions toward the cabin where I hid just on the other side of the wall.

"Oh my god…" one lost his breath to speak. "He's dead…the captain is dead!"

"What?" another Deliverer yelped and swore. "Who the hell killed him?" he asked with such fury. "The cops? Are the God damned cops here?" In unison, with the cue of the Deliverer's raging voice, they raised their guns.

One step closer, and they examined the captain's body even more. Shattered glass was spread around his figure and over his face. There were several bloody dots on his chest from where I had fired.

"No…" a Deliverer said like he had seen himself in the future, laying on the ground with a bullet between his eyes and a bloody tear being the only sign of emotion he ever had. "It's *him*…"

They all swore softly to themselves, saving their last breath before a ghost would possess their lives and take them to the feet of a grave. All together, the Deliverers crept closer to the body.

I swapped one of my rifles for a knife with a deadly edge, slick enough to cut callus as tough as any of them on the boat.

Unable to gather enough courage, four of the five Deliverers forced one of their own toward the cabin. He resisted as much as he could, but eventually had to raise his gun higher and approach the captain's body.

I heard the clattering of his teeth, the thumping of his heart trying wildly to break through the bones it was trapped beneath. I could smell his sweat, his fear pushing out of every pore.

First I saw the barrel of his gun, rattling around in the Deliverer's palm. As soon as I saw his wrist, I brought the tip of my knife straight into his skin. He wailed when it pierced him, and with the knife wedged into his wrist, I pulled the Deliverer fully into the cabin and took a shot at the side of his head.

With a single squeeze of the trigger, my automatic rifle shot several rounds at a time. The man's body lurched to the side before falling, and a flick of blood hit the wall aside of him. I heard more cursing popping out of the Deliverer's mouth as their friend fell.

"Christ…" spewed one with their words. "Go get him!"

"You go!"

"*You* go!"

As the Deliverers argued about whose death came first, I returned the rifle to my hand and twisted out from behind my cover and out of the cabin. Their distraction had lowered the guns in their hands, but as soon as they saw me, they brought them back to attention.

And everyone began shooting.

I pulled both triggers of my two rifles and pointed each one at a different person. Every gunshot was a firework exploding on the deck. They all launched single bullets at me, while I sprayed them with mine. My guns shook violently in my hands as I let loose their power.

The first Deliverer fell backward over the rail and into the frigid water. The next ran across the deck toward a crate where he believed cover would protect him. I shot at his legs and he collapsed before he crawled fully behind the crate. Another made a successful shot at me—his bullet landed itself in the Kevlar vest over my chest. I hopped my aim to him and waited until he too fell dead. The last was braver than the others...

He charged at me with a blade in his hand, swiping it through the air like a conductor's baton. As soon as I noticed the sword wielding Deliverer, I moved my gun in his direction, but before I could fire, he knocked it to the floor.

The blade dug into the skin over my shoulder. He pulled it out and drove it back it. I sprung my fist to his temples and made distance between him and me.

He bent at his knees and tossed the knife back and forth between both hands. His teeth flared like an animal's—a cheetah waiting to pounce. He sounded a battle cry and charged again with his knife raised. Though I was sure my knuckles would be useless, I held up my fists.

Before the rabid Deliverer could stab me again, I grabbed his forearm and together we struggled to get the knife. I yanked him to the left and he pulled back to the right. I held the knife away from my face and he tried his best to cut my skin.

We struggled and maneuvered all around the deck—running into crates of ingredients, nearly falling over rails of the boat and trampling over the bodies from before. Soon, my muscles began to grow tired, and the Deliverer showed no sign of retreat.

The Borm in his system must have made it impossible for fatigue to affect him.

With great strength, I brought my knee right into the man's groin. He grunted and groaned, then hunched just a bit, trying to ease his pain. Only half of his strength was trying to bring the knife into my body, but the other half was focused on his jewels, buzzing with pain between his legs.

I inhaled deeply, and slammed the Deliverer's hand against the metal railing over and over again until the knife fell out of his hands and was taken by the Pacific. He looked up at me and into my fireplace eyes. I grabbed the hair on the back of his head, and cracked his skull against the railing. Unconscious, soon to be dead, he fell.

The entire vessel was dead now. No life boarded it...not even me. I stood there just as cold as the people who lay. Though my heart was beating in my chest, and theirs was paralyzed, I was dead...or at least not alive.

I stood there for a moment while all the other boats began to dock, unaware of my arrival. And I stood there wondering how I could feel nothing, not even the missing chunk of meat on my shoulder. My blood soaked through my hoodie, even in the places where my hoodie wasn't torn. How could I take lives and yet, keep mine? And the worst part was I didn't even care. Complete apathy numbed my pain, sustained my life.

I walked over the bodies and to the cabin, pulling a grenade from a pouch at my hip. The ship had to be sunk, but I couldn't damage the ingredients onboard if we expected to discover the recipe to Borm.

Once I was inside the small boxy room, I pulled the circular pin from the frag and released it from my hand then twisted my body around. I ran across the deck, over the bodies, and just as the grenade exploded, I leaped over the rail and into the water.

All sound was muffled and distorted underwater. The explosion up top was more like a gurgle from underneath the waves. I had sunken far below the water, and when I looked up, a ball of fire was trying to make its way deeper into the ocean. The burning ship began to sink, and every second, more and more of the vessel fell underwater.

Not a spot of skin on my body was smooth. Small little bumps pushed up from the dropped temperatures of the water. It was nearly impossible to hold my breath, for the chill nearly stole it. When my puffed cheeks deflated and the oxygen in my blood depleted, I began to swim up toward the rippling surface.

Below and almost entirely above me was blackness. All but

the flame of the sinking ship was consumed by night's unyielding shadow. In a way, I took my time before coming up out of the water. It was like for just a second (if not a tiny split of a second) the water distinguished my flame. I thought that maybe steam would begin to rise out of the ocean. In the silence, the chill and the solitude, my anger was missing.

Everything was opposite on the surface.

As soon as my head broke out of the water, the noise and chaos returned to me like a mob. The crackle of flames! The screaming of Deliverers! The voice of death whistling into the air a melodic lullaby before their permanent nap...

I took a moment, treading on the surface of the waves, to reclaim my orientation. There were three more boats lurking around. I kicked my legs and paddled with my arms and started swimming toward a second boat.

A man on the vessel's deck raised his gun and shot several rounds at me in the water. The salt water splashed up in my face every time a bullet landed nearby. I forced myself back under once I had taken the deepest breath.

I could see where the bullets had gone. Lines like footprints traced their paths in the water—corkscrews twisting on after the bullets. None of them touched me, and soon the shooting stopped.

I was afraid to resurface, so I tightened my breath and swam underneath the boat to the other side. When I came back up, I had to eat as much air as I could.

A small ladder hung off *my* side of the small vessel, and after noticing it, I swam near. The focus of every Deliverer was toward the side I was previously on. Together they watched, waiting for me to surface, wondering if I had been hit by any of the rounds fired.

Slowly I took hold of the ladder and ascended one wrung. A man's ankle was right at the level of my eyes. Careful not to make a sound, I unsheathed my remaining blade and tightened a grip onto its handle. I pressed the blade to his heel, and slid it across his tendon. His skin parted to a deep gash as soon and his tendon snapped like a strained rubber band.

The Deliverer's natural and inevitable reaction was to collapse, but before he could, I wrapped a hand around the other ankle and pulled. He lost his balance and fell backward over my head and into the water.

I brought myself fully onto the boat and charged the nearest man. He turned just as I collided with him. The Deliverer caught my knife but couldn't touch my inertia. We sailed over the edge of the vessel and back into the ocean as well.

Like an anchor we sunk, taking turns slinging fists at each other. Under the water, our punches and strikes couldn't travel nearly as fast, so each punch was like it came from a toddler. The Deliverer and I sunk farther down into the Pacific, as if we were being swallowed for our sin.

I pushed away from him and headed quickly toward the surface in need for air. My head had just been exposed to oxygen when the Deliverer, from underneath, grabbed my ankle and yanked me back down.

I returned to his level underwater and had to wonder how he could hold his breath so long. He was charging his arm back, but like a lashing whip, I tailed my arm with the knife in hand, and slit his throat. His entire expression widened, shocked. His fist never left its charge, and the Deliverer began floating away from me, still upright in the water.

His blood grew into a huge violet cloud which spread in the water endlessly. The Deliverer disappeared into the bloody fog and the water's darkness.

Immediately I swam back up. There were still three more men on the ship. Each one of them searched the water for me or their friend. I ducked back under and swam, again, for the ship.

I sprang out of the water and onto the ship like a mad shark. I thrashed my strength upon every Deliverer on the ship—throwing my arms around, pulling every trigger I could, making every stab I desired.

One to my right was knocked with the hard metal of my gun. Another to my left was stabbed by the point in my hand. I would block a punch, then send one of my own sailing into the skull of the nearest Deliverer.

One Deliverer broke past my defense and threw a pair of dirty hands to my throat. He squeezed and tightened his choke. Blood was forced to my head, herded by the man's unbreakable strength.

I turned my knife upside-down and dropped it into the man's forearm. His grip loosened just enough for me to break away from the choke, and acquire my own. I grabbed his neck and charged forward with him in my hands. I ran so fast and so hard, that by the time we reached the vessel's rail, his spine snapped and bent around the unbendable metal.

I heard his back crack, snap, and break. His eyes popped open and nearly fell out of their sockets. On his own, the man fell to the ground.

Behind me, I heard heavy footsteps sprinting in my direction. I turned with my rifle up and shot as soon as I saw the final Deliverer.

One shot. Two shots. Three shots and the deliver was down. There was more blood on the deck than saltwater.

Same as the last ship, I rolled a grenade inside the cabin, and turned to make my quickest escape.

The last two ships were side by side now, both docking together. In my head I ran the slimmest, most vague equation to calculate the stunt I was daring to take.

There was no space of time from when I pulled the pin of my grenade, rolled it into the vessel's cabin, and sprinted for the end of the boat. When there was only a foot more of solid ground beneath me, I jumped and aimed for the crumpling wooden dock.

While I was in the air, the vessel behind me exploded, and I could feel the fire's heat groping at my back. The shockwave of the explosion forced me farther across the water and landing hard on the dock. The beams supporting Port Lybric's dock buckled when I crashed on to it and rolled to my back.

But I stood just as quickly as I fell, and picked my pace back up again. There were only a few feet of water between the dock and the next boat. I leaped with one last grenade in the bend of my fingers and the mold of my palm.

Even before I landed onto the next vessel, Deliverers were raising their rifles, ready to shoot the hawk swooping down. Time slowed, and, in midair just as before, I gripped the pin of the grenade, pulled it, and let it fall out of my hand and bounce along the deck.

The boat rocked when my feet made impact. The Deliverers began to open fire at me. I felt the heat of their whizzing bullets skimming my neck. A few collided with the armor on my chest, and each shot—even with the Kevlar—felt like a sucker punch to my chest. Each nearly knocked the air out of me.

I didn't bother to pick a greater fight. I ran through the flying bullets and prepared myself for a final leap. My body took the hits of several bullets as I passed across the vessel's deck. The grenade exploded right as my feet left the boat, and lost its temper. The explosion took care of the Deliverer's shooting at me. The cabin was torn open by a ball of unstoppable energy and fire.

I was thrown onto the next vessel and flopped across the deck. On my back, I shot as many bullets as I could at the Deliverers approaching me. One by one they fell. But wave after wave they charged me.

Over time I made it to my feet. I pulled back on my rifle's trigger, but all it did was make a dry clicking sound over and over again. I swung the rifle around and it collided with a Deliverer who was about to strike me from behind.

One Deliver, much stronger and faster than the others, swiped the rifle from my hands, and it clattered on the deck. With two flat hands ramming me in my chest, knocking me off my feet.

From a pocket inside his dirt colored jacket, he revealed to me a revolver. The Deliver took a closer stand over me. A smirk of satisfaction drooled from his mouth. The man had beaten me, and he knew it. He would kill a ghost.

The Deliverer took a second to collect an aim over my head, and as his finger began to pull on the gun's trigger, I closed my eyes tight. I heard a gunshot, then a loud thump. But I hadn't been shot, and when I opened my eyes, there was no fiery gate to welcome me.

The Deliver lay dead on the deck with a small hole that broke clean through his skull. The officer back at base had just saved my life.

On the ground, I ripped open my hoodie and looked at the vest underneath. Like Swiss cheese, it was covered in holes and spread over by sticky blood. I tore the vest from my body, but my skin didn't look too much different...

All about my pale chest and stomach, purple, circular bruises blossomed. It hurt just to look at them, let alone get pounded by bullet after bullet. I rolled to my stomach and pushed myself to my feet.

As soon as I turned around, thinking that the battle had been won, the last Deliver tucked down and threw himself into my waist. Together we flipped over the railing and into the Pacific like many others had.

I was too weak to swim...I let my own buoyancy deflate. I depleted my lungs of air, and closed my eyes. My body floated between the bottom and the surface. Never did the Deliver return to me. I didn't feel his hands grab my ankles. I didn't feel a thin blade scratch across my skin. It seemed he had been ingested by the ocean.

Then, through the thin layers of skin over my eyes, I saw the glare of a bright light, but never cared to open them. The light got brighter and brighter, until I fell asleep, and everything went black.

For a quick moment I opened my eyes again. The sky was above me, and I was being dragged out of the water by an officer in a diving suit with an oxygen mask on his face. The next time I woke up after falling asleep, I was back at base, and Barrette was hunched over me, calling for my consciousness.

"Kid! Kid you awake? Answer me, kid! Answer me!" Through the barely open splits of my eyes, the commissioner was a blur. His voice was echoes and hard to listen to. "Wake up kid! They're coming! They're coming!" I almost allowed myself to fall into sleep once more. But Barrette spoke again, and I could hear the urgency in his voice. Before his speech faded, my eyes shot open. "Kid!" he cheered. "You're alive God damn it! You're alive!" Barrette laughed and looked around at the officers surrounding us.

I then asked him what had happened. My voice was hard to make loud enough for any pair of ears to hear, but the commissioner leaned in. I repeated, "What happened?" and he understood.

"You did it!" he cheered some more. "You stopped the shipment!"

"How...how did I survive?" I asked him lackadaisically.

His eyes traveled to someone standing aside him. It was the officer in the wetsuit. "He saved you," Barrette said. "And the rest of the divers collected all the Borm that you sunk. The crates are being transported back to the station for Ed to analyze. But right now," Barrette pried me off the ground with his arm, "we gotta go. The Traders are going to be here any minute."

I was carefully brought to my feet, and I was able to see the aftermath of the resolution. Several officers stood around me— some wore their everyday uniforms while the rest were squeezed into wetsuits. Every head was bobbing, nodding at me like I had done a good job. There was a silent congratulations passed to every person in the ruined building.

With his long rifle lugged over his shoulder, the officer who had previously saved me stood and clapped as best as he could. The other officers joined, and eventually all the congratulations were directed purely to me.

I pulled the silver zipper back up my hoodie and flipped the hood over my head.

"You're lucky to be alive," Barrette patted me on the back. "Now let's just hope you have equal luck to make it through the rest of this night."

"Is everything ready?" I hurriedly asked Barrette.

"Um..." he was surprised I didn't savor my third chance at life. "Um, almost," he answered, then turned to half of the officers. "Get to your positions, and good luck!" Barrette faced me again. "Are you sure you want to do this?"

"It has to be done."

"I know," Barrette told himself. "It's just...how can you give up everything you have? How can you compromise so much?"

My answer was nothing but sour meat freshly cut from my thigh. "I don't have anything left to give up. Even when I consider the obvious, I have nothing to compromise."

"You still have your life, kid."

"Yes," I agreed, "but I've lost my identity to Big Rich. Now I'm just a body..."

Barrette continued to argue: "But you've created something new here...you've become something new. You do have an identity," he said. "Alexander Hale might be dead...but there's something left. Like a Phoenix born out of its ashes."

Half of the officers had already exited base while the other half were suiting up, out of their wetsuits. Barrette and I proceeded outside.

Several large crates—identical to the ones sunken with the vessels—were set out near the dock. The Traders were coming to pick them up, and I had to stop the rest of the operation. Barrette was insistent on expressing his own concern.

"Kid...the slightest mistake can make this whole operation turn on you. I mean, if they *really* get ahold of you, then...who knows if you'll be coming out alive?"

The concern I had for my own self wasn't near as expressive as Barrette's was for me. "I won't let anyone stop me from getting to Big Rich. When this is over, there are two more people in the way before I can finally end this thing."

Although Barrette wasn't the slightest bit convinced, he shook his head saying, "Sure...right. You'll finish this thing just like you started it." His focus was shining on the guns they may have had, or the conscience they didn't. Barrette walked away from me and got into his own position.

It wasn't long until the sound of several large truck engines overwhelmed all silence. The trucks shook the distance, and soon, I could see their bright lights climbing down the hills. When they finally reached the harbor and Port Lybric, their engines died down.

Several men, dressed in apparel that shared the same color palette as any grime or dirt, stepped out of the trucks and gathered around each other. The Traders looked around the property for the Deliverers who were meant to be there.

"Where the hell are they?" one asked to another, who passed the question on until it returned to him.

There was no evidence to give our operation away. The boats had sunk, the bodies sunk with them, and several large crates just as expected were waiting for the Trader's to retrieve. Eventually, after a brief discussion, the Traders began loading the packages into the backs of their trucks.

I looked for stencils on the sides of the vehicles that spelled TOY PALACE or BIG'S INCORPORATED. But there was nothing to give Big Rich's involvement away either.

While all the others loaded the remaining crates into the backs of their trucks, one Trader wandered off away from the commotion and lit a stick of Borm. He put it in his mouth and inhaled all the toxins and blue gel. It looked as if the Borm was massaging his insides. He sighed from ecstasy and took another deep breath.

He heard something rustling in the darkness and peered in. I could see him, but he couldn't see me. I unsheathed my last knife from its holster and sprinted out of the darkness with it raised.

The man's condition changed immediately after he saw me. Suddenly he stood on his toes and widened his eyes. "It's him!" he yelled, stripping me of the option to make a silent kill. "It's—" I ridded him of life's grace and stole his final words as I struck him with my blade.

It slid right into the side of his neck like he was made of butter.

He couldn't speak or scream or make a sound with the knife wedged into his flesh. But by the time he fell to the dirt, every other Trader was aware of my presence.

I made no attempt at sneaking my way into an entrance. I ran around the truck with my fists raised and my temper gruelingly hot. The closest Trader took the blunt force of a sprinting punch. His jaw snapped to the side and I was on to the next.

He swatted my first punch out of the air, but was hit by my second. He stumbled backward, and continued to deflect and attack. Another Trader threw his fists at me from behind. Then another from the side, and one more to my right.

Soon I was surrounded and forced to the ground with several pairs of limbs swinging at me. The group closed in around me, and soon I was watching the bottom of a boot sailing down onto my head.

And again, it was dark.

FOURTEEN

WITH THE CLOSEST THING TO A LIMP, I HOBBLED DOWN THE FAR stretch of the department's hallway, heading for the elevator, and after that, Ed's company. There was a woman slouching on a small bench pressed up against one wall to my left. Her long, greasy, bacon-colored hair covered her face, but as she heard my footsteps near, her eyes traveled to my face. Suddenly, the woman sprung from her seat, plummeted into me until there was no more room for me to fall. While my back was flattened to a wall behind me, she clung to my chest, standing on the tips of her toes.

The woman's words were breaching the border of insanity. I could only understand bits and pieces of her sentences shooting out of her mouth like bullets. She wanted desperately to tell me something, but couldn't restrain her thoughts enough to make anything understandable.

Her long, painted nails nearly broke through the skin of my shoulders as she gripped my arms with both hands. Every now and then she shook me, trying to concentrate my focus and emphasize what she was saying.

"I swear…it's not…he's…just don't…!"

I only understand shards of what the woman was telling me. Everything else just shook out of her mouth and landed on the floor. Just by the tone of her voice, the forcefulness in her movements, I could tell the woman was desperate.

She tried to fit as many words as she could between every

sob. Her breaths were taken in and released quickly, and she never got enough air. Over the span of our conversation, her eyes grew increasingly blood shot.

The blue of her irises popped out from the red backing of her whites. It was evident that woman had been living on the streets and making her living in different hotel rooms, or in the back of some scumbag's car.

Her hair had been neglected: It was knotted, greasy, and was denied of the opportunity to be brushed. Bright red lipstick was slapped sloppily across her lips, looking like a child had applied it. Her teeth were crooked and turning yellow, and veins webbed her hands and arms since there was no meat on her bones to hide them.

"Barrette!" I called for the commissioner to come over. His head jutted out the door of his nearby office. He looked at me and began walking down the hallway toward us. "Who is this woman?" She was still holding onto me by my shoulders. "She just came right up to me as soon as I entered the place..."

"She said she knew you," Barrette explained. "Why? You don't know her?"

"No..." I looked at the woman to second guess myself, but no recognition of her face came to mind. Though, the color of her eyes reminded me of my formal eye color.

As Barrette and I conversed, the woman was trying to articulate, sharpen and refine her words. She wanted desperately for me to listen, though there was nothing to listen to but her scrambled speech.

There was a word she was trying to pronounce. The only reason she couldn't was because her voice was trembling. She tried so hard to speak so I could understand.

"What?" I asked her. "What is it? Tell me..."

"Huh...huh...Hale," she finally got out. "Alex...Alexander Hale..."

I was surprised and confused. I looked at Barrette who just shrugged. "How do you know my name?" She tried to continue, but trembled too much. "Here," I helped her back over to the seat and sat the woman down. "Calm down...what do you need to tell me? How do you know my name?"

"I..." She took a wise while to calm herself and breathe. "You can't kill him, Alexander...you can't kill Richard Lucifer..." Those mere words were enough to increase the temperature of my attitude greatly.

I aimed my rage toward the commissioner, asking meanly, "Who the hell did you let in here, Barrette?" I stood and snipped at the commissioner, offended that another skeptic was in my presence. "I don't need any of this sh—"

"Alex!" the woman spoke up. "Listen to me, Alexander!"

"How do you know my name?" I asked again, more aggressively this time.

"Just listen to me..." The commissioner and I watched for an answer. I remained silent and she took the room to speak. "He wants all of this madness," the woman spoke with such ambiguity. "He wants you to kill Richard, he wants Los Angeles to fall!"

"Who? Who wants that?"

"*Him...*"

"Who?"

"Just...just don't kill him, Alexander. Don't kill him and you won't have to live with it for the rest of your life. All of Los Angeles will die! You know that, don't you?"

I said, "They deserve to die. Big Rich deserves to die..."

"No!" the woman cried. "No he doesn't!"

"Ma'am, who are you?" I asked the woman for the last time. "Tell me, or I'm not going to hear any more of what you have to say."

Her head dropped and shook. "You don't understand...I loved him once..."

"Who? Who are you talking about?"

"They took me from you! They took me from you!"

"*Who, are you?*" I screamed at her angrily!

"My name is Tabatha..." she said like that meant something to me. But then she finished, she told me her whole identity. "Tabatha Hale," she said in a heavy exhale.

"What?" I stood higher from my seat and directed my confusion toward Barrette. His mouth fell open—he too was speechless. "What did you just say? What did you just say?" I picked her up violently by her shoulders and forced her to the opposite wall of the bench.

She shrieked and told me again, "I swear! My name is Tabatha Hale...I'm...I'm your—"

"Shut up, woman! My mother is dead, my father is dead! What do you want from me? Why are you here?" I shook her. "Tell me, or I'll break your neck!"

"Hale," Barrette tried to calm me, thinking that his relation with me could ease and clog my pumping anger.

"Don't make me hurt you, Barrette! Stay out of this!" I turned back to the woman, foam in my mouth, baneful spite in my voice. "Tell me!"

"I'm sorry I haven't come to you sooner! I just...I could never find you! But you came to the club and I saw your face...and then it made sense. I've been hearing about you, what you're doing... what you want to do..." The woman was talking about my plan of ending both Project Home and Big Rich. "I had to find you! I came here to the commissioner," she looked at Barrette who stood a distance from us, "and I tried to explain myself..."

"I swear," Barrette defended his own innocence in the situation, "I didn't know what she was talking about! It was all nonsense!"

"He said he knew you and that I could wait here until you came..." the woman said. "I am your mother, Alex..." the woman said to me, so desperate in breaking my refusal to accept what she was trying to convey.

"I'm an orphan!" I hooted. "My mother, my parents are dead!"

"No," she opposed. "No, they took you from me, Alex! I'm so sorry...I'm so sorry..."

"You're lying, lady. Get the hell away from me!" I ripped my arms free of her grasp. She refused to step away. The woman lurched back toward me.

"Please, Alexander! You have to believe me! How else would I know your name, Alexander Hale? How else would I know what you're planning on doing...?" She fell to her knees, looking up at me with eyes that could not bear anymore tears. Her fingers were hooked to the bottom fraying ends of my hoodie, tugging it down from my throat.

I lowered my hostility for a moment and disregarded both options of believing whether or not she was my mother. "What... do...you...want?" The woman still hadn't answered my demanding question.

She looked into my eyes, my dark, coal-colored irises. Her eyes were so electrical like mine had been...And maybe, just maybe I could see myself in her. "You can't kill him," she begged me once more, calmly this time. Her voice was most sincere and concerning. "You can't kill Big Rich. It's not what you think," she promised. "Take that hood of yours off and look at things from a different angle."

I shook my head and pounded my perception into her's. "Big Rich is a guilty man! I'm going to bring his whole, God damned business to ashes! That's where it belongs!"

"No...no..."

"Tell me why the Drug Trade doesn't belong in the ground... Tell me why!"

"You don't understand," she expressed herself hopelessly.

"No," I fought, "it's you who doesn't understand. It's this entire city that doesn't understand!"

"Please," she pleaded, "please don't kill him! That's what he wants! You'll live your life in hell if you go through with this! Don't kill him...don't kill him...he's...he's *innocent.*"

"Ah!" I screamed and threw her violently to the side. She fell to the ground and I kicked the woman in her ribs. "Get out!" I screeched. "Get out before I kill you!"

She hurried to her feet and nearly fell out the door.

"What the hell, kid?" Barrette lifted his hands and dropped them. "What was that?"

"Shut up, Barrette…"

"No, you need to hear this."

"I said shut up!" I turned toward him and picked up a fast paced march with my fists sharp and mean.

He reached inside the left flap of his coffee-colored suit jacket and removed a revolver from its hidden holster. The commissioner held its aim right over my head and sent me a look that said he would shoot. He would shoot, and kill me.

I had no choice but to stop in my tracks. "Are you going to kill me, Barrette? Huh?" He just stared at me with a concrete expression. "Huh? You're just gonna shoot me down right here?" He said nothing, but held the gun between me and him. "Go ahead!" I tickled his temptation. "Shoot! Kill me!"

"You don't want to die, kid. Don't pretend you do…"

"I'm already dead!" I hollered. "I was murdered, remember? I'm a ghost! A fucking ghost!"

"You're standing right here!"

"No…" I said quietly, forcing him to listen. There was the moisture of tears soaking my eyeballs. "No, I'm lying dead at the bottom of a cliff. I'm lying dead with all the other kids of the orphanage who refused to join the trade!"

The elevator doors dinged and opened. Ed came walking out with his eyes scrounging about a manila colored file. He took a quick glance up, looked back down, but then double-took. "What…" was his first response of what to say. "What's going on? Barrette, put your gun down…"

"No!" Barrette opposed him. "This maniac has gone too far…I should arrest him! Better yet, I should shoot him down." Barrette's eyes became so evil, that I thought maybe I was looking into my own.

I was on the other side of the gun now. Our roles had shifted, and for the first time I felt what it was like to stand in justice's grimy animosity. I couldn't find comfort in my own body, and I was paranoid about every action I made, hoping that Barrette wouldn't fire his gun. I could smell, feel, and taste his own temptation.

Why not just kill him? Barrette must have been thinking. *He has hurt me; taken from me…He deserves to die…He, deserves to die. Just like Big Rich…*

"Barrette, put down the gun!" Ed tried again while slowly approaching the commissioner. "Barrette…"

I knew he wasn't going to lower his anger or his firearm, so, quicker than his itchy finger, I dashed my hand into my pocket for Jay's pistol…but it wasn't there. I had reached into the wrong pocket.

I paused as my fingers made contact with the spotless, cold glass of Raine's necklace. I had forgotten about it…about her. Slowly, I removed it from my pocket and held it in the callused palm of my leather-gloved hand.

The reflection of everything on the droplet was bent to match its shape. I saw the ceiling above my head, and the monster looking at me. I wouldn't have recognized myself if I were living from a third-person-perspective.

*Raine…*I thought. In the mess of my depleting life, I had forgotten about another. She was taken from me. She gave me such strength, such anger, such sadness, something fight for and not to die for. Who knows what would've happened if I came into her house that one night.

My skin wouldn't be peeling from its skeleton, my innocence would have had a fighting chance, Big Rich would have had the rest of his life to live. But Project Home would take its final step across the finish line. Big Rich would spread his Borm across the world, and when the day would come that death would shake his hand, Earth would die with him.

A loud, unwarned noise made me jump. It was a gunshot…

I looked at Barrette who held his gun toward me. But his face was as equally surprised as mine. When I looked down at my chest, there was no blood, no bullet hole or scratch. Barrette hadn't shot me, and I hadn't shot Barrette.

Then, all in unison, Ed, Barrette and I knew exactly where the shot came from. Simultaneously, we raced out of the department. Lying in the street was the woman I had tossed out.

Her chest was red with blood, and she gurgled and coughed up even more. I looked both ways, up and down the street until I saw the suspect. It was the mysterious man I had seen several times before.

As soon as I looked, he was fitting a large handgun into the pocket of his pitch coat. He tipped his head and covered his identity in a shadow, turned, and disappeared into a nearby alleyway. I wanted to chase him and hunt the man down, but I knew the woman at my feet was dying.

She grabbed my ankle, wasting the last of her strength. Her mouth tried to form several, bloody words that were inaudible from where I stood. I lowered to her level on the street. In the background I heard Ed calling at the commissioner to find a doctor or call an ambulance. We all knew she would die, though.

Blood, like drool, spilled out of the corner of her mouth and down one cheek. I slipped my arm underneath her head and lifted it from the pavement.

"Don't..." she managed to pronounce. "Don't kill him... *please*..."

"I...I have to..." I didn't want to crush her life's last chance at hope, but I didn't want her to hear a lie as the last thing she ever would. "I have to..."

"If you do," the woman began telling me with blood in her mouth, "then everything you know will come to an end..."

"If crime is merciless..."

"Then we must do what we can..." She gurgled. "...to defend those with mercy, against those without it..." Her last words were naturally wise and well-conceived. She hoped I would listen, not just hear. "Take off that hood, and see this for what it is..." Her hand slowly reached up to the hood on my head, but didn't make it. It fell to the ground and her head grew heavy.

"Ma'am?" I called for her. "Ma'am...?"

Her eyes never closed. I slowly set her head down on the street, and laid her to rest.

Far behind me in a faint voice I heard Barrette commonly apostrophize, "Jesus Christ...Hale," he raised his voice, "come inside. I'll have someone take care of her..."

I rose to my feet, and looked into my mother's eyes for the first and last time. Then I stomped them to the horizon of urban stubble—the city growing like a weed in the distance, against the orange hues of a rising sun.

FIFTEEN

THE MAN'S CONDITION CHANGED IMMEDIATELY AFTER HE SAW ME. *Suddenly he stood on his toes and widened his eyes. "It's him!" he yelled, stripping me of the option to make a silent kill. "It's—" I ridded him of life's grace and stole his final words as I struck him with my blade.*

It slid right into the side of his neck like he was made of butter. He couldn't speak or scream or make a sound with the knife wedged into his flesh. But by the time he fell to the dirt, every other Trader was aware of my presence.

I made no attempt at sneaking my way into an entrance. I ran around the truck with my fists raised and my temper gruelingly hot. The closest Trader took the blunt force of a sprinting punch. His jaw snapped to the side and I was on to the next.

He swatted my first punch out of the air, but was hit by my second. He stumbled backward, and continued to deflect and attack. Another Trader threw his fists at me from behind. Then another from the side, and one more to my right.

Soon I was surrounded and forced to the ground with several pairs of limbs swinging at me. The group closed in around me, and soon I was watching the bottom of a boot sailing down onto my head.

And again, it was dark.

When I awoke, my arms were numb and my skin felt stretched and bound to tear like dry hide. There was no ground beneath my feet—I was suspended, weightless like a ghost's body. My head hung harshly from my neck, and just to bring it up took more strength than I could afford to waste.

I heard talking around me, but none of it was clear enough to register in my mind. It felt as if metal razors were cutting at my wrists, rubbing my skin raw. My arms were stretched to their capacity above my head.

Finally, my eyelids parted and I could see a plain landscape around me. It became clear that I was hanging from my wrists above the ground. My upper body was completely bare of clothing, so I hung with nothing but a tattered, gossamer pair of jeans on my legs. Even my shoes were ripped off my feet.

One Trader noticed my lucidity regaining. He called all the others' attention to me, and slowly each member of the group began to assemble around me.

"Wakey wakey!" clowned a Trader who was standing just below and in front of me. "Sleep well?" he asked facetiously. He bent over his knees and looked at my sagging face. "Come on," he perked, ""wake up! Look around! Do you know where you are?"

I lifted my head with a painful motion and peeled open my eyes fully. Slowly, every one of my senses regained its health. I could hear the grinding of rusty gears, smell the odiferous stench of gasoline, feel the numbness in my arms, the shredding skin of my wrists, and my stretched muscles. I could taste the iron in my blood that had seeped through the spaces of my teeth.

I was in an industrial junkyard. The entire warehouse was occupied by the metallic limbs of machines and the stretches of conveyor belts. There were mechanisms in the warehouse that I couldn't ever begin to explain. I was in Gray Moss, the birth place of Borm.

The series of machines started simple: First there were a few dispensers that released different ingredients onto the belt, then furnaces and mechanical arms swinging in every direction.

To my left there was a horribly loud hissing sound, and when I looked, I saw fiery teeth in the open jaw of a mammoth furnace. I was tied to a rotary of chains that I knew would pull me into the furnace.

The Trader recognized my own realization. "Oh yes," he spouted, "you've made a mistake. But before we kill you, we want to know who you are…" I found it foolishly wise to keep my silence. Quickly, the Trader caught on. He smiled at me—two rows of stained, holey teeth, and breath *that could suffocate bitterness itself. "Boss told us about you..." I looked at him. "That's right, he knows you're going after him. He knows your plans...he knows about your friends and that pretty little girl..."*

Right as the Trader mentioned Raine's description, I tried to lash my legs at him. He simply stepped back and laughed. I couldn't afford to move too much, for my shoulders were bound to pop right out of their sockets.

"Save your energy...you're going to be squirming a lot more when you're being baked alive!" The Trader turned around to the others and together they all laughed. "So...tell us, who are you? Huh?"

I piled a wad of spit in my mouth, and launched it at the Trader. My saliva landed right in his left eye. He flinched backward in a similar motion to a twitch. he wiped the spit out of his eyeball and walked close to me with a balled fist. He socked me in the gut, and grinned with satisfaction.

"You make another move like that and I'll roast you even slower!" the Trader threatened as an attempt to rebuild his masculinity and surely dominant stance. "Now tell us! Who are you? You've gotta have a story..."

I finally opened my mouth. "It's not a story a piece of shit like you could follow..."

He was amused. "Did you hear that, boys? I'm a piece of shit! And I bet you all are too!"

There were over a dozen Traders who stood around me with rifles resting in their hands. They all had emotionless eyes and stone expressions. Half sucked on the butts of Borm sticks, but the other half was wishing they had some Borm of their own. They all glared at me, waiting to witness this public execution.

"Oh well," said the Trader conclusively. "When you come out on the other side of that furnace like a damn steak, I'll make sure to piss on you... you piece of—" For a second time, I spat in his face. He had dropped his patience and replaced it with utter irritation. He made his way over to a control panel to begin my entrance into the furnace.

He flipped one switch and then another. The Trader hovered one hand over a giant red button. "Do you have anything else to add to that?" he asked me.

"I do..." I told him and said without any matching context, "Now!"

Out of the crates the Traders had picked up from Port Lybric, several squads of officers burst out with their guns drawn and their targets perfectly chosen.

"Get down!" the officers ordered. "Get down now!"

But every sedulous Trader raised their guns and picked a fight with the outnumbering police officers. Having given a chance of grace, the officers didn't take one more moment of serenity before beginning the seize of the warehouse. Both sides opened fire.

The Trader chef twisted around to the commotion running wildly from every gun. He reached for his own rifle, but an officer's bullet caught him in the chest. He fell backward right into the control panel, and the weight of his body pressed down on the red button.

The rotary I was chained to jerked, and began slowly moving toward the furnace.

There was only one thing my adrenalin told me to do: PANIC!

I began swinging my legs in all different directions and tugging on the chains to try and free myself before being cooked alive. With a background noise of gunfire and the presence of grim nearing, it was impossible to think clearly.

The furnace's heat was beginning to creep close. It was only warmth at the moment, but I knew that a few seconds later it would be a scolding heat. Screams scraped past my ears and bullets sped around my body.

The chain wouldn't budge and my lonely weight wasn't enough to collapse the rotary bar. I looked into the mouth of the furnace. In it was nothing but bright orange teeth dancing around inside a metal jaw, just waiting to devour me.

I gave one last try to breaking free of my chains. Nothing was loosened enough to free me.

Without warning, the heat intensified. I felt it boiling blisters on my skin, burning it away into little shredded peels. I screamed loud, but it wasn't a match to the shooting inside the warehouse. The closer I moved, the more my skin felt like it was melting off my body.

I tightened my teeth and even felt my molars crack under the pressure.

An officer dashed over to the control panel and hit the red button, *stopping me before fully entering the furnace. But I was still in reach of the fiery spikes eating away at my flesh.*

After a point, the side of my body that was burning away felt cold—the flames were cremating the ends of my nerves. I could smell my own flesh burning, and my gag reflexes were scrambling about from the pain and the odor.

The first layer of my skin had burned away, and by that time I was completely disregarding the small battle taking place around me. The flames continued to gnaw at the next layer of skin, and eventually the beginning layer of muscle.

I heard a loud pop, and I was falling from the rotary. I landed on a conveyer belt and rolled off onto the cold ground. My raw flesh and tissue and muscle hurt when anything touched it. I screamed and rolled around, trying to find a way to lay that wouldn't shoot endless amounts of pain across my body.

"Stay down!" a fading voice yelled. "Just stay down and we'll get you through this!"

The sounds of the battle began to sound distant...and before long, I was lost in a near coma sleep...

..."Stay down"... "Just stay down"...

"I have had the privilege to be part of this great movement," Ty Eval praised. He stood next to Big Rich who stood in between him and Mr. Ill. "Project Home is what this city needs, and what its people want. Thousands of orphans are living on the streets after their parents have been murdered, or after the children have been abandoned. From around the world I have had the cooperation and friendly assistance from an uncountable amount of sources. Last night, Big's Incorporated coordinated a shipment of goods that has allowed me to supply Project Home with its greatest gift yet!" Mr. Eval smiled a kind, harmless smile. He raised his arms and shook them in the air to raise his audience's enthusiasm. "Next week, Mr. Lucifer, Mr. Ill and I will be celebrating Project Home's completion, and the grand opening of Toy Palace! After years into the making, Project Home will no longer be a vision, it will no longer be an ambitious dream. Project Home will be a blast of hope that the City of Angels deserves!" There wasn't one mouth in his audience that didn't open wide and let loose the most exciting scream of joy and pleasure. They all bounced up and down, turning the audience into an ocean's current.

"Thank you, Mr. Eval," Big Rich stepped close to the microphone, clapping. "Thank you! Yes..." Big Rich began his own dialogue. "Project Home is nearing completion. In addition to Mr. Eval's conduction, Mr. Ill will be visiting a source along the east coast. If they accept our business proposal, Project Home will become a nation-wide collaboration. We all deserve its grace! We all deserve its mercy! So when Project Home is open, our streets will begin to clean themselves, and children will grow to benefit this society! It will be a Renaissance of its own—a new beginning for this city and this country!" His voice was omnipotent. It boomed from the Heavens without the help of a microphone. "It's time we take our city back from the indecency and cruelty that has scared us back into our shells. Our country was once a place where people would compromise everything to be a part of, and now people will compromise everything just so they can escape its immorality. Project Home will light the fuse; it will lead the way to a new becoming. So we hold our hopes high as Project Home is coming to its completion! And we continue to fight the current, to climb the slope, to light the darkness! We are not slaves to corruption! We are not weak, and we are certainly not fools! Stand beside me so we can rid the evil that has rotted this nation! Stand beside me so we can clean the mess we helped make! Stand beside me, and we'll prove to never start what you cannot—"

The period to Big's sentence was a loud gunshot that erupted somewhere behind the audience. One of Big's guards in a white suit fell backward with a single bloody dot on his chest. Another gunshot roared, and the Officials' second guard fell dead.

The audience shattered and people spread everyone outside of

Big's Tower. All three Officials ducked to try and dodge the bullets buzzing past them and in their direction. Lucifer and Ill made an immediate dash to their black SUV waiting in the street just a few feet from where they were speaking.

Eval tried to run with them, but a bullet caught him in the leg. He buckled and fell to the ground whining in pain, clawing at his wound. He tried to hold the thick warm blood from spilling out of his circular chunk of missing skin, but his blood seeped through the spaces between his fingers.

He cried aloud, and one of his guards was racing to his rescue when he too was shot. The white-suited-guard fell to his face only feet from Eval. Ty rolled around on the ground, clutching his leg.

The audience had diminished, but the shooting continued to pick off each of Big's guards one by one. Big Rich and Ill had raced off in the black SUV, but Eval was left to die. "Help!" he cried desperately. "Help me! Help me!"

An officer slid up next to Eval and spoke loud over the distant shooting. "I'm here! I'm here! Come on, sir, we need to get you out of here! Can you stand?"

Eval lifted his head and looked at his leg now soaked in blood. He wailed his voice again, then told the officer, "Help me to my feet! I can't use my right leg!"

"Okay," the officer cooperated and began scooping Eval up into his arms. With rusty movement, Eval was eventually to his feet, leaning on the officer like a crutch.

Bullets were smashing into the walls of Big's Tower right aside the officer and Eval. Brick powder blew out from the walls each time a bullet would strike. Little whizzing sounds flew past their ears, and both the officer and Ty would flinch, ducking their heads even lower.

The officer escorted Eval to a police cruiser on the other side of Big's Tower, opposite of where the shooting was occurring. "Okay," he said to Eval, "get in, and he'll take you somewhere safe. I need to go see if I can apprehend the shooter." Just as he said so, a gunshot sounded and a bullet hit him in the back.

He fell limply into Eval and then to the concrete. Ty shrieked and took no time to get into the police cruiser. "Drive!" he commanded as if the commissioner was a chauffeur. "Drive!" As Barrette began to press heavily on the gas pedal, a bullet struck the side of the cruiser. A metal on metal ding rang from the side of the car. Eval panicked even more. "Drive! Drive! Drive!"

The tires screeched and nearly rolled in place until the car was in motion, zooming through the concrete forest. Eval was slouched, as far as he could be slouched, in the back seat. His tie was loose on his neck, and his chocolate covered hair hung before his rattled eyes. Each breath Eval took was deep and frantically accepted.

Barrette looked back over his seat. "You okay, Mr. Eval?"

"What...who...who was shooting?" he asked the commissioner all while trying to contain himself. His leg was bleeding all over the leather seats of the cruiser.

"I don't know," Barrette answered. "But we need to get you to a hospital." The commissioner grabbed his transmitter off the dash and spoke into it. "This is commissioner Barrette. I'm on West Fourth Street approaching South Broadway." He took a quick glance at Eval through his rearview mirror and said into the transmitter, "It's time..."

He made the turn going Northeast onto South Broadway Street. The cruiser was approaching the next block when Barrette shifted uncomfortably in his seat. He wrapped all his fingers around the steering wheel and cracked his neck just by swiveling his head.

Barrette opened his mouth to speak to Eval again, but as the cruiser began passing through an intersection, another vehicle came out of nowhere and crashed into the left side of the cruiser's hood.

Eval and Barrette were whipped to the left and the car was forced to the right. The collision was quick, and neither of the two cars moved very far. The commissioner and Ty stilled in their seats. White steam was hissing out of the hood of Barrette's cruiser.

"God damn it!" He slammed the heels of his hands on the steering wheel and cursed. Again, he looked back at Eval and asked, "Are you alright?"

Eval checked himself. Aside from his already-injured-leg, he was fine. "I'm alright," he confirmed. "I'm alright."

The driver of the other car opened his door and slowly, menacingly stepped out. His clothes were dark and filled with bulk, and on his head he wore a simple black mask with two eyeholes cut into it.

"What...the...hell..." There was nothing else, no other words that came into Barrette's mouth. Barrette turned back to Eval who was stunned in his seat still. "Sir, stay in the car, I need to have a word with this guy." Barrette faced forward, but the man was gone. The commissioner looked all around, searching for the guy, and suddenly there was a knock on his window. Barrette jumped and looked to his left.

The man in the mask stood there with a pistol in his hand. He tapped on the glass with his gun's metal barrel, wanting Barrette to open up. He paused, and Barrette lunged for the door's lock. The masked man ripped open the door before Barrette could lock himself and Mr. Eval inside.

There wasn't even the tiniest crumb of hesitation before the masked man raised his gun, and fired into the car at Barrette's head. In the compact space of the car, the gunshot was deafening. Eval cried aloud when Barrette's body fell to the side.

The hijacker and now murderer pulled Barrette's body out of the car and took his place in the driver's seat. He leveled his gun's aim over Eval's terrified face and locked the doors once he closed his.

Leaving Barrette's body on the street, the masked man put the car in reverse, pulled away from the accident, and squealed on. Eval continued protesting in the back seat. He tried to open the doors, screaming at the masked man, gripping his leg.

"Where are you taking me?"

"Shut up!" the driver shouted.

"Tell me!"

"Shut up!"

"You'll never get away with this!" Eval swore. "Do you know who I am? Do you?"

The driver laughed evilly at the idiotic question and confidently said, "You're Ty Eval. You work for Big Rich..."

"Exactly," Ty smiled, then grunted from pain. "So you know what I'm capable of...what *he's* capable of."

"Be quiet," the driver requested again with a little ounce of patience.

"No! I won't be quiet. I'm going to—" The masked driver slammed on the breaks, turned around, and knocked his handgun over Eval's skull. On the first try, Eval fell unconscious.

He woke up with a heavy amount of blood sitting in his head. His orientation was deceived, but it didn't take long for Eval to realize he was hanging upside down. "What the..." The cow about to be butchered tried to part his hands, but they were bound at the wrists. "Hey!" he screamed. "Hey!"

All around him was darkness. Impenetrable, unsinkable darkness. He couldn't see anything but his own body hanging from nowhere. The ground five feet below his head was dusted in ash and littered by burnt wooden beams lying all about. And slowly his eyes began to dilate as an environment began building around him.

He was in a sort of building or warehouse...or at least what was left of one. A majority of the structure's walls and ceiling had fallen over or collapsed in. Eval was hanging from a rope tied around one of the last remaining beams, then tied tightly to his ankles.

He struggled and thrashed his body like a mutant worm suspended in the air. "Hey!" Again and again he called out to no one. "Hey! Somebody! Help me!" Eval grunted to himself, and then remember the injury on his leg. Suddenly his bullet wound hurt again. "God damn it!" he whined and wailed.

Slowly, from out of the darkness, the masked man came. He held his hands behind his back and sauntered in circles around Eval.

"What do you want?" Ty finally asked the man. "Why did you bring me here?"

The man started immediately. "I know what Project Home really is..."

Eval didn't seem to understand the thesis of his kidnapper's words. "What?" he asked, astonished. "What are you talking about? You say that like it's some sort of conspiracy..."

"And it's not?" the masked man asked hastily.

Eval claimed, "Of course it isn't!"

"Hm..." The masked man continued to walk in circles around the suspended worm. "And what about Toy Palace? What about the orphanage homes? Are those just the blessings of a charitable man?"

"I don't understand...Let me down and we can talk about this. I'll pay you," bribed Eval.

"Don't play dumb with me!" the shadow-appareled man growled hostilely, and I ripped off my mask.

Eval knew he had seen me before. By the changing and shifting expressions on his face I could tell he was trying to figure out where his recognition came from. "You..." he said. "I've seen you..." I waited until it came to him clearly. "You, you tried to attack Big Rich at one of his conferences, didn't you?"

"Mm..." I hummed behind my closed lips.

"Why...why are you doing this? Why did you bring me here?"

"I know, Eval! And I'm not the only one who does!"

"You know what?" Eval played clueless.

I curled a fist and launched it into his stomach. He grunted and coughed, and his body swayed weightlessly. "Damn it! I don't understand!" I hit him again, and he vomited all over his own face, nearly choking on his puke.

"The Drug Trade!" He was still vomiting as I spoke. "I know you three oversee the operation...I know Big Rich is in charge! And I also know this..." I took Eval's head by his hair and pulled his face close. "I know that Project Home is his way of spreading the business across America. The orphanage homes—they're recruiting centers. He wants to gather as many kids to be future members of the trade. Toy Palace—it's another factory and a place to sell and buy Borm. I know, Eval! I know everything!"

After spitting and coughing up more vomit, he made eye contact with me. "I don't know what you're talking about...you have a problem with Big Rich, you settle it with him! But believe me... you won't get anywhere!"

"Really? I stopped your shipment of Borm last night..."

"My shipment?"

"...I burned down this damn factory! I think I've gotten pretty far...and when I kill you," I leaned in closer, "I'll be another step ahead."

"Kill me? Why do you want to kill *me?*"

"Don't take it too personally," I advised him. "I'm killing all three of you. Next it'll be Mr. Ill, and then Big Rich himself. I can't expect to fully kill the Drug Trade if any of the Officials are still around..."

"Kid, I don't know what you're talking about!" I could smell his bluff. "I'm not a part of this...*Drug Trade.* I swear on my life!"

"That's a pretty bold thing to do...seeing how you're going to die because of it."

"Please! I swear! I'm innocent!"

"Nobody is innocent, especially not you, Mr. Ty Eval. You've helped raise Project Home since its birth! You were going to allow it to spread the Drug Trade across the nation!" Little flings of spit landed on Eval's face from my mouth.

"Project Home has nothing to do with any of this!"

"Don't lie to me!"

"I'm not lying! I swear!"

"There's no point in swearing," I said. "You're already dead. This is just a matter of you dying honorably or not..."

Eval began to shred tears. He whimpered and whined like a little baby. His true form was finally crawling out of his skin. "I swear," he said with a trembling voice, "I have nothing to do with any of this...please, just...let me go..."

"I don't think so, Mr. Eval..." My voice was chilling and dragged coldly across his ears. Besides his own chopping whimpering, my voice would be the last he would ever hear.

I made him look at me, at my blistering skin and my burnt flesh. I made him smell the stench of my raw meat, the putrid scent of burnt hair. My face and body was as monstrous as my insides. Several teeth were missing from my mouth, and now, a third of my body was seared and peeling off its skeleton.

His eyes widened and his breath was taken. He was horrified, and it pleased me to know that fear would be his last emotion.

I bent down and wrapped my fingers around a wooden beam that had fallen from the ceiling the night of the fire. Half of it was burnt away, leaving a sharp, charred tip on the end of the beam.

I twirled it so the pointed end was at its tip. "If crime is merciless..." Without any lacking strength, I forced the sharpened end of the beam into Eval's stomach and pulled it out. He began vomiting blood from his mouth. It drenched his face until I couldn't even see his eyes. "Justice must be too!" I spoke the last breath of my chant, pulled back the beam in my hands, and cracked it like a baseball bat across Eval's skull.

A variety of sounds exploded from the hit. It was first the crack of his crushing skull, then the squish of his mushy brains. His face was automatically deformed, and thick, syrupy blood began to spill out of his head and puddle on the ashy ground.

I was left standing in the ashes with a dead man. In the silence, I could hear each beat of my heart, the waves crashing in the Pacific, and every drop of blood splashing in the deepening puddle.

After navigating out of the ruin, I found my way to the street cutting through the tiniest, most vacant neighborhood California had to offer. Gray Moss was always lonely. No one roamed its streets, no light combated its darkness. It was easy to find my ride; it was the only car around.

Every house was just a hollow box with black windows and grassless lawns, broken gates and mutilated mailboxes, locked doors that wouldn't stop a thief from stealing anything inside.

I walked around the police cruiser to the passenger side door, opened it, and got in. For long, I never said a word. I stared at the dashboard while he drove us all the way across town. In my ear, I could still hear the dripping of Eval's blood.

Drip...

Drip...

Drip...

I would look out the car window and see him hanging from the air with his impaled skull and disfigured face. When I looked at my feet, I thought I saw blood leaking into the car and slowly rising to the level of my knees. No matter what I did, I couldn't get him out of my head.

"It was that bad?" Barrette asked.

All I said in return was, "He had to die..."

The commissioner didn't have the slightest idea how to make me feel any better. "Did he?" Barrette looked at me straight and didn't blink. He wanted me to answer, but knew I wouldn't...I couldn't.

I leaped to another subject. "How's your ear?" I asked him.

"Oh..." He faced the road again. "It's alright..." Now that I had brought his attention to it, Barrette brought his left hand to his left ear and cupped it. "I think a bruised eardrum is better than a bullet in my head. Thanks for using a blank," Barrette thanked me.

"At least now Big Rich won't suspect the police to be involved with any of this...looks like you're safe," I observed.

"It was a good idea," he credited. "It's best we keep our hands clean until he's out of the picture for good...who knows what Lucifer would have done if he knew the Los Angeles Police were involved..."

[My plan for abducting Eval called for a single officer sniper to make base across from Big's Tower. I could have had him kill both Big

Rich and Ill, but I needed my message to ring loud and clear. I told the sniper (the same one from Port Lybric) to only injure Eval. From there, a second officer would escort him to the back of Barrette's car. Big Rich would notice the police's aid, and his suspicion toward their involvement would be completely eroded. I waited at the intersection, waiting for Barrette's call. And from there, it was only a masked madman kidnapping the infamous Ty Eval.]

We had already dug our way through the city and broke out the other side to the eastern outskirts where the station was. He came to a stop at the curb of the department and Barrette turned the car off.

I began to step out of the cruiser but Barrette stopped me. "Kid...I hope you know what you're doing." I just looked at Barrette. I didn't have to tell him that I did. "Once this is over, there's no going back. Your innocence will be forever lost...people will come after you..."

"My innocence was lost when I was born, commissioner. And when people come after me, I'll be waiting." I stepped out of the car.

As I boarded the sidewalk to head for the entrance of the building, Barrette rolled down the window. "Kid!" Barrette threw his voice after my attention again. I turned around once more. "Just...don't let your flame grow too hot." He didn't leave room for a response. Barrette closed the window and drove off into the city.

Night had fallen over Los Angeles, but there was a dawn breaking. Ty Eval was dead, his shipment was destroyed. Project Home was limping now, and it was just a matter of time before day would rise, and I would kick its legs out from underneath.

Inside the department, I made my way to its very end and entered the elevator which lowered me to Ed's basement. The ding of the opening doors never brought Ed's attention up from his work. He saw me, acknowledged me, but said nothing.

Never to make any form of eye contact, Ed snidely assumed, "You killed him?" Unlike when Barrette asked me, this time, I said nothing back. "You killed him just like you're going to kill the others." Then he looked up.

"What else is there to be done? The only way to stop Project Home is to kill them…"

Laughing beneath his breath, Ed shook his head. He then fed me his opinion. "I feel like…like you're losing sight of things, Hale. Why you're doing this, what it's for. Ever since Raine was taken…" He checked to see if I was boiling with rage. I only stood there, feeling his words pass me. "You're getting lost inside that hood of yours."

"That's not true," I defended myself.

"Isn't it?" Ed stepped up to me and quickly pulled the hood from my head.

My reflex told me to look away. I did. He grabbed my chin with one hand and forced me to look at him. Ed examined the burns and injuries on my face and neck. Every time he rotated my head around, he shook his own, appalled by what he was seeing.

"It's infected," Ed said, and held up a mirror to my face.

It was torturous to look at my own reflection, but I had no other choice. On the whole right side of my head and neck, a burn stretched from beneath my tattered hoodie and crawled its way all the way up to my ear and the back of my head.

Hair was missing where I had been burned, and my raw pink flesh was literally peeling like old wall paper from the rest of my skin. Yellow puss seeped out of the cuts and splits amongst the giant burn. Bubbles of blisters rose out of my flesh, and were soon to pop.

And where my skin wasn't burned, it was still marked. My lips were the same color as my pale skin. What were once fresh cuts and scratches were now crusty scabs. Along my neck like skid marks, were the streaks of bullets that had skimmed me in prior fights.

"You see?" Ed asked. "You see what you're doing to yourself?" I should have been the one disgusted by the way I was rotting alive, but Ed was more upset. "God damn it! At what cost are you willing to kill that man?"

"It's not just about killing him, Ed."

"Yes it is!" Ed promised me my own truth. "And don't you dare try to say otherwise. Maybe at some point in the past there was more to your plan, but not anymore. This is about you carrying out Jay's chore."

I was taken back, insulted. "You think that's what this is about? No, there's—"

"Don't kid yourself, Hale. We all know that this is a scheme of revenge. He took Jay and Raine from you, and now you're getting back at him!"

"He killed me! He took my identity!"

"And you had a choice!" Ed claimed. "You had a choice to rise above the temptations, or to crumple beneath the weight. You chose this identity, Hale! Not Big Rich, not the Drug Trade, *you*! You chose this…"

"You don't know the beginning of it!"

"Then tell me, Hale! Tell me what happened, tell me about the day you came back to life!"

It was days of swollen feet and lousy bus fare before I made it back to Los Angeles. My clothes were stiff from the salt water which had dried onto them, and my mind was rattled by the chaos that had been crammed into it.

I noticed when I got back that the city did not, in even the tiniest bit, move differently. It was accustomed to losing the weight of people each day. I was just a piece of dust which landed back on the city; it didn't notice me at all.

After I took a lunge off of an eighty foot cliff, I made it back three days later. Beyond the layers of pollution which never left the city, the lights of the skyscrapers lit themselves up like man-made galaxies.

It was night, and criminals were nocturnal. Amongst the noise of traffic flying by and in the dark heat which gathered around me, I walked, and walked, and walked. I walked until the city itself began to fall asleep, and soon I was the only person with their eyes open.

Feet bleeding, skin raw from the rubbing of my stiff, salt water drenched clothes, I watched my shadow begin at my feet and end on the wall of a building across the street. The hood on my head made me a menacing form, and my broad shoulders intimidated it.

After long, I was back into the neighborhood which tossed me out. In all doubt of my return, the orphanage home sat in its normal position. No light escaped the home, and in fact, it seemed that darkness came through its brick walls of the building.

The car that had brought me north and dumped me off was parked back behind it. From the construction-site nearby, I noticed a building beginning to rise like a zombie from a grave.

Big Rich's work was nearing completion. Dirt which had been stirred up from the numerous bulldozers and vehicles began to fill out around the toy store's grounds.

My first thought was to go see Raine, but then something happened...

From the shadows, a man emerged. He took step by easy step toward me with his arms proudly crossed in front of his bloated chest.

"He was easy to kill," the man spoke. "A pathetic old man. He begged for his life like a starved dog...I looked at him, spat in his face, then killed him." The man was amused by his own words.

"What...?" I was so dazed by my trip home, that I couldn't conceive what the man was telling me.

He grinned and continued to spoil his role: "That's right," he said without the aid of any occult abilities, "I killed him. I murdered that old hag...I needed a couple bucks to buy some Borm." He seemed so pleased with his kill, so happy and cocky that he couldn't help but share it with me. "Man, he was pathetic...the way he begged me for mercy before I shot him. It was hilarious!" Obviously he wasn't aware that I would be so pleased to strangle him to the ground.

The man began opening his mouth to rant again, but my hands shot for his throat, my fingers wrapped around his neck, and my strength squeezed the two factors together and began choking the life from him with the force of rage.

As terrifying to him as it was, he knew I would never let go, never release the ankle of his life. The only escape he would ever be able to reach is *wrestling away my strength, which meant assuaging my anger until it was less than a unstoppable force.*

His hands grabbed my wrists; I could feel him tugging at my grip, trying to pry my palms from his airway. I choked harder, and slowly I lowered him to the ground and took the time to watch him die.

I heard myself screaming, and I knew it wasn't him. Over and over I screamed to him, and the murderer inside me, "If crime is merciless, justice must be too! If crime is merciless, justice must be too!" Over and over again until the man's struggle died as he did. His thrashing and wailing slowly became less and less as his blood flow demised from a red river to a shallow stream.

It felt good to kill him.

SIXTEEN

"**T**HE FINNIGH HOTEL," BARRETTE SAID WITHOUT ANY PREVIOUS context. I had just walked into his office when he threw me the random information. "I had a couple of my men follow Mr. Ill after the conference yesterday. He's flying to DC tomorrow for a second conference. I can have my men arrest him right now if you want…"

"No…" I shook my head. "The less it looks like police are involved, the better. Plus," I added, "nothing can keep him behind bars. I need him to end permanently…"

Barrette shot down his pen that had been sketching notes and plans on paper. Sweat moistened his flabby cheeks and the balding lobes of his head. "Then what do you suppose we do?" he asked me, very frustrated.

I stood there, silent, raking together the flakes of my thoughts. Barrette's office was a boxy cave, and no figure more luxurious than a prison cell. The department's beige skin continued into the room—paint like a molded mold. Though the color was dull and thirsty for any variety or brightness, the paint was uneasy on my eyes. And no matter where I looked, jaded perspective seemed to be given to me.

Behind Barrette's desk framed with leafy engravings, and past his red leather throne, buttoned with circular plastics, a row of cabinets stored away the remaining files and records the police had.

In the far left corner, above rosewood a dresser, hung the elastic, wide-spread leaves of an artificial fern. But my eyes gravitated toward something that I would never own myself. Nearest to the edge of Barrette's desk was a framed photograph facing toward him, away from anyone else.

I disregarded the picture's implicit secrecy, took it, and placed my eyes upon the family portrait. Barrette (near the age of ten) stood in front and between both his mother and father. His father looked like him. A gaunt man with round cheeks freckled by tiny black dots that seemed to have been sprayed from a can. The gentleman had all the buttons of his crimson plaid shirt buttoned up, and had a perfectly pressed collar without one wrinkle on it.

His mother—a woman of tradition—held a brilliant smile on her mouth, and around her neck was a band of pearls, complimentary to the opal-colored dress she wore so elegantly.

"How exactly did your father die?" I knew that Barrette wouldn't mind me asking, and also that he would answer without the slightest bit of hesitation.

"A drug raid," Barrette said without looking up from his papers. He had completely accepted the fact that his father's life was stolen from him by a couple of addicts. I don't know how he did it. "He and his squad entered the house where a few guys were making Borm on their own. Shots were fired, and the fuses were ignited..." He narrowed his eyes upon the picture in my hands, then, very slowly, began shaking his head. I agreed with that action more than any of his others. It seemed that Barrette was much too casual toward his father's murder and his mother's preceding demise. "His entire squad was caught in the fire," Barrette resumed. "Though, only one of the suspects lost their life. The rest got away...they were never caught," he told me.

I continued to paste my eyes upon his father's face, picturing him burning in a jaw of flames—his skin peeling away, his blood boiling, his head falling bald. Then I saw his mother's fresh smile which would soon sag low, her eyes to fall dark, and the skin of her body never given the chance to grow wrinkly. I imagined her neck bruised by the noose that killed her.

"I'm sorry," I said to Barrette. Though, I couldn't expect him to accept it, especially from an 'insincere' mouth like mine.

But he, unlike me, accepted the forgiveness, and continued to share the rest of his story. "I felt horrible," he said. "I felt sick and constantly nauseas. And so did my mom. She was left with the bills, the media, a son in school and a crumbling economy. There are times when I hold more anger toward my mother's suicide than my father's murder."

As Barrette was opening up, I thought that maybe the leather wrap around me could pull apart. I said to him, "I was abandoned too. Although, I don't remember them…I lost my parents when I was three. When I was sent to the orphanage, I met my new father…"

"Jay?"

"Yeah," I answered. "He took me in as his own. Jay worked at the orphanage as its janitor, and when I grew up, he introduced me to the brutality of the Drug Trade. Over the course of fourteen years, he became my mentor, teaching me all about the trade's mechanics." As I re-placed the picture back on the surface of Barrette's desk, I added, "In order for the Drug Trade to fall, we must kill Samuel Ill. We cannot have any of the Officials around if we expect it not to rise again."

"How will you get to him?" Barrette asked me, possibly doubting my ideals. He looked at the face of his father, and I could tell he was losing himself in the memories of his past.

"I have to get him before he heads east to promote Project Home," I informed the commissioner. He, though, was already ahead of my knowledge.

"He'll be leaving tomorrow morning," Barrette said. "My sur-veillance has been keeping all eyes and ears on him. The Finnigh Hotel is in East Los Angeles. Mr. Ill will be taken via helicopter back west to the Los Angeles International Airport. I guess Big Rich is being extra vigilant," Barrette assumed with evidence. "Mr. Ill is secured tight. There are four guards at the hotel's entrance, two by the elevators, and the entire top floor is reserved." Barrette looked at me to ask if any of that was a problem.

"I'll be fine," I assured him. Then I had an idea. Once more, I took the picture from the commissioner's desk and looked at his father's face. "I need to talk to Ed," I said. "Have a car ready for me outside. Samuel Ill dies tonight…"

I left Barrette's office. The hallway outside held no great form to a police station's home. Instead, the walls, ceiling and floor resembled the covers of tattered books, battered crates and, most realistically, a small hallway that had held the battleground for a war. Holes that had been blown through the walls were now patched with wooden planks. The wiring through each light had been repaired though, so a steady stream of florescent filled the hallway.

I opened the elevator, and it lowered me to Ed's basement. He had an assembly of ingredients laid out upon one of his granite topped tables. His spine was, as always, arched over the mess. His hands rummaged through the sorts of roots and powders and herbs. It appeared that Ed was compiling the ingredients to create Borm on his own, and before I spoke one word he eased my suspicion.

"I've almost got it," he said, and resumed to holding his tongue out in a habit of focus. "I've almost got Borm. I can see why Big Rich has it factory made…" Ed leaned up from the table and removed a pair of clear goggles from his face. "It takes a lot of time and effort to create from scratch. But I've isolated the effects of every ingredient. It looks like Borm does a lot more than replace the blood supply."

I asked Ed, "What do you mean?" While I walked closer to the table, he continued to explain.

"It prevents its user's neurons from firing, thus disabling the brain's ability to receive pain signals." Ed spun around to a table sitting parallel to the other. He sorted through a mess of photos and notes until retrieving a surveillance picture of Mr. Ill.

In it, a wrap of Borm hangs from the corner of Ill's mouth. The blue gel burns into black smoke, and never is Ill without his precious habit. The dark glasses over his eyes practically filtered out all of his emotions. Mr. Ill was a monster's external form and its internal persona.

"Mr. Ill is a heavy user of Borm," Ed said to me, though I was plenty aware. "If you confront him directly, he'll be a nearly impossible enemy. He won't feel pain, and he'll feel stronger than he really is. I suggest," he began, "that you attack him with something big, and I suggest you get out of his way."

We had thought alike: "I already have a plan." Then I proceeded toward fetching a favor from him. "Do you have any explosive natural gasses?"

Ed thought without questioning the mere morbidity of the idea. "Hm…" While rubbing his fingers against the scruffy skin of his chin, Ed's eyes wandered over to a hidden cabinet beneath one of the lining countertops around the basement. He quickly hobbled over to one, bent down, and opened a cabinet. "Methane gas," Ed roughly murmured while hauling a metallic cylinder out of the cabinet. It clattered loudly when it touched the ground. "One of the most sensitive and explosive natural gases there are. A single spark can ignite this stuff…"

"Perfect," I said with a grin beneath my hood. "I'll take three."

Without a license in my pocket or a clue of knowledge in my brain, I took a seat behind the wheel of an undercover cruiser— beige like Barrette's. The Finnigh Hotel was far east of Downtown LA, far east of the department.

As the sun lowered beneath the city carved horizon of the sky, I drove into the spawning night of the east. The hotel was the neighborhood's most opulent, stuck-up building. Nearly every inch of all four walls was made of glass, framed with black metal.

The transparent building held the smell of chlorine from a centered fountain surrounded by several looping levels of hotel rooms. A rectangular glass case encaged a stainless steel, boxy elevator. A sandstone marble was spread out across the bottom floor, and from far outside of the Finnigh, I could spot the white dots of Ill's guards.

At the very top of the hotel was a palace of its own. The penthouse sat atop the Finnigh like an individual manor rather than a suite. It opened to a far stretching balcony recapping the sight of the distant City of the Angel.

The front bumper of my car faced the entrance of the hotel where two white-suited guards stood with an obvious display of threat in their arms. Each of the guards held loaded rifles that were sleek and black—dangerous looking.

A dark vehicle pulled up to the curb of the hotel where Mr. Ill, his Borm wrap, and two more guards unloaded from it. The men at the entrance stepped aside, but the other two escorts followed Ill into the hotel where they took the stainless steel elevator to the hotel's penthouse.

I was two blocks away from where the Finnigh sat at the end of my road which met another perpendicular. The night was made lonely by the streets' hostility, and illuminated with vomiting streetlights. I was watching from beneath my hood, through the windshield of the cruiser. And until I twisted the key in the car's ignition, I was sitting beneath a drape of shadow.

The car's engine rumbled and groaned, and the lights opened their eyes brightly. At first, neither of the guards gave any attention toward my vehicle. But as I pressed my foot to the gas pedal while the car was still in park, and as the engine began humming loudly, the two guards slowly passed each other looks of worry.

I pressed harder on the pedal. The engine hummed louder and louder, and soon, wisps of smoke began rising through the cracks of the hood. I curled my fingers around the steering wheel, and placed my other upon the gearshift. Without ever lifting my foot from the pedal, I shifted the cruiser into drive, and, after a violent lurch and deafening screech of the tires, I was rocketing toward the hotel's entrance.

It seemed that, at first, the guards were urging a game of Chicken with my two ton vehicle. They widened their stances and lifted their guns nearly to their faces. But as the speed of my vehicle never slowed, and as the hotel's front doors were just meters from the bumper of my car, the two guards leaped to the side and rolled out of the way.

When my vehicle made impact with the two glass doors, the entrance shattered into an irrevocable, undone puzzle of glass shards and splinters, all tinkering down across the front and roof of my car. Every time a blade of glass would touch the ground and shatter into several more slivers, they produced individual tones, and it was like the sky was raining notes.

Two guards on the inside of the hotel were nicked by the sides of my car. Their bodies were thrown into the air, but quickly smashed to the marble floor.

The collision didn't weaken the speed of my car at all, and by the time I blinked, I was fully through the shattering entrance, zooming toward the hotel's center fountain. I skipped my foot from the gas to the brake pedal (not that I expected, nor wanted, to slow down before crashing into the glass caged fountain). The tires screeched against the sandstone floor, but only when I made impact with the center of the glass fountain did I stop completely.

Water began streaming across my vehicle's hood when I broke through the fountain's glass barrier. But as the water poured through the cracks and made contact with the scolding engine, white steam began violently hissing from underneath the hood. Soon, all visibility was cut short by the fog-like steam building around my vehicle.

Two guards by the elevator stood from their crouches, and, with all caution and vigilance, began stepping foot-by-foot toward the car now completely possessed by steam. I heard their voices chattering back and forth from each other. It was obvious that my attack was ambiguous—either I was a drunk behind the wheel, or indeed a blood thirsty killer looking to slay their master. Without the slightest sound, I opened the car's door and crept into the steam's density, waiting...

They had their rifles raised, and one was soon stepping into the fog. I saw the barrel of his gun, and before he could immerse himself completely in the steam, I lashed out and recoiled my hand which took hold of the gun. The guard was yanked into the steam and I took him by the back of the head, and cracked his face against the metal of the cruiser's top. The bridge of his nose broke, and, unconscious, he fell to the marble floor.

By then, the steam had thinned, and the unconscious guard's partner was transferring his aim from no target at all, to the hooded man who now possessed his own weapon. I took the quicker aim at the man and pulled back the trigger of my rifle. The gun blasted a series of involuntary bullets toward the man who was rugged backward by each bullet, and eventually fell to his back out of the cloud of steam. The bullet shots were deafeningly loud and echoed up every floor above the lobby.

"We have an intruder on the bottom floor!" called one of the guards at the front door through the transmitter on his chest. "Get Ill away from all entrances!"

He and his partner retrieved their rifles from the asphalt and crept around the jagged corner of the torn-open entrance. He placed both hands on the handle and barrel of his weapon, and together, the two guards approached the thinning cloud of steam.

Their steps were long, stretched far and exaggerated. Both of the guards spotted the dead and unconscious guards, the destroyed fountain and the foreseeable destruction of every corner and pane of the hotel, and every broken bone that would snap within their bodies. The guns shivered on their own, and every step closer to the car, the guards would wish they could step back two.

And before long, the steamy cloud had thinned and dissolved completely, and the guards were creeping close to an inanimate vehicle. I was nowhere to be seen. The guards looked at each other, confused.

One asked with much frustration derived from fear, "Where the hell is he?" The two twisted themselves around until facing, again, the vehicle. The cruiser's front was crushed, mangled and deformed like it had been trampled by a surge of steel bulls. "Where'd he go?" he asked again with a louder voice, hoping that maybe he was a bait to lure me out. Unfortunately, his hopes were right.

I had slipped beneath the vehicle as the last of the steam vanished. I saw both pairs of feet on either side of the car. The rifle in my arms was held close to my chest. Slowly, without making a sound, I rolled to one side while the two guards continued to ramble their questions. I took an amateur aim at one pair of feet, pulled the trigger, then took a shot at the other.

Both guards bawled their own acclamations as they tottered and plunged to the ground. They rolled around the cold marble of their own deathbeds, and I returned my aim to both, pulling the trigger twice more.

I rolled out from beneath the car and stood over a guard's body. His eyes never shut, and I looked up to where his line of sight ended. The bottom of the penthouse was the closest thing to heaven he would ever see.

Upstairs, an organized scrambling of guards and security had been shaken. They hustled Ill to the farthest point of the outside balcony overlooking the city skyline. "What the hell is going on?" Ill asked the man forcing him to the balcony.

"I'm sorry sir, but he's here, and we think he intends to kill you," the guard responded.

Ill tilted his head to the side, then removed the shades from his eyes. Like every pair of eyes I had killed and intended to kill, Ill's eyes were of black irises and faded white. His eyebrows were thick and coal black, rigid and overhanging.

The first words out of his mouth were nothing close to the farthest edge of easeful. "What happened to the guards downstairs?" His question was more of an encouragement for the guard to admit the obvious truth.

"Um..." He was staggered by Ill's unsharpened blade of voice. "They're..."

Ill threw up his hand and twisted around to face the balcony's end. "Whatever," he fastened his voice tight. Without even looking back he ordered the guard, "Go take care of this. Don't you dare let him up here or I'll make sure he kills you before he gets to me."

The guard dipped his head and hurried around back into the penthouse. At the mouth of a hallway which ended at the elevator's doors, a line of armed guards stood with bent knees and palms drenched with salty sweat. Their mouths were dry and their lips were chapped. The sweat around their necks and chests made their suits soggy, feeling like a sauna with no exit.

There was an electronic, modernly fashioned dial above the elevator. It was number with the twenty five floors the Finnigh had to offer. They waited for the dial to begin moving. "Don't give him any chance," said the guard. "As soon as the doors open, let him have it." A high tune dinged from the dial, and slowly, its arrow began brushing past one floor...two floors...three floors...

"What if it's not him?" another asked the man who seemed to be in charge. "What if it's not him in the elevator?"

Immediately, the other responded, "We have to keep Ill alive! It's him," he said. "It's him..." They waited, and very swiftly the dial swept closer and closer to the twenty fifth floor where they stood. "Remember," continued the guard, "don't give him any chance at all. As soon as the doors open..." He waited until the dial wiped over twenty four. "Kill him." Once more, the dial dinged and the elevator doors split open just enough so that the light inside the box gleamed out. "Now!" the guard screamed, and in unison, all the others ordered a storm of bullets to drown the hallway in explosive noise and tattoo the metallic door with lines of bullet-holes.

All guards vociferated with mouths opened widely. Though, their voices were utterly defeated by the screams of their guns. Not the chinking of the metal door or the hissing of adrenalin was heard over the blare.

The doors were opening wider now, and the main guard saw not me inside the elevator's cage, but three metallic cylinders pressurized with the maximum capacity of methane gas—the most sensitive, most explosive natural gas offered. Only *he* lowered his gun, both in shock and defeat. But none of the others saw what he saw, and as he tried to scream for them to stop, several bullets had already pierced the cylinders.

"No!" he shrieked away his last word and breath.

But none of the guards seized fire until the methane gas ignited with the spark of a bullet, and the containers burst open, loosening a fiery beast which clawed through the metal, tore out the elevator doors and shredded apart the hallway. The guards were immediately lost within the flames—their bodies boiled and melted into nothingness far less than dust. Even after the guards' deaths, the explosion continued raging, and charged all throughout the penthouse until it was bursting through the west facing glass wall and out onto the balcony where Ill stood.

He faced the beast in the quickest movement, and in the reflection of his dark glasses, the fire rammed him with the curls of uncountable fiery horns. His scream couldn't make use of one entire exhale before he was being digested by the heat.

From far below on the street outside the Finnigh Hotel, the explosion's echo was a shower of hollow howling, a fierce rumble that shook the ground beneath my feet and sprinkled the top of my hood with splinters of glass and debris. But the plume of fire quickly retreated and curled into invisibility, and Samuel Ill's life was over.

At my feet, a pair of melted framed glasses landed, and more of the lenses broke apart. I looked down, seeing my own reflection in the dark bounce back of sight. Far above me was the rendering remains of the explosion—little tails of thinning flame and sprays of spark too hot to exist, even in the Californian air.

I could see my chin and lips emerging from the shadow of my hood. My jawline was sturdy and cornered sharply. My lips were chapped, peeling like the old wallpaper of the orphanage home I grew up in.

In the far distance, the last lingering sound of an echo drifted beneath the horizon. I stood there in the street as the distant sirens wailed closer and closer, thinking about the life I had erased. He was a middle-aged man, a creature composed of accumulated years, developed by the mistakes he made and the experience he took and lost.

There wasn't a single bloody drop of regret in my conscience for killing Samuel Ill. *But what a waste*, I thought.

It took a miraculous process to spawn the existence of that man. It took love between a man and a woman. It took the marvel of biology to create a life form so intelligent, yet so stupid and ignorant to find logic in the business he sold his life to. And there I was, basking in the acid of his own reverberations.

The entire layout of the Drug Trade, schematics of Project Home and biological reasoning for Richard Lucifer's life was not only the self-destruction of Eval's life, Ill's life (and my life), but a corrupted train of utilitarianism heading toward the end of its tracks where it would fall into the shadowy abyss of Earth's most intelligent species' stupidity.

Mankind has created empires, cities, elements and the ability to wage war against itself. Dogs chase their own tails, but men murder themselves with weapons they created. And then they're buried in the ground they helped make.

Big Rich now stood before me—the last person I had to cross before my life's purpose would come to an end. When I realized that, I realized my fear of death. Jay had told me that man fears most what he cannot escape. But I didn't think that death was inescapable. Society's foundation is built upon the corpses of its makers. Certain individuals would die, and both their bodies and souls would rot. And then others would die, but only their bodies would rot. Their characters, though, would remain on Earth.

Death, I believed, was indeed escapable, and that made it all more terrifying—knowing that when the Reaper would come for me, I would have to face the unavoidable truth that I had a choice somewhere along the line to immortalize myself. Somewhere along the line I had the choice to give my life a purpose, to force the world to remember what I stood for.

I had partaken in the act of erasing life and its purpose. No one would remember Samuel Ill and what he added to the world and took from it, but everyone would remember the murderer who took his life and never gave it back.

But at least what I stood for would be remembered. At least I wouldn't completely die…

The crush of Project Home would mark my legend. An idea that could have destroyed an entire nation was burned to ashes by the hands of a single individual.

SEVENTEEN

TOOK A STEP INTO BARRETTE'S OFFICE, UNWILLINGLY PLACING MYSELF amongst his ricocheting words. He was speaking to someone on the phone, asking over and over again, "Jom Atitya? *Jom Atitya* was murdered? By whom?" He waited for the response, and when it came, Barrette was even more distraught. "A man in a mask? God damn it," he cursed. "What the hell is going on?" A few mumbling words made it through the speaker of the phone before tickling my ear as fuzzy noise. "Thanks for letting me know anyway," Barrette thanked the man on the other end, and hung up the phone.

I asked the commissioner, "Who was that?"

He waved the question away. "Just some of my police friends down in Miami. It doesn't matter," he swore, and proceeded with more important news. "Here, look at this."

Barrette pushed a glossy, very opulent postcard across his desk to where I stood.

"What's this?" I asked the commissioner as I picked it up. The card was exuberantly decorated with the loops and spins and flips of golden cursive writing protruding from the thick paper. I ran my fingers across the words PROJECT HOME.

"Big Rich is celebrating the completion of Project Home..." Barrette was as 'thrilled' as I was. He shook his head and lay back in his squishy throne. "Christ," he sighed, "we've done so much damage to the operation, and it's like he isn't affected at all by it. He's celebrating Project Home's completion for Christ's sake! I mean...we stopped that shipment, that trade..." He thought. "You killed Mr. Eval and Ill...was it all for nothing?"

I easily guessed, "It could be a trick. He doesn't want the public to know that he's falling...he doesn't want *me* to know that he's falling."

"But why go through all this trouble?"

"I don't know, Barrette..."

"It's like...it's like he's innocent," Barrette said to me with every drop of courage on his tongue.

"If he's innocent, then I'm innocent..."

Barrette snickered to himself. "Then I'm also innocent..."

At the end of Barrette's sentence, an officer threw all his weight into Barrette's office. "They're dead too!" he informed us urgently, though neither Barrette nor myself had any idea what topic the officer spoke of. He recognized our cluelessness and aided. "The Traders we arrested from Gray Moss! The ones who made it out alive—they're dead!"

Barrette stood from behind his desk, and all three of us hustled to the holding cell room. The officer stood outside, having seen enough already. The commissioner looked at me and I nodded.

There was a faintly noticeable smell that lofted in the air of the hallway. And when we arrived outside the last cell, we knew where the scent was emanating from.

Like a morgue, the cell was filled with nearly ten dead Traders. All of them had colorless, pale faces and deteriorated muscles. Their bones showed through their skin and the veins in their arms were dried and crusty. Every pair of eyes was missing, and each cheek was sunken in toward the jaw.

Barrette turned away and covered his mouth. I heard him gagging behind me, but I just stood there imagining a nightmare far worse than any Elm Street.

I pictured thousands of pale, meatless, eyeless corpses lying in the streets and gutters all through Los Angeles. I imagined the smell, the inescapable stench that would burn away every hair in your nose. The city would become a dug up graveyard, and eventually a city of ruins.

And though this next thought was in complete opposition to everything I had surrendered, compromised and lost, I wonder if Big Rich's life was worth so much filthy death.

Barrette was already thinking my thoughts. "This is LA's future," he said between gags and coughs. "This is what's in store for us..." He walked out of the hallway.

I followed quickly behind him. "Barrette!" I yanked him backward with one call. "Big Rich dies tonight!"

The commissioner spun himself around in the most hasty, uncoordinated movement. He marched up to me, talking right in my face. "Do you not see that? Do you not understand that *that* is LA's future?" He was pointing behind me at the room full of corpses. "You kill Big Rich, and our streets will be filled with thousands of bodies just like that! Fuck you," he abruptly cursed at me. "Fuck you and your plan to kill that son-of-a-bitch!"

I couldn't believe the seriousness in his voice. "After all of this...after all that you've done, all that you've sacrificed, you're going to stop now?" He never responded to my question, even if I expected him to. "What about your father? What about Jay or Ed's parents?" I continued pressuring him with such morbid, guilty questions. "What about justice?"

That one word snared his attention. He protested hard and strong. "What you're talking about is not justice! Killing Big Rich will not bring justice, don't you understand that? Thousands, maybe even millions of people will die. You talk about my father, the people you and Ed loved, and yet you don't realize that if you kill Big Rich, tomorrow morning will bring the dawn of people like me...people like Ed...people like *you* mourning and fighting for the deaths of their loved ones!" After twisting back around and hauling himself forward, Barrette stood at the doorframe of his office and said to me, "I'm not going to stop you from killing Big Rich, but if you go through with this, I will hunt you," he swore. "*We* will hunt you." The commissioner, upon our last encounter, brought himself fully into his office and slammed the door shut.

EIGHTEEN

THIS IS WHERE MY LIFE BEGAN TO UNRAVEL IN ONE WAY, BUT ITS chapters twisted together in another. There was no happy ending to my life and my story. My dream ended as a nightmare. But I guess there was never any dream in my life… only dreaming, really.

After all this, there was no sunset I could walk away with Raine in. There was no rejoicing as much as I wanted to see Jay again, and wished he was alive. Most of all, there was no satisfaction of killing Big Rich. Not even any guilt of killing the many people I did. Numbness had taken over my body, but even with it layering all the pain I had, I never felt greater misery than what I felt then. It was the pain of slowly killing myself.

I missed her, but yet, constantly, my urge to believe I could find her shrunk. In replace of Raine standing at the end of the tunnel, was Big Rich. When I thought about securing her in my arms, taking her from wherever she was, I then thought of shooting Big Rich in the heart.

I had to kill him; I couldn't let Big Rich live and Project Home rise. I had to forget about Raine…

Space in Ed's basement had been thieved by even more boxes and crates, the crates that were taken from Port Lybric. When I entered the room, Ed was slouched in a chair, cupping his hands over his head. He muttered a few words to himself, and massaged his temples.

"Ed? Are you okay?"

His head jolted up and he rebuilt his posture. "Yeah," he said, "I'm fine!"

Even the dumbest fool could tell he was lying. I walked through the only space of the basement not consumed by crates until I got to him. Heavy bags were drooping under his eyes, and his face was bright red and misted with little red dots of acne.

I didn't except his pseudo, conversation-avoiding answer. "What's wrong?" I persisted on knowing.

"Nothing..." he answered in a different form.

"Ed...what's wrong?"

He had to consider something first. Ed looked at me straight in the eyes and took a breath. I could tell that his news was going to be just as pounding on me as it was on him. Ed stood and tugged on the bottom of his collared shirt. He brushed aside his hair and adjusted the pair of glasses that aided his sight.

One piece of his sentence was short and abrupt. He said, "The boxes." I asked for more, and Ed elaborated: "The crates from the shipment. Look..." Ed pulled open the hatch to a crate and I looked inside. There was no Borm or weapons or any tools of mass destructive that alluded to Project Home's corruption.

Inside the crate (and all the others), were sorts of children's wear, children's toys and decorative items for the rooms and space of Project Home's orphanages. There were stuffed animals, dolls, pajamas, chairs and pictures.

"I don't understand..." I said, and dropped my thoughts to Ed's same level of frustration and confusion. "Where's the Borm? Where are the drugs?" I thought about the possibilities that had been drowned deep in illogic. "Maybe it was a set-up," I concluded vastly. "Maybe they knew we were coming..."

While shaking his head, Ed replied with a straight forward "No." He thought some more...He then said, "That can't be it..."

"Well," I shrugged my broad shoulders, "...I don't know what else it would be. There's no way Ty, or any of the Officials are inno-cent. Let along Project Home. Tell me, how does any of this make sense?" There was an idea running in circles around Ed's mind, but he was too timid to share it with me. Until I caught onto his knowledge, Ed tried to reason different logic. "What do you think, Ed?" I asked him, suspicious of his answer.

He neatly composed the exposition to an explanation. "Remember that lady from a couple days ago? The crazy one who told you not to trust *him*, who said *he* wants you to kill Big Rich...?"

"My mother?" I clarified.

"Yes," Ed affirmed. "Well...who is *he*?"

"I..." There wasn't any thought in my head that brought an answer. "I don't know..."

"I think I do," Ed told me. "I think she was talking about Jay..."

"Jay? Jay is dead...he was murdered, remember?"

"How do you know?" he dueled reality. "How do you know he was really murdered?"

"I...because...the man who killed him...he told me...he told me right before I murdered him..." I threw the little reasoning I had to the floor like a crumpled piece of paper. My voice rung loud when I let my words topple off my tongue like a rock slide. "I watched him be buried, Ed! I knew Jay my whole life, and I was the only one who could pay any sort of respect, the only one who could acknowledge his death. His *murder*!"

But Ed loaded his gun packed with questions, took no time to soak in my sobs, and began firing. "Why did Jay want you to kill Big Rich?" Ed questioned my motives. "What was he expecting to come out of one man's murder?"

"He...he wanted me to stop Lucifer from destroying America with his drug," I said simply. "He didn't want the Drug Trade to spread across the nation."

"But killing Big Rich will only kill the people of Los Angeles," debated Ed with Jay's and my reason.

I threw away my temper and attacked Ed with aggressive speech. "What are you saying, Ed? Tell me, what are you saying? You seem to be so sure of your theory, so tell me now!"

Ed shied away a bit, sheltering himself with cautious words. "I'm saying that maybe Jay wants you to kill Big Rich so he can kill the city...maybe he knew everything from the very beginning... that's all I'm saying."

"That's all you're saying? You think that Jay, my best friend, a man who I looked up to like my father, would use me like that?" I brought my height over Ed's. He shriveled down into a little, ter-rified ball of coward. "Don't you dare try to pretend that's what's happening! Don't you dare! I haven't given up everything I owned to fulfill some madman's plan! This is about justice! This is about saving the city!"

"No it's not, Hale! No it's not!" Ed forced his words into my ears. "This is about you, and your ignorance, fulfilling a madman's own revenge! Have you ever considered that?" I reached toward Ed with my hands, but he pushed me away with the strength of his legs and stood. "Think about it, Hale!"

"There's nothing to think about!"

"Open your eyes! Take off that hood!"

I did as he said, and ripped the hood from my head. Ed could hardly stand to look at my uncovered face. "You're the blind one, Ed! You can't see things for what they are!"

"You're wrong," he insisted. "You have nothing, no evidence, no proof that Big Rich has anything to do with this God damn Drug Trade!"

I spoke a trivial question, one that I didn't think Ed had any answer or guess to. I asked, leaning on my last bit of defendable argu-ment like a crutch, "Who else would be running it if not Big Rich?"

Ed looked away...

"Tell me!" I blurted at the top of my lungs, the peak of my volume. "*Who?*"

"I told you, Hale! But it doesn't matter, you won't listen to anything I have to say..."

"Why would Jay be running this entire operation in hopes that I would bring it down? That doesn't make any sense at all, Ed.

Why are you even telling me this? Why the hell would you want to hurt me like this?" I cried. My voice began stirring with my only desire to cry. It wasn't that I believed Ed, but after everything that I had been saturated in, I just wanted to bawl. I asked Ed again, "Why would Jay do that?"

"I don't know, Hale! But I think you do," he began saying softly, dropping out of all our yelling and screaming back and forth. "I think you know why…"

I thought about any explanation, but nothing made sense. I looked at Ed and told him, "I have to kill Big Rich…"

"*Why*?" desperately, hanging onto the last, unwinding string of hope, Ed asked me with a ball of air in his throat.

"Because he's all I have left…he's all I have to live for…" The answer broke free straight from my heart and its deepest pit. It was the truth's concentrate. The only reason I was living, was so I could kill Richard Lucifer.

The only conversing of sound was Ed's and my panting of breath. Everything else was silent and dead. He had fallen back into the chair he was first in. Ed sighed and re-brushed his hair. He had given me a chance to listen, to see the gray.

"Not everything is black and white…" Ed spoke with exhaustion quieting his philosophy.

I looked at Ed with the most distant response. "Justice must be merciless…"

"That's not justice," he spat. "That's revenge coming straight from revenge's mouth. You kill Big Rich, Alex, but I won't be there to pity what's left of you…"

There was something I had to say but nothing I could pronounce. Ed had claimed the final sentence. So I flipped myself around and left the basement, and Ed's diamond truth picking at my leather denial.

Just as I was exiting the department, Barrette's voice tugged on my shoulder and turned me around. "You burn in your own fire," the commissioner caveated me for a final time before I would complete the deed of necessity. He watched with his eyes just beneath the bushes of his eyebrows.

Barrette backed into his office and shut the door. I was standing alone in the colorless hallway. Once I had returned the hood, my true face, to my head, I took a step outside, and scaled my eyes up the tower of Big's palace.

Beneath my breath like a snake's hiss, I said to Big Rich and Project Home, to the corruption of the city and the injustice that murdered Jay, "I'm coming for you."

NINETEEN

UBBLING CHAMPAGNE, COMFORTABLE TEMPERATURE, WHITE TABLE 'clothes hanging just above the floor like the legs of a ghost. Free food of a buffet, chatting smiles and busy servants. Guards petrified by duty, weapons readied by force. Hair that had to have taken hours to curl and dress. The party's population didn't match that of the city outside.

Silk dresses swayed breezily alongside the ballad tempo of the live band. Women cuddled bouquets handed to them by their clean-cut men. Bow ties and pearls around necks. Jewel-dazzled watches and rings around wrists and fingers. Over the soft lips of females, bright red lipstick hid the tender pink underneath. Teeth scintillated behind the arcs of smiles which I presumed to be artificial, only to please their powerful host.

Even with Big Rich out of sight, his guards stood like white statues, completely obvious to pick out from the colors of Big's party.

Colors like satin red, deep crimson, earthy brown, greens of the lushest palette, yellows from the sunniest day, and of course Richard's suit like a piece of the night sky standing beneath a roof.

The party was an excuse for its every puppet to pretend their strings had been cut—a chance to mock reality as if truth were to lie. With the fizzy alcohol hissing in tulip-shaped, crystal glasses, and powdered with sweet illusion that they actually matter, the party-goers would participate in the darkest scandal beneath the shadow of Lucifer's potbelly. If sprinkled enough by the magic-like affair, they would smile in a time of grief, they would fight when peace was the cure, and they would die when their own life hadn't opened its eyes.

And still, the ties around men's necks fell like silky colored water from their pearly collars, and the bells of women's dresses were so elegantly ruffled that each individual layer could sway on its own.

Stationed at the front doors were a couple of doormen. I'm sure they were just more guards wearing bright red coats and hats.

I saw all of the party from outside whenever the automatic doors slid open, then through the glass when they shut. I was too under-dressed to enter the party with the doormen's permission, so I waited longer before the streets dried of visitors. Soon, pointless, but a tactic to pass time, conversation was thrown back and forth between the two men.

I took a step into the street, then another, advancing the doormen with a steady, aggressive walk. My pace gained speed, and by the time one doorman noticed my rapidly nearing presence, I was already bounding my hands toward his neck.

Like talons, my fingers seized an unbreakable, inescapable grip around the back and front and sides of the man's throat and neck. He tried to call out, but my choke had severed his ability to speak.

The second doorman was reaching for a small firearm on the inside of his coat. Big Rich had assigned extra security to keep guard over the party. As soon as I saw the silver glint of the doorman's pistol, I maneuvered the one I was choking, throwing him in front of me like a flesh-ridden shield.

The second doorman—out of pure, brainless and terrified instinct—pulled the trigger of his gun, shooting his partner in the back while I hid behind him, untouched by any of the bullets.

I snatched the first doorman's gun from his inside pocket before forcing him into the other. The two fell to the ground—one was dead, but the other was still scrambling to preserve the last strands of his life. With the small, diminutive looking handgun, I put one single bullet between the two watery eyes of the last doorman. The shot rang loud, but died quickly in the spoiled air. I looked around as his head hit the concrete. There was one man on the corner of the street. When I looked at him, he pretended not to see anything, turned, and walked away in the opposite direction.

I ditched the gun in the sidewalk's gutter, and stepped through the doors of Toy Palace—immersing myself in a toxic amount of perfume and cologne, cigar smoke and the potent aroma of wealth.

When the doors opened automatically, Big's voice was already blabbing to his guests who opened the deep dug canals of their ears clogged with infected earwax. As always, his voice was large and prideful, made fat by the confidence he pretended to have when, really, he knew Project Home was nothing more than a flabby cripple, whimpering behind his back. I knew who he really was, and his words were more devilish than anything else could ever hear them to be.

"Ladies and gentlemen," Big Rich started his speech with an appropriate greeting, "I want to thank you all for coming. It is a pleasure to have you here celebrating a dream come true." He was speaking from a level above, on a grand balcony met by two staircases on either side. "For my whole life, I have wanted to spare the innocent children of our city from the grief and agony so noticeably present in our world. Until just recently, that vision was unattainable." Big Rich was tossed and buttered in the blissful ignorance that Project Home was not, indeed, terminal. "But here we are," he brought a smile to his face, "and here I am, finally fulfilling my dream. *Our* dream, now! Each and every one of us has a debt to pay to the City of Angels, and now, we will all be able to finally pay this city with our graciousness. We have gathered to celebrate the coming reality of a dream, mourn the passing of Ty Eval, and pray for the health of Samuel Ill, wishing him a quick and full recovery. They made this dream come true—I could not have done it without them. Mr. Ty Eval, bless his soul for he is no longer with us, donated a miracle's worth of goods to complete the construction of ten orphanage homes across the state. Though the shipment was...

postponed, soon, fully furnished, fully equipped orphanage homes will open their doors tomorrow morning." The crowd was pleased and their hearts were filled with warmth, though fake warmth— warmth that was just barely thawed by the heat of Big Rich's arm-pits. "It was his final action, and now we let him rest in peace with his name always remembered. Ladies and gentlemen," he raised his arms to amplify the celebration, "in honor of Mr. Ill and Mr. Eval, of Los Angeles and this great state, and in honor of all you and all the people we will help, I present to you..." Big Rich leaned over the balcony to cut a red ribbon strewn across one set of stairs to another. "...the highly anticipated completion of Project—"

Before he could cut the ribbon, I shot my voice into the air, screaming with such blood drenched tone and deafening volume, "Stop!" My scream burst open like a firework released indoors.

Every guest in Toy Palace shifted their big-eyed sights to me. Big Rich never cut the ribbon, and pulled himself back onto the balcony. His white-suited guards lifted their rifles and scanned the crowd for me.

"It's all a lie..." I said, my voice ringing from somewhere beneath the ocean of people, though Big Rich could narrow his eyes. "Project Home, Toy Palace, even Mr. Lucifer himself. It's all fake!" I wasn't sure how else to begin the prologue to his demise. I never once expected the people of Los Angeles to immediately believe my words.

Big Rich swam his eyes through his audience. "That's an outra-geous thing to say!" Big Rich protected his baby he was fat and preg-nant with. "What kind of person would ever assume such a thing?" he asked anyone within the crowd. "Show yourself!" he commanded.

A circle of audience members drew around me, and Big Rich was able to narrow his choices to the hooded figure who stood with his head tipped down. He saw me standing there; fists curled tight, hood on head, deadliness with a watering mouth.

"I know who you are, Big Rich! I know what Project Home really is!"

"I don't understand," he said, rattled by the chaos and struck with dumb confusion. "What are you talking about?"

"I killed Mr. Eval and stopped his shipment…and I sent Ill half way to his grave! I would've had tried harder to kill him if I knew he was to survive…"

"*You…*" Big Rich awed. "You're the ghost everyone has been talking about!" His audience's eyes pointed inward toward me. "Who are you?" he asked. "Why are you doing this?"

"I know everything!" Then I directed my voice to the crowd of people around me. "This man is not who he says he is! And Project Home is a cover-up…"

Big Rich interrupted me, leaping toward shutting my mouth before I could completely reveal his true plan. "A cover-up for what?" he asked me, still pretending to be taken aback by my claims.

"For the Drug Trade!" I finally clawed off my chest.

Big Rich laughed, throwing his hands on the bulge of his belly. He snarled back at me, "That's insane to think! I have nothing to do with that *myth*!" Meanwhile, the guest mannequins of Richard's party were fetching their eyes back and forth from me and him.

"It's not a myth!" I began rotating around in slow circles to reach every person surrounding me. "I know it's real, and I know that this man is overseeing the entire operation! He's been using you all, working right under your noses…"

Untranslatable sentences of gossip began rising from the ground. Nearly every person around me was debating with their neighbor whether or not I was telling the truth. Most returned their faces to me, shaking their heads.

"Lies!" Big Rich claimed. "It's all lies!" He cued his men with the flick of his fingers, and slowly, they descended the two sets of stairs. "Ladies and gentlemen, leave for your own protection…"

As if a giant plumber came to the front door and plunged out the party, a clog of guests left the toy store as the drain was cleared. An even number of Big's guards were split in half around the store;

five on one side, and five on the other. Of course here and there a few lonely Drug Trade members watched the entire thing.

Step by easy step, Big Rich walked down one of the staircases, getting closer, and closer to me. His hands were in his pockets, but his thumbs hung out. On both sides of him, his guards assemble neat and evenly.

When he stopped about twenty feet from me, he parted his legs shoulder width apart and crossed his arms, relaxing his giant neck and shoulder muscles. No guns had been ordered to take aim at me, so for now his guards held their weapons by their waists. Each one of them was silent.

"You know, kid. I've lived by one rule: Never start what you cannot finish. I started this project, and nothing is going to stop me. Not even you. If you think you can stop something far mightier than God himself, you have obviously no idea what you're dealing with. This is going to change our entire society!" he applauded his own work.

I could smell the sweet, rich cologne on his neck and wrists. It reminded me of a mansion dipped in pure silver, or a fleece of golden wool.

This was the first time I had the opportunity to talk to Big Rich one on one. Everything I knew about the lord of LA was all from what I had heard, and his character existed nominally. It was shocking that I resisted insulting him to a point where any ego he might have had would be sagging to his knees.

He was the reason for so many things: Jay's death, Raine's kidnapping, and the murder of Alexander Hale. But here he was, as fancy and classy as always, just like I was watching him behind Jay's old television screen in the small attic. Nothing moved him, nothing touched his emotions.

"I have to say," Big Rich resumed his verbal engagement with me, "I never actually thought you would be capable of killing Mr. Eval... but he's dead, Mr. Ill is half way there, and it's all thanks to you."

"I'm capable of a lot of things. Like killing *you*." Jay's pistol in my pocket became heavy, calling for my hand to dip down and take it by the handle.

"I would hate to see you die trying..." Now his men raised their guns. "It's a shame that you came so far for nothing at all." He shook his head, laughing with his breath. "I'm going to walk out of here, and you're not going to do anything about it. Shame on you for thinking you could ever beat me..." With a flicking motion of his hand, his men took more accurate aim at me. "Take care of him," he said, emotionless. With that he walked around his wall of guards and left the building. At his closest point to me, I could smell the cologne on his neck even more. And with a stronger waft, it was the scent of a snake's venom.

With the butts of their weapons to their eyes, each guard closed one eye and placed a finger to their triggers. All moving closer, I had seconds before a tidal wave of bullets would come crashing into me.

What do I do now? I had to ask myself. I had one bullet loaded in the chamber of one gun. Not even the most dramatized ricochet could strike all of them dead with one discharge.

Like too much oxygen to take a breath, the amount of humil-iation, shame, guilt, and pain I was experiencing, there was too much to handle. I was choking on my past and all the promises I had made to the ones I loved. Knowing that the vision Jay and I shared would only ever be a dream, was more torturous than a flame-dipped-dagger slowly breaking the skin over my stomach. And Raine—knowing that she would die without any closure to say why, or if she was alive, knowing that no savior would come to take her away...it was monstrous.

Just before I shut my eyes for the last time, I saw the myste-rious man tipping his black hat and covering his face with the flap of his jacket. He pushed through the doors of the back room full of winding mechanical arms, and disappeared. His signal was inscru-table with my death ready to take me away, but as the men took one last final aim at me, the loudest sound ruptured behind them.

The walls and the floor below my feet shook madly as if the

building lost its temper. Heat, unrealistic heat, seared my face, burning the flesh beneath the layer of my hoodie. An untouchable force threw me back away the men, but they too were tossed from the explosion. Blazing flames jumped out of the back room like they were escaping a cage. The brightness made us cover our eyes with our hands, and the heat made it hard to watch.

A second explosion rocked through the walls and trashed holes into the brick. Debris was scattered through the air—chunks of brick, burning toys. Dodging them was a focus. My senses were ripped from my head after the first explosion, and I was being played with by the ferocious explosions.

Big's guards were as unprepared as I was. They tried to get to their feet but every explosion sent them back down. I crawled on my stomach toward Toy Palace's exit as it collapsed around me.

One more explosion was enough to make the entire structure of the toy store crumble. Now pieces of the ceiling broke apart and crashed like small meteorites next to me. A few chunks of brick caught me in my shoulder blade and back. It made it hard to stand.

Once to my feet, I turned toward the back of the store. There was no wall to separate the toy store from the factory of burning metal and malfunctioning hardware, torn apart by the explosions.

The hairs on my arm burned away. I caught the sight of one last stuffed animal, burning in a pile of flames around it. Its black beady eyes melted into liquid plastic, looking like black tears, crying.

The sound was horrible. Nothing else could be heard but the roaring of the flames and the stomping of explosions. But there was the slight hint of a terrible crunch that I heard above me. When I looked, I saw a giant piece of concrete hurling toward me. I dove and rolled away, and the chunk of ceiling shattered when it hit the ground.

A few of the men had been crushed under other parts of the ceiling that fell. For the rest, the intense flames burned them away into dust. Black smoke was already winding through the entire building. It filled my lungs, scratching at their insides, feeling like I had drank the world's strongest acid.

I saw the exit ten feet from where I stood. Only a wall of flames flickered in front of it. I took no extra time to wait in the arson. And it was time that my lungs were full of black, heavy smoke eating away at them even more.

My hand reached for the doors, but I never reached them. A dump of sparks warned the collapsing of more structure. I was trapped beneath hundreds of pounds of brick and building that had landed right on the lower part of my leg.

I felt parts of my bones splinter and crack. The debris caught me, and sent my head cratering into the floor. My jaw smacked shut and both rows of my teeth collided with each other. I tried to pull my leg out from the chunk of brick, but it was too heavy. When I looked around, there was nothing but weighed blackness and dancing flames. My whole body was sweating profusely, but as each drip lost its grip from my skin, it was evaporated before even hitting the ground.

After the burning of my leg and the smell of sizzling flesh, I could only imagine, and feel, it disintegrating beneath the fallen object. The burning became even more of an overwhelming pain, but I couldn't free myself from the wreckage. What was even more disheartening, and aggravating, was the exit of Toy Palace only inches feet from me. I could see the street outside, but no one or nothing to help me.

There I was, burning in the crash I brought to be, the fight I picked, the war I waged and always thought would win. There I was, burning in my own fire.

I couldn't allow that be the end of my life, but no one was there to help me, and I was helpless myself. Had everything finally caught up to me? Was I lost in revenge, in my own self-glory? This was never supposed to be what would happen, or the reason for my madness.

The lower legs of my jeans had burned away, leaving only my naked skin to fend for itself against the unyielding fire.

Even with no one to hear it, I screamed the most painful noise any human ever could and began tugging on my leg. Whether they were tears from the stinging smoke or tears from the amount of failure I felt, I didn't know. I screamed some more before the muscles and tendons in my limb were ready to pull apart, tear, and rip. It felt like my leg would soon be severed from the rest of my body, but before it could detach from my hip, it came free.

I jolted forward to my face. The ground of the store was as hot as an iron pan held over a blue flame. My right leg was useless, and as I pulled myself to a broken stand, I was forced to hop out of the collapsing building.

Compared to the temperature inside, the night air was numbing. Exiting through a blast of flames, I rolled out into the middle of the street, clutching my leg. From below the knee, my jeans were shredded and smoking; they might as well have been half shorts. And underneath them, my skin was the color of raw flesh—a reddish pink, bleeding, blistered, scolding hot. Wherever my jeans were burnt open, my skin was as well. It hurt just to move my leg, but I knew by now Big Rich was on his back to his tower. That's where everything would end—on the top of the world for all of Los Angeles to witness.

There was a bright light in front of me, nearing quickly. I held up my hand in front of my eyes to shield them from the blinding white.

The car, at first, honked loud, but stopped before rolling over me. A man stepped out of the driver's side and hustled to where I laid. "Are you okay?" he asked me urgently after noticing the building flames inside Toy Palace. He bent down and hooked his arms beneath mine, pulling me to my feet. "Are you okay?" he asked again.

I held myself up over the hood of his taxicab. Without ever looking the man in the eyes, I felt for his head. When my fingers made contact with the thick strands of his hair, I tensed my muscles, slamming his head down onto the hood of the vehicle. He grunted loudly before falling to the ground.

"What the hell?" he asked, returning to his feet as I limped over to the driver's side.

His hand landed on my shoulder, trying to pull me back. I

whipped around with Jay's pistol drawn. "Get away from me!" I said weakly, trying to sound strong.

The driver held up his hands and made distance between us as I continued into the car. I sat myself right behind the wheel, and without even closing the door aside me, I stomped my crippled foot on the gas pedal. A terrible groan came from the taxi's engine as it launched out of rest and into a most fast-paced pursuit.

It was harder to keep my eyes open—to keep my mind alert—than it was to wind between the many cars ahead of me. Far in front of me, I saw the polished black SUV escorting Big Rich to 'safety'. It drove no faster than the law advised—Big Rich had assumed that his men could handle me.

Chopping and buffering air from a helicopter made me bend forward and look up through the cab's windshield. Blinking lights indicated the helicopter making a landing on top of Big's Tower, and I could only guess it was a ride for Richard.

I slammed the heel of my hand to the car's wheel, blaring the horn at all the other cars in front of me. I swerved around one, swiftly swooped beside another and speared in front of one more with rolling speed. Several of the cars I passed honked their horns as well, but now I could see the back bumper of Richard's SUV. The passing buildings and cars were no more than smears of flashing images racing by the windows.

The closer I got to Big Rich and his SUV, the harder I pushed down on the pedal. I ignored the temperamental groaning of the cab's engine, and soon the front of my vehicle's bumper was parallel to the SUV's back tire. No face could be seen on the inside of the SUV—the windows were tinted completely opaque. I could only assume that the driver had not yet noticed me soaring beside them.

In a whisper to myself, I cursed Big Rich saying, "Time to die you son-of-a-bitch!" My vehicle jolted and tucked sharply to the left when I jerked the steering wheel over.

A loud crunch chomped its way from the moment of impact when the front left side of my vehicle collided with the back of Richard's.

At the speed we were traveling, the slightest nick would have made it impossible for any driver to maintain control of either vehicle.

When I rammed the SUV, its front end jerkily swiveled to the right, and soon after it was skidding down the street sideways. The tires left thick black marks across the asphalt until they were caught on a chink in the street, and the SUV tipped. It plunged to its side, crushing the SUV's doors and shattering its left line of windows. Though, the speed we had acquired kept the vehicle tumbling upside down, across its other side, and back on its wheels.

I had veered off the road, wrecking through a single light post before meeting a brick wall face-to-face. The front of the cab was immediately mutilated and its engine was deceased. My head convulsed forward, straining my neck with whipping force.

When all the speed had been crushed, I was left with my head lying upon the top of the steering wheel. I could hear the engine's last breath—a long lasting hiss, slowly fading as time slugged by. I heard the tings of shattering glass and the crunching of bent metal. Though, my consciousness was quickly dimming like an ancient light losing its brightness.

Reality began to bend as a dream or hallucination of sort stirred the environment around me. I was no longer in the car, rather atop Big's Tower, holding the barrel of Jay's pistol to Richard's head. Everything else was black; an infinite void. Big Rich held up his meaty hands and his blubbery arms in the air. Slowly, the lord lowered to his knees and my shrouded-self stepped closer, pushing the tip of my pistol against his head.

In a quaking voice, Big Rich cried and looked up at me, begging, "I know I'm guilty! I know it! But...but please..." He sniffled wet snot. "...don't kill me..."

And then I spoke right back at him, more hateful. "You killed *me*, Lucifer. You killed my best friend, the one girl I could have loved. You were going to kill this entire nation!"

"I know..." he cried, finally realizing his own guilt. "I know... but...have mercy!" He looked at me with his black marble eyes.

I laughed at him. "There's no room for mercy! If crime is merciless, justice must be too!" I put my finger to the trigger, and pulled back. The gun clapped loud and sent a heavy lead bullet right into Richard's skull.

At the point of impact, his bones broke in and a spray of blood left his head. The lord looked at me, though dead, and fell, from his knees, to his back. I stood there, a curl of smoke twisting from the gun's barrel. And suddenly, the blackness around me began to lighten.

And in the shine of a distant glare I could see two figures, walking side-by-side. One was tall and gaunt, but the other was small and gentle. Soon, they walked outside of the glare and details on their faces grew.

I saw Jay, and I saw Raine. They were walking toward me out of the light, smiling.

Jay reached me first, and slid his hand and arm across my shoulders. "Thank you," he said firstly. I nodded at him, smiling a set of white teeth. "You did it, you're a hero."

"Looks like you didn't die for nothing..."

"No," he smiled happily. "I didn't. But, I suppose I was a sacrifice. I had to die if anyone ever expected you to kill Big Rich and stop the Drug Trade."

"I wish it could have been different..."

Jay was nodding his head as I was shaking mine. "Sometimes..." Jay was beginning something. "...people need to see what's worst in order to see what's best. We're all blind, Hale..." Jay only knew that I would agree to that. "When people's worlds are tossed into darkness, it takes a lot of light for them to see anything else."

"I just...why did you have to die?" I asked him.

"Like I said, we're all blind. Open your eyes a bit..." Jay turned, brushed by Raine's side and returned into the bright light.

Raine, and her size half of Jay's, replaced where the old man was standing. Part of her weight rested more on one leg than the other. While one hand sat in her pocket, the other was busy being nibbled by her white teeth.

"Hi Raine..." I said softly.

"Hi," she said equally shy. Raine didn't speak, but reached her hand up to my hood.

Suddenly, as the hood fell from my head, our black void world twirled into a completely new environment. As I blinked my eyes and opened them again, Raine and I were standing on the surface of a glacier floating in a sea of ice and below a sky of brilliant blue.

There was a cold, tickling breeze that blew across my face. I was dressed in a white collared shirt and clean black pants. My eyes were back to blue, my hair was full of volume and color, and my smile was finally smiling. Raine stood before me in a white, ruffled dress that blew in the icy breeze.

"You killed him to save me, didn't you?" Raine asked me and stepped closer. She flattened her hand over my heart and looked into my eyes.

I couldn't determine one answer from another. I thought I had killed Big Rich for Jay...maybe I killed him for Raine...maybe for the city.

"Yes," I possibly lied to her. "Yes."

"I knew you wouldn't let him take me, Alex. I knew it!" She hopped once and laughed, then threw herself into me. I hugged her back, and a heavy release of air escaped my lungs—stale, grungy air that was growing old sitting there.

Over her shoulder, I saw the icy horizon. We were standing at the very bottom of the world, the very opposite end of the spectrum. There was a yellow sun drizzling its warmth over us, but when it got too warm, the artic breeze would cool our skin.

"I did it for you," I whispered into her ear and hugged her tighter. But it seemed my grip broke her apart, because not long after I tightened my arms, I was hugging myself. I opened my eyes. Raine was gone, and, again, my world was changing like it was inside a blender.

And there I was, standing atop Big's Tower again, looking out across a fire of buildings and people, looking across the City of the

Angel. I heard a loud roar echo into the air from the cracks between skyscrapers filled with the people of Los Angeles. They cheered to the hero who had just slayed their enslaver.

I did it for the city, I said to myself. *But I did it for Jay…no, I did it for Raine…*

Suddenly, the bluntness of reality slapped me in the face, and my head sprung up from its tenuous nap. I looked around, out the shattered windows of the cab. A small crowd of people had gathered outside my vehicle. Strangers' voices scurried into the car, asking me if I was okay or if I was hurt.

The door didn't open easy—I had to invest a great amount of strength I didn't have to free myself from the wreckage. Once out of the cab, I teetered against the building I had collided with. My vision was defamed and foggy. The images around me held to defined outline or shape, no details or anything close to that. But I was able to spot the black blur of Big Rich's destroyed escape.

I shook my head, though it hurt miserably to even think. Slowly, my vision was becoming less floppy and vague. Big Rich and three guards were hustling toward the doors of his tower which was only one block away. I took one step away from the totaled taxicab and stumbled as my foot landed back on the ground. The crowd around me was beginning to realize who I was, and slowly they faded away.

I doddered and lagged toward the crushed form of the SUV, sitting lifelessly in the middle of the street. Once I reached it, I threw myself up against its jagged side. Every muscle and bone in my body hurt. Places that I had never regarded before were throbbing with pain. I dreaded each breath, for every time my lungs expanded, my cracked ribs would pull apart. But I couldn't let Big Rich get away, and by then, they were nearly inside the tower.

Foolishly ignorant toward the warnings my body was giving me, I stepped forward once more, and a meaty arm lugged me in the head. With my already battered composure, it took no effort to send me to the ground.

One of Big's guards who had stayed behind emerged from

around the vehicle. He too was limping and scratched and bruised from his own accident. I had landed in a spread of glass, and as the man shuffled toward me, I felt for a larger piece.

He lifted his foot, but I rolled out of the way of his stomp, and brought myself to a stand before he could strike my jeopardy again. In my hand, I held a glass dagger, and began slashing the man's skin open. He squealed like a suffering animal as parts of his skin broke and the tendons beneath could be seen. The glassy imitation of a blade cut through him like he was butter, already melted. As a final attack, I slashed the glass across his tender throat. A tide of crimson blood vomited from the open wound, and just as his face turned the same color as chalkstone, he fell dead.

"Richard!" I called after him and his men without even taking a breath. My own hand was gashed and cut from the glass, so I dropped it and returned my legs to a wild sprint. I could feel my heart throbbing the last of its time. "Richard!"

I was muddling along the side of the tower's base, but when I saw my reflection in the reflective glass walls, I wished I had taken a more frontward approach. If anything in reality were to compare to a zombie, I would qualify. The shear destruction of my body was painful to look at, let alone to comprehend the rapid descent in self-preservation I had taken.

From way up top of the tower, the chopping of helicopter blades was slowing, and the copter itself was lowering onto the tower, waiting to retrieve Big Rich who was on his way up.

I had dragged myself to the front doors of the tower, and fell inside like slime without a skeleton, but before I entered, my eyes climbed up the trunk and through the branches of the green-canopied tree, still lavishly looming in its place.

The sound of my entrance echoed through the cavernous ceilings of the tower's entrance. Crystal chandeliers hung from the hollow ceilings like crystal stalactites. Sandstone colored marble crawled all up and down the walls and floor. My vision continued to fall in and out of clarity. While at first I would see giant, watercolor portraits of Big Rich, I would blink again and be planting my eyes upon a photograph of him handing toys to homeless children.

The clap of every step I took bounced around the marble hall before coming back to me. Directly ahead of the entrance were two elevators, one of which had just closed shut. The pants of my heavy breathing reverberated back to me. I was completely alone in the grand hall of Big's Tower.

Taking the elevators would have usually been too risky—not knowing what was on the other side once you were in—, but on that very night, it was the quickest option.

The elevator opened in front of me, and I stepped in. Every wall on the inside was a square mirror, and closing my eyes was the only way I could help not to see the rotted face beneath my hood. Besides the dark of night, my eyes were now just as black as Big's. The skin on my face was pale and full of a dead man's description. Like a fiend, the scar on my neck and part of my face was scabbed over, but cracked in spots leaking blood. On the back of my hood, a hole was cut in by the flames. The gloves on my hands were ashy, and their palms were well worn. No longer did I see any innocence in my eyes. Across my shoulders were the tons of guilt I toted with me. I could practically see the thick, warm blood dripping from my fingertips and filling in around the souls of my boots—a blue puddle my life would forevermore wade through.

Rusty and ancient, the handle of Jay's gun waited in my pocket, patiently watching its use creep closer and closer, until I would finally pull its trigger.

Spotless and pure, Raine's necklace was in my other pocket— its glass and water droplet shape free of any smudge or blood.

In its reflection, I saw myself, but not the city's ghost or a ruthless vigilante. I saw myself the Raine would have seen me. Clean black hair fully covering the top and sides of my head. My eyes were not like clouds before Armageddon's storm, but blue and crisp of color, a perspective of only justice and unattainable innocence.

It hurt more to look at the false reflection than it did to look at the one of reality. I always knew that the poison of anger inside of me would slowly rot my body, but it had never been more than a thought.

A small slit, from when the elevator doors opened, let me dread a glimpse of Big's remaining three men inside the hallway on the last floor. They all loaded their weapons and fastened their ties tight to their necks. A harmless chime of the elevator doors turned out to be the most fatal note. Each face of every guard whipped toward me in the elevator, the square cage.

Time didn't slow like I thought it would, and with just barely enough time to react, I was being eyed by not only the irises of the guards, but the deep pupils of their guns.

There were uncountable triggers being pulled, and many shots being fired, but when the guards all unloaded their clips, it burgeoned into only one sound of deafening ringing and roaring.

Just enough space aside the door in the elevator was my only cover. I hurled myself against the side wall, while the back wall of the elevator shattered into fractures and shards of glass when the shower of bullets rained upon it. Every shard caught the reflection of the onslaught just outside of the elevator. I could see the flashes of gunshots winking violently in each tiny reflection.

When the shooting stopped and the guards had to reach to reload, there was an aftertaste of sound that was bitter and unpleasant. With only an amount of time tinier than any one of the shards of glass, I twisted out from behind my cover, scooping a handful of glass powder upon my exposure.

With a glance, I threw the handful of tiny glass grains into the closest guard's eyes. He shut them tight when the tiny shards touched the squishy surface of his eyes. I leapt off the ground, brought both of my knees to my chest, and at my closest point to the guard, I shot them outward. The kick combined with both of my legs sent the man backward into the wall, then to the ground where he held his eye sockets as the glass pieces slowly blinded him.

I managed to land on the tips of my feet and fingers, and in a constant duck, ran toward the second guard. He bulleted two separate punches toward me after abandoning his rifle. He had the lost the opportunity to reload. I blocked both powerful strikes with the meat of my forearms, then clawed at the collar of his jacket and hasted him close. His nose broke under the impact of my forehead. The stun clouded his sense of reflex and loosened his body.

I combusted the fastest speed for a punch, and landed the sharp tips of my knuckles directly over the fragile bone of the guard's esophagus. There was no doubt that the bones would snap, and the untranslatable strike stunned him with even more shock. When I released my hands from his collar, he fell to the side without any extraneous force and a collapsed windpipe.

The last guard had just jammed a new clip into the chamber of his rifle and lifted it toward me. As I approached, quick like an eye's blink, he had pulled back on the trigger and soared three separate bullets into my chest. But before I could acknowledge the burning sensation, or the crushing pressure of my wounds, I took hold of the rifle's barrel and steered it away from my direction.

He continued firing the gun, blasting little trails of bullet holes along the walls and ceiling of the compact hallway—much like the one at the police department. I slung the point of my elbow backward into the structure of the guard's face. His head snapped back each time I struck him, and on the third blow, he released the rifle and buckled to the floor.

Now I stood over him, playing with his life as if the gun's aim was a marionette. I never pulled the trigger, though. He flashed his hands, waving surrender. "Don't kill me," he begged, putting forth the remaining pity he had. "Please...don't kill me."

I lowered the gun to my side. As I stepped over him, he awaited a sign of mercy, but I merely raised the rifle like a sledge, and dropped the metal butt of the gun through his skull. By then, I had become used to the sound of squishing brain and the sight of oozing guts.

Ahead of me were the remaining steps to the top of Big's Tower.

I released the elongated rifle from my grip, and stepped over the carcasses strewn across the hallway's width.

With all the strength in my body, I climbed up the stairs like hiking up the side of a steep mountain, but regardless, I made it to the door where I stopped and imagined what would happen on the other side once I walked through.

I would walk through the door, and shoot Big Rich right in his heart. My work would be complete, the pain would desecrate, revenge would be served. Big Rich would fall to his back and die right on top of the world where everyone could see him. Project Home would only ever be a vision, and Jay's dream would become reality.

A blast of rain and light pushed against my face when I burst through the door and stepped out onto the roof of Big's Tower.

"Richard!" I howled loudly, competing with the buffering helicopter hovering above, and the grind and click of the pistol's slide as I pulled it back, pushing the hammer out. The sound rattled across the rooftop and heckled Big Rich with its pending deadliness.

He never turned around. Instead his feet remained pressed to the rooftop, his arms widened away from his body (as if he was afraid of touching himself), and ponderous pants inflated and deflated his body. A little, dotted trail of drops of crimson blood followed Richard's path to where he stood in the middle of the rooftop's helicopter pad. Above, the copter was trying to land, but my presence and the conflict I provoked prevented any such thing. A bright spotlight, with surprise, capped both Big Rich and me in a cone of white glare.

At first, Big Rich only turned his head halfway over his shoulder. I could see the scratched and bleeding skin of his cheek and the flab beneath his chin. None of Richard's words were dauntless enough to exit his mouth or hop off his tongue. He was looking right into the depth of a gun's eye. I held my arm out straight, ignoring the fatigue of my muscles and their burning pain, begging me to lower it.

The helicopter above pulled higher into the air, and entered a slow orbit around Big's Tower. There were the strobe patterns of lighting, flashing in the distance, yet quickly approaching the city. Soon, a shower of rain would wash away the blood in the streets and on the roof.

Big Rich was waiting for me to speak, to let him hear his last words before executing him atop the entire world. The whole time I held out my arm, my finger was just barely making contact with the curve of the pistol's trigger, molded to fit my fingertip.

I began, unsure how to capsulate everything I had wanted to say to Lucifer: "You didn't think I would be here, did you...?" My voice was just loud enough for him to hear it over the cluttering noise around us.

As he spoke, Big Rich rotated his bally body fully around to face me. His black suit was tattered, as if its age was prehistoric. Smears of blood were wiped across his face, crusted around his nose and lips, and bruising the soft flesh around his eyes.

"No," Richard admitted at a slow speed of breath. "I didn't. How did you escape?" he asked me, using the last of his airless breath to speak sarcastically. "Did you turn into plume of smoke? Did you walk through the walls...?"

"I burned down your store, Richard," stated the lack of ceremony within me. "Your men burned with it," I stung him with the addition.

The bridge of his nose wrinkled, his eyebrows fell inward and Big Rich flared both his teeth and nostrils when he asked me furiously, "*Why*? Why are you doing this? What do you want from me?" he screeched his voice.

There was no hesitation when I told him so plainly, "I want you dead, Richard! I want your life ripped from this world!"

"But *why*?" he asked again, looking for the most specific answer, as if he could not assess his own guilt. Overhead, the helicopter was still circling, casing the climax of my plot in light. I was unable to see anything outside the cone of glare we were under.

I never answered his question with a direct onslaught of words. Innuendoes slowed my words as they muddily crept from my mouth. "I know about Project Home; I know about the Drug Trade and your plan to spread it across the nation."

"*What?*" Big Rich seemed appalled that I knew of his plans.

"I know about the orphanage homes—how they're recruiting centers for your trade," I specified. "And I know that Toy Palace is just another factory, another place to distribute your *Borm!*"

Realization had finally widened Richard's eyes. He shook his head while the words of his wheedling bounced right off my ears. "No," he said, "you have it all wrong! You have it all wrong! I don't have anything to do with the trade...I don't have anything to with Borm..."

"It's too late," I told Big Rich. "You've taken everything from me, Richard. You murdered Jay, an innocent old man! You kidnapped a harmless girl like ransom!—an innocent girl!" I loudly judged the innocence Big Rich was claiming to possess.

"Jay?" Richard asked, catching only that name from my burning sentences. "*Jay?*"

"He was like a father to me! He was my best friend, my mentor!" I explained our relationship through a desperate yell.

"No..." the fat lord persisted on repeating beneath the hiss of his breath. "No, you don't understand!" he claimed. "You can't kill me! I..." Big Rich considered the words he was about to speak. "I'm innocent!"

I was hacked apart by his words worth no more than spit. "Don't give me that shit!" I ordered him, mixed with a great hint of threat. "I know who you really are, Richard Lucifer! I know you're true intentions!"

Again, he screamed, "No! No you don't! You don't know the beginning of it, kid!" Big Rich once again claimed, "I'm innocent—I have nothing to with the Drug Trade anymore. I pulled myself out of that life when I was just a kid," he told me.

A rush of wind from the approaching storm, and whips of air lashing from the helicopter's blades threw the hood off my head, pushing back my remaining hair. Right then, with Big Rich caught in the aim of my one bullet, the length of his life was my choice.

"You..." he formed the single word in his lips, and backed away from me. "It's *you*..." Like the simple sight of my face brought bare reality just before his eyes, Big Rich was weakened by a sudden lapse of revelation.

It seemed so distant from me—the truth that I was actually there, holding Jay's gun to Richard's head. I had the power, the chance and will to shoot him. Or so I thought my will was as unbeatable as my body.

The pain in my chest had increased from where I was shot. I could feel the led caps burning away the flesh, dug deep into my body. My lungs, every time they filled with air, would touch the bullets' crushed tips, and a stab of pain raced to my head. I flinched, cringing my face every time I had to take a breath. I could feel my organs punctured by the bullets—the acid from my stomach slowly dripping down the insides of my legs, my intestines ready to burst open. If my stomach wasn't as impaired as it was, I would want to vomit, but nausea only induced more pain.

Slowly, my posture was collapsing inward, but every time I noticed, I brought myself back up, neglecting the pain my body was gorging me with. A sudden surge of readiness overtook my mind, and I stiffened my arm then stepped one foot closer to Big Rich.

"If crime is merciless," I began dispersing my life's only wisdom, "justice must be too..."

Big Rich could tell I was ready to kill him. He held up the white palms of his meaty hands and continued shaking his head. The fat beneath his chin, I noticed, jiggled with his every motion. "Don't kill me!" he begged helplessly. "Don't kill me, Hale!"

The sound of my name ringing from Big Rich's mouth added a hundred pounds to the pistol I held. My arm fell down by my side, and I tried over and over again to bring it back up. No matter how hard I tried, or how heavy the gun *really* was, I couldn't return a killer aim to Big Rich's head. It took inhuman strength to return the gun back up, but before blood was forced out the pores of my face, I was again trapping Lucifer in my opportunity of murder.

"You can't let him win," Big Rich struggled to say in between the quivers of his every word. "He wants you to kill me so the City of Angels will fall! He wants all this madness...all this death and chaos! Ever since I threw him out, he's been looking for a way to take revenge..."

"What are you talking about?" I asked him. My own fury was growing impatient, and the mouth of the killer inside me was watering vigorously.

Big Rich said, still with much ambiguity, "It's all part of his plan, Hale...this is exactly what he wants..."

"How do you know my name? And who are you talking about?" madly, I asked Big Rich. It wasn't that I was prepared to believe his answer, though.

"Jay!" Big Rich clearly pronounced the old man's name. "*Jay!*"

He was using my own words against me, pretending to actually know Jay, pretending to understand the extent of the situation. It was a fool's last attempt at saving his own worthless life. I said to him, "Don't you dare try to convince me of such lies. You don't know Jay...you don't know me."

"Yes I do," Big Rich swore. "I know who you are, and I know everything the old man is capable of..."

"How?" I asked, challenging the outlandish claims he was defending.

"Because," Big Rich advanced, "he is my father! I deceived him all those years ago—I burnt down Port Lybric and turned him into the police," narrated Big Rich with a voice washed over by the terrors of his past. "I couldn't stand his business!" he added. "The Drug Trade was more important to Jay than I—his own son—was. He neglected me! He abused me!" His breaths were even heavier now, sticky with clots of saliva in his throat and tears in his eyes. Big Rich ripped the dark glasses off his face and threw them to the ground. Though, there was no more color in his eyes than there was in the black lenses. "One night," he continued on telling me the false, fictitious story that was all an act of his cleverness, "I snuck into Port Lybric, and burned the whole place down. I hoped that maybe it would weaken his business…that maybe he would notice me. But even when he discovered that it was me who sparked the flame, my father had me killed!"

The quakes of my every emotion—the struggle to believe Richard's story—sent tremors across my arm, seizing my hand and once motionless aim. Again, my vision was fogged by an uncertain doubt. My aim toward Big Rich was starved of confidence, and my eyes couldn't look straight forward. I noticed things to my side, things that were once made invisible by my hood.

"I came here after the war, opened a shop of my own, and made the best out of the worst. I opened a pharmacy," Jay said, trying to sound happy. "It was only a matter of time before the city found out what I did and tossed me out. I was locked up for years until my case was unable to be policed. When I was released, I had so many enemies. Everyone knows what I did…so I found refuge in the orphanage home. No one there knew about my past…" Jay looked at me. I was one thing good that came out of his retreat.

"You went there to hide…" It made sense why Jay lived in a dusty attic above an equally ignored orphanage home.

"Yes. To try and run away from everything…but then I see Big Rich, doing exactly as I did but with no intent of doing right! He knows he's killing millions, but he doesn't think twice about it. What heart is that cold? I learned that your closest friend can be your closest enemy…Big Rich's father, the man who started the Drug Trade, stole my formula and…"

"No!" without warning, I blurted loudly and sharply, the most staccato scream ever. "I know this is just a trick—I know that you're lying, Richard!"

All the while, Big Rich shook his head back and forth in heavy motions. "No," he began sobbing. "No, please…don't kill me… don't kill me and let him win…" The fat lord—out of both physical exhaustion and an empty cellar of chance—lowered his rounded, fat-plumped body to his knees. Both of his arms he held outward, flattening his two palms to the ground. Thunder's bellow rolled in a nearer distance after a flash of lighting dove through the black clouds. While I held the pistol over his head, Big Rich bowed to me, hailing me. "You have the chance to kill me, so why don't you?" Only because he knew of my doubt did Big Rich dare to ask. "I beg of you," he spoke as if he were praying, "don't kill me. Not for my sake—for your sake. If you kill me, you will learn of my innocence, and you will be punished…"

My feet were spread to the width of my shoulders, and the arm that didn't hold a gun hung at my side, though far from my ribs which were constantly parting from the huffs of my breathing.

I was standing on the peak of my life, the only moment of my existence when free will would not just influence, but dictate the embers of my life's conclusion. How quickly my flame would sputter into a twist of smoke, and how long after my embers would stay hot. Either way, whether or not I would kill Big Rich, I would die again. I was reborn only to hunt down the man who killed me. After my poach's end, any purpose clinging to the fraying ends of my hoodie would lose their grip.

"Tabatha Hale," spontaneously, I pronounced the name to test the liability of Big Rich's tears, waiting for any reaction to stir him.

His head lifted with the quickest, most involuntary spasm. "Tabatha?" he asked, his voice soaked with the blood of his heart.

The helicopter was circling the tower, still blinding us with its spotlight's bright eye. Stronger than the one before, each breath of the wind blew stronger and stronger. My balance was bullied by the gusts from the copter and storm. Still, though, the city had not been graced by the icy droplets of rain.

"Who is she?" I asked. I had to fight the high volume of the lowering helicopter.

Big Rich looked up at me. "She's your mother. My w—" His own silence cut, short, the continuation of his dialogue. "Just believe me, Alex!" he leaped over the topic of my mother. "Believe what I am telling you!"

I continued to wear the topic even further. "She's dead!" I blunted. "Tabatha Hale is dead. She was murdered a few days ago." I made my voice as apathetic as possible. It seemed that murder was a casual subject worth only casual words.

His eyes fell away from me, all the way to the rooftop's floor. Big Rich drooped even closer to the ground from his bowing position. He set his heavy, black-haired head upon the tops of his folded hands, and a choppy sound of crying wormed away from him. The fat, almighty, indestructible ruler of Los Angeles who had mangled the good and morality of so many beings, who had taken an overgrown population by his hand and crushed it with no more energy than it would take to crush a can, was crying on his knees before me.

And either Big Rich held no respect toward his pride, or the tears chapping his cheeks were as sincere as a human's true emotion. Slowly, he pulled his hands out from beneath his face, set them beside his head and curled both into tight fists. At first, he brought himself up to one knee, slugging his body over his thigh.

"What have you done?" Big Rich was blaming the murder on me. "What have you done?" he shouted the question while bringing himself fully to his feet. His height was equal to mine, but his mass was unmatchable. "You're just a *kid*!" Big Rich wailed, and charged a curved punch at me.

His strength was that of a speeding semi-truck. The strike caught me in the side of my cheek, snapping my head to the side and spinning my body halfway through a complete rotation. I was thrown to my stomach, but caught myself with my hands. Turning around, Big Rich was stepping close to me, lofting his giant, beastly form over my diminutive self.

"What do you know about me?" he asked, fed up with the game he was being forced to play. "What do you know about Jay? What do you know about the Drug Trade? You fell for the lies of an old man!" cried Richard, now standing directly over me. "You are an ignorant fool!—a blind child who believes everything he hears, everything he sees. Project Home was not a conspiracy, Hale. It was not a scheme! It was going to save the lives of thousands of people like you! Orphans, homeless children, mislead souls..." The release of anger and pressurized emotions was draining his stamina. He was breathing heavily. I just laid there, caught in the stun of what Big Rich was telling me. "He lied to you, Hale, just like he lied to me."

"Why would he want me to kill you...?" I asked Richard, defending my last, unwinding strand of faith in everything.

"I stabbed him in the back," Big Rich answered. "Even if he did deserve it, it was still deceit. I turned him into the police when he had me killed at Port Lybric. When he lost his power, I started a plan of my own and built an empire from the ground up! My incorporation was going to change the world," he told me, now saddened by its sudden lay back. "I was going to show the world, the city and my father what one abused, neglected child could grow to be. I was going to take my seat in a throne that this world needed! Then, my father would regret the way he treated me. Project Home was in retribution to everything Jay put me through, everything that every child like me would have to endure. And here you are," Big Rich focused on my own act of retribution, "ready to put a bullet in my head." His hands grabbed my right wrist, and he pulled the barrel of the gun close to his head. "Pull the trigger," Big Rich jibed my restless urge to kill him. "Pull the trigger, Hale, and kill a man who was trying to save this city, just like you thought you were. If you knew who I was, you would know how alike we really are."

I attacked Richard's words—"We are nothing alike!"

"And thus," he said slowly, "more proof of your ignorance. Shoot me," Big Rich dared. "Shoot me...if you're so confident that the words out of my mouth are all lies. Shoot me, if you're so confident that no consequence will follow." He stepped away, removing his stand from over me. I slowly brought myself to my feet, keeping the aim of Jay's gun nailed to Big Rich's forehead.

The helicopter that had been circling around Big's Tower had made a descent close to the rooftop without actually making contact. While it hovered just inches above the ground, a side door slid open, and out of the helicopter's chamber, a white-suited guard hopped out. In his hands he steadied a sleek rifle, bringing it to an aim over my head.

Big Rich, without removing his eyes from mine, threw a flat hand up and said to the guard, "Don't! Don't shoot!" The guard's obedience (though obedient beneath a salary) lowered his gun, and waited for his next command of action.

I watched Big Rich, waiting to see if the move he had pulled was a trick or illusion. He did nothing but watch me, waiting for my own response. "What are you doing?" I asked Richard, as if I would be happier in the company of his retribution.

"I'm not who you think I am," Big Rich simply said back to me. "And this is my way of proving it. I know his power," Richard finished.

A loud sound clashed behind me, and Big Rich's eyes focused on Barrette who had broken through the door to the roof. I didn't look back, but as Barrette laid his eyes upon me holding Big Rich in an aim, he called over to me.

"Don't kill him, Hale! Put the gun down!" I could tell by the sound of his voice that Barrette had his own gun drawn and pointed toward the back of my hoodless head.

Between the truth that Big Rich had presented, and the choice within myself to believe, I was caught in a net. The only thing that could extricate me was either the loud roar of a gunshot and a bullet between Richard's dark eyes, or the lowering of Jay's gun.

My eyes struggled between the guard who had lowered his gun, and the aim of my own. Big Rich just stared at me, still and silent amongst the rush of motion and noise. It was time, I knew, to kill myself, my identity.

"If crime is merciless," I began reciting, tightening Big Rich's body and cracking the faith he had held in me. But I never closed the words that had brought me to the top of the world. In the most defying movement, I lowered Jay's gun.

Big Rich didn't make any move. He didn't order his guard to kill me. He didn't lunge at me or strike me with any sort of attack.

His eyes, though, remained stuck to mine. Something in the look on his face told me that, soon, I would be given the whole truth. There was still a piece missing in my own sagacity, my own plot that had been thriving on that moment ending the way it was never supposed to.

Nearly unnoticeably, Richard Lucifer dipped his head downward, loosened his stand, then twisted around to face the awaiting helicopter. He hurried toward the guard, ducking beneath the invisibly spinning blades above him. Big Rich climbed into the hovering helicopter, and as the guard followed, it pulled away from the tower.

Behind me, as I had thought, Barrette was standing in a stiff stance with both hands supporting the weight of a silver revolver. And just as I had lowered my gun, the commissioner lowered his. He tucked it away into an inside pocket of his nut-brown suit jacket.

As I stood still, Barrette walked toward me, retrieving something else from his pocket. In his hands, as he finished the stride over to me, was a gleaming pair of handcuffs. "Jesus Christ," he muttered. "You're under arrest."

He wasn't expecting any resistance from me. I held out my arms with wrists close together, and when Barrette tightened the cuffs around them, he took me by the arm, with both hands, and guided me to the rooftop door.

In the hallway, amongst the three corpses bleeding red, were the officers of Barrette's squad. All eight of them stood in their navy uniforms and golden badges, watching Barrette fulfill the task they felt should have been executed long ago.

One of them pressed the button to open the elevator. Four stood on one side, and four stood on the other with Barrette still gripping my arm in between them. Below our feet were the shattered reflections of reality's images—the images of our faces, our thoughts, our sights and senses. Through the whole descent, no one spoke. I could hear the breathing of every officer, and see each stump of whiskers growing out of their cheeks and upper lips.

With the hood off my head, they were able to see the bald

patches of my head from where the hair had burnt off. They were able to cringe at the cracking, splitting and peeling burn conquering the skin of my neck, jaw and part of my head's backside. And my eyes (which wandered all around their sockets) were black; black like coal and all other colorless evils that, from a wider perspective, were not so evil.

The escape of heat beneath a night's shading darkness—the ink of words that build nations—the paint of an artist's delicacy—the color of rest—and the coal used to sustain a kindle, used to thaw a pair of frozen hands.

Outside of Big's Tower, a line of siren-topped cruisers were parked both on the sidewalk and street. Barrette's car was the beige sheep of the flock. He said to the officers who kept their formation around us (an even split on both sides), "I'll take him back to the station." Opening the passenger door of his car, Barrette lightly pushed my head down and sat me inside. He began fitting a key inside the hole of my cuffs. "I won't be needing these, will I?" I shook my head, and Barrette removed them completely.

He walked around the front of his cruiser and took a seat behind the wheel, setting Jay's gun (which he had taken from my possession) on the dashboard. The car's engine groaned softly, and Barrette pulled away from Big's Tower. I looked over the shoulder of my seat, watching as the lushly-canopied tree of green, fiery leaves shrunk with distance.

Until a drop of fallen rain flicked the windshield of Barrette's car, my eyes were watching the boots of my feet. I was waiting for blue and red blood to fill in around them. When the raindrop hit the windshield, I jerked my head and eyes up. I could see the splattered mark where the water had hit. A second raindrop soon followed…then a third…and a fourth. Soon, the storm that had been sitting in the distance was finally overhead. Barrette looked, from over the steering wheel, out his windshield to the dark, churning clouds in the sky. The occurrence (of which was mended naturally, and naturally expected) was surprising to me, Barrette, and every other witness in the city.

Only a few blocks ahead, just out of the city's density, was the yard of Crown Cemetery. I could just barely see the black iron gates spired with pointed tips. And when the car was surrounded by the lines of falling raindrops and the hiss of their noise, two thoughts of unmatchable merit were suddenly mixed into a gray tide of revelation.

Jay's watery eyes made me look away. One more sentence and Jay might as well have been balling. His lips quivered, hands shook, but his body was still. When he blinked and wiped the tears from his eyes, he shook his head and cleared his throat. Smiling, his acting didn't fool me.

I fiddled with Jay's small gun in my hand. He looked down at it and said with a drip of venom on his tongue, "Don't waste this, Hale...don't waste this..." Jay graced himself with a breath of life and said, "This is where everything ends, Hale. One way or another, it will all tie back to this. This is where it all ends...this is where it all ends..."

I broke the trend of silence between me and Barrette and spoke, without any previous prologue, "He has her."

Barrette looked over at me, skipping his eyes between mine and the road. "Who?" Barrette asked me. "Who has whom?"

"Jay," I answered. "He's still alive, and he has Raine. It all makes sense," I said to the stubbornness of my comportment.

There was surprise in the tone of Barrette's voice. "What? What the hell are you talking about?"

"Jay," I said again. "He's behind it all..."

"I thought Jay was dead."

"No," I spoke lightly, hollowly. "It's all him—everything that has happened...it all makes sense..."

"I don't understand!" Barrette shared his puzzlement. "Don't tell me that all that's happened, all that I've done is all a part of a God damned illusion! A God damned trick! What is going on, Hale?

What did Lucifer tell you?" The panic inside Barrette was surfacing. He, truly, was realizing that every one of society's member held the weight of their own guilt, and of the entire world's culpability.

"I'm sorry, Barrette, but we have all been blinded. We are all fools," I theorized. "Jay is alive, and he is waiting..."

"Where is he? Where can you find him?"

Barrette was driving alongside the iron bars of Crown Cemetery's perimeter. I looked out his window, watching as every black bar passed. "This is where it all ends," I said to Barrette. He followed my gaze.

In a snap-of-a-motion, I took the pistol from the dashboard of Barrette's car. His reflexes told him to reach for it, but by the time he could react, I had it pointed right toward the side of his head. "God damn it, Hale! What are you doing?"

"Pull over," I said. "Pull over now!"

"No," Barrette refused. "I'm taking you to jail! You're done with all of this! Put the gun down."

When Barrette still didn't cooperate, I filched his control over the vehicle and forced the steering wheel to the left. The cruiser veered off the street, quickly, and boarded the sidewalk, unwelcomed. It came to a rough stop when the car's front end met the stone basing of Crown Cemetery's iron perimeter. Behind and in front of the crash site, the four other cruisers came to a scratching halt, and while I had just swooped beneath the iron arch, the officers were exiting their vehicles and entering a pursuit after me.

Barrette's head was forced into a collision with the bend of his steering wheel. I threw myself out the car door, and sprinted, with a limp, beneath the iron arch of Crown Cemetery. As I was ascending the slope of the hill leading to Jay's grave, I could hear the voices of calling officers. They sprawled out across the cemetery's yard calling, "Find him! Find him!"

But as Jay's grave came into sight, my sprint was slowed. Standing there, over his own grave, was Jay. He was doused in dark apparel, and the black hat and coat of his outfit resembled that exactly of the mysterious man who I had encountered several times prior to that night. And in his grasp was Raine, bound by the wrists and heavily soaked by the storm. Her golden hair hung heavy, and the thin layer of makeup around her eyes was streaking down her cheeks like black tears.

I brought myself to a walk, and eventually a still stand when I was just feet from the man who had raised me, and the man who I was ready to kill another for.

"So," he began saying sweetly, "the deed is done. You killed Richard Lucifer, otherwise you wouldn't be here. And now," Jay continued, "I thank you for killing the one person who has ever stood before me."

"I know everything, Jay." The old man didn't seem to be threatened or staggered by my knowledge.

"Oh," he said, and brought a smile up from his wrinkled lips. He spoke with a sugary tone, "Then I guess there is nothing to discuss. My son is dead, and now the city will throw you out. I told you, Hale, your closest friend can be your closest enemy."

I waited not a second before asking, "Why did you want me to kill your own son, Jay? Why did you want Richard dead?"

At first, Jay pretended to have no remaining spite toward his son. He started with a chilling laugh, then a killing stare. For a while, he held the smile on his face before letting it go completely. "Because he threw me out!" Jay bellowed suddenly. "The entire city threw me out!—just like they're going to throw you out. I should have known better," Jay expressed his shame. "I should have known that once you show people a glimpse of your own marvel, they'll want it for themselves. They'll do anything to have it! As soon as my son turned me into the police, all my loyal slaves suddenly turned their backs!" Raine flinched and her whole body jolted every time Jay shouted. At last, Raine knew who it was beneath the hood. "My own *son* turned me in...and no one cared. All he wanted was revenge for his piece-of-shit childhood, and all *they* wanted was the drug I gave them! The drug I created! Out of the kindness of my heart, I shared Borm with them...and look how they repaid me. I was locked up for thirty God damned years before I was released. And when I got out, everyone pretended like nothing had happened. All they cared about was the Borm... the *Borm*..." I had never seen Jay's eyes compromised by hate and anger, nor had I heard his voice pronounce such spit and animosity. He said some more, "So I found you, Alexander Hale. I took you from your home—your mother and father. I chose *you*, the prince of the city..."

My eyebrows crumpled up. "...Prince?" I queried, stumbled and lost in the comprehension of the label he put me under.

Jay snickered through his nose, snickering like he still had tricks up his sleeves. "Then I guess you don't know all of it," he patronized. "You don't think I'd just pick a random kid in an orphanage home, did you? No," he explained, "I'm not that generous. You were just so...*perfect*. All you needed was a little push and I could make you do anything. You are just like us!" He paused, filled with suspension, antagonizing me with the knowledge he locked away under his bald head. "You have our blood, Hale. You have the blood of *kings*. You had no hesitation killing an entire city. I made you take control just like we did. You see, grandson, you're no different than us," Jay said to me just as Big Rich had. "All I had to do is make you hate Richard as much as I did, and you would stop at nothing to kill him. I walked you through everything..." Jay began to peel away the layer of lies that had built me: "I framed my own murder; I prevented you from seeing the truth. The ambush out front of Toy Palace, the death of your mother! I kidnapped Raine because she was a distraction," Jay justified his horridness. "Mr. O, all those dealers—they all worked for me. I told them what to say, what to do to make you think that Big Rich was in charge of the very thing he tried to destroy. Don't you see?" he asked me. "It was all *me*. Now that my son is dead," he immediately proceeded, "and the city is dying, it's time that you lose everything just as I, and just as your father did." He gave me a chance to speak my own bitter words back. I let a canyon spread until he spoke again, completing and polishing the revealing of his master plan. "When I got out of jail, I rebuilt my business and began spreading Borm across California. I wanted every person to have a taste of it, that way when you killed the only other man who I wanted dead, I could kill the rest of Los Angeles! But I needed someone to destroy my own business for me—someone to blame everything on. Like father like son," he jingled. "Richard tried to kill me, and you killed him."

"Why make me kill Big Rich?" I asked. "Why did you make me destroy Project Home?"

"For simple, sweet revenge!" answered Jay without so much as a thought. I looked at Raine who was standing, shivering and wishing she could escape. Lightning and thunder were making their presence known in the sky. Jay continued and said, "He tore me from power once—there was no saying he couldn't stop me again. If I couldn't have power, *he* couldn't have power." Jay was a completely different character than I had ever known him to be. It was pure melancholy that built his demeanor. "I hated that child! But it's okay, because you killed him…"

And just as he had, I snickered. Raising his own gun toward him, I said to Jay, "But I didn't kill him."

"*What*?" he asked.

"I didn't kill Big Rich, but I'm going to kill you." I pulled back the top of the pistol, and Jay practically leaped backward at the grinding sound of the loading bullet. "Like you said, Jay, your closest friend can be your closest enemy."

"Don't kid yourself, Hale! You won't kill me!—you're nothing without me!" Behind me, the shouts of police officers were growing louder and louder—steady crescendos climbing over the hills and meandering around the tombstones. "If you kill me," he continued desperately coaxing me, "then all of Los Angeles will die! Everyone will come after you!"

I came back at Jay with the truth that had excused my every action. "Thanks to you," I said, "I'm already dead." While Jay's words continued to scramble past me, I fed him the last words he would ever hear—the words of irony. "If crime is merciless," I prepared a golden aim over Jay's head while he tried to hide himself behind Raine, "justice must be too!"

The gunshot rang loud and echoed through the entire cemetery. Raine shrieked from behind the tape over her mouth as a mist of Jay's blood sprayed her face, and the old man's body fell limp to the ground. She jumped and closed her eyes tight, hoping that maybe she hadn't seen any of it.

The distant voices of the officers hollered, "Shots fired! Shots fired!" And slowly, they narrowed in on my location. The glares of flashlights were passing behind the silhouettes of tombstones all around me.

Quickly, sure not to waste any time, I removed the tape from Raine's mouth and the bindings from her wrists. But as I reached my hand toward her face, she flinched and took a step back.

Amongst all the chaos and stirring noises, I managed to still myself and focus all my senses on the angel who stood before me. "Raine," I gently said as I walked close to her. She flinched even more when I touched her arm. I pulled back and took a step away. "Are you okay?" She looked at the old man lying at the surface of his grave. No words shook out of her, though her body quivered. "It's *okay*," I promised her. "It's all over." I took all the courage in the remaining human part of me to allow her eyes the scorn of seeing my face. They practically shrieked when seeing my peeling burn, my rotted flesh, and my colorless eyes. "Raine..." I offered my hand once more. She froze, terrified from the monster reaching his claws toward her. I pulled in my reach and my hope that Raine would accept me after my blood ran cold and my compass shattered.

Caught in the understanding that she would never again take my hand, or press her lips to mine, I reached for her glass necklace in my pocket. I held the necklace in my palm. A nasty crack had taken a well pronounced chink of the glass. For a while, I looked at it. The silver chain was dirtied and had lost its shine, and the glass of the droplet was hardly transparent now. Raine's eyes focused on the air, as if her mind couldn't conceive the intensity of the graphics scripting before her.

While my left hand held the weight of Jay's murderer, I held the shattered representation of Raine's necklace in my right. But the choice was not a choice at all. I dropped the gun next to Jay's still body, and curled my fingers around the necklace.

I never again tried to soften Raine's understanding. A whip of lightning cracked in the sky like an impermanent scar, and a loud mumble of thunder rolled through the graying clouds. Every second that passed was a second granting the approaching officers more of a chance to capture me.

I brushed passed Raine, heading for the ever-expanding grounds of Crown Cemetery. From behind, Barrette's voice bound me in order. "Don't move, Hale." Slowly, I turned around to see Barrette, once again, strapping me in an aim of his gun. He quickly looked at Jay's body, then back at me to make sure I hadn't yet vanished. "So it really was him all along…" Barrette thought without sharing any of its details out loud. Though, he lowered his gun and said, "The city will survive."

"He was the only one who knew how to make Borm," I said, admitting the inescapable truth to Barrette. "Without Borm, every user in Los Angeles will perish."

"No," Barrette rephrased my sentence with one word. "Ed devised a formula that counterattacks Borm's effects. Once it's airborne, every user's dependency to Borm will be broken. So it looks like all the trouble you went through paid off," he said to me. I was lightened by the information Barrette had graced me with. "I should arrest you," he added, contradicting the connotation of his previous words. "If crime is merciless, justice must be too, right?" he asked in a mockery to my foolishness.

It should never have been about me killing a man, or even saving another, but, instead, doing what had to be done for mercilessness to become a bit more merciful. Because of the lives I took and the hood I wore, people saw the truth and how ruthless it was. And because black and white came together, we were all allowed to see the gray. There was no good and bad, wrong and right. The blue blood of every criminal was no different that red blood of every other human on Earth. There was only necessity—what had to be done to make something become. Whether it was to kill or bring life, it was what needed to happen, and it needed to happen without mercy or compromise so we all could see what came from the ignorance thought to be innate in all of mankind.

But the hood came off my head, and my most unnoticed, insignificant bend of nature proved to every closed pair of eyes that ignorance is nothing more than a habit you choice never to get rid of.

"Commissioner!" the officers were calling for him. Barrette could have called back and fetched them all on me like hungry dogs. But Barrette never did. He looked at me beneath the strobes of lightning which allowed us to see each other's faces for only split seconds at a time.

Before I turned and disappeared into the unending shadows, Barrette spent his last words toward me. "You're not the only one," he said over the rushing rain and calling officers. He knew I wouldn't understand his spontaneous sputter-of-a-sentence. But he only elaborating saying, "A storm is heading for Miami. If you so happen to find yourself there, I think you'll find someone who is searching for the same thing as you."

"And what am *I* searching for?" I asked Barrette.

Barrette replied, but his words were beaten down by another boom of thunder, and there was no time for him to repeat it. He turned over his shoulder and called to his officers, "Over here! He's over here!" When he turned back around, he nodded his head and said, "It's time to spread you wings, Phoenix."

I nodded back, and in the decaying flash of another whip of lightning, vanished into the shadows both behind and ahead of me. The officers had finally caught up to Barrette. They noticed, first,

Raine standing with shivers trembling her body, then Jay who lay dead, motionless with the deceit of his own deception.

"What the hell happened here?" an officer asked Barrette who wiped the streaming raindrops from the ridge of his brow bone. "Where did he go?"

Barrette never responded, but instead focused his eyes on the drape of shadows before him, and as he looked beyond the darkness blinding his perception, he could see me, winding my way through the garden of stone gently rising and falling upon the rolling hills of the cemetery.

I had reached the end of Crown Cemetery's yard. Through its black iron bars was an expansion of the decaying city of short neighborhoods and cluttered communities, and beyond that was the sun always sinking. When I turned around, I saw Big's Tower hoisted above the city's skyline—the City of Angels. The bars were just barely bent apart, lending me enough room to squeeze through.

The neighborhood I entered was a branch of street scorned by the refuge of acknowledgement and rotted by the departure of care, thus the immigration of walking mold. I had only traveled one block east of Crown Cemetery when a single man (made of expectation no different than the next) proved to me that I could never truly kill the crime society praises, but I could strangle it to near death.

As I passed by him, a man on the corner of the block asked me, with a voice indistinguishable from a woman's or man's, or a genderless friend's, "You wanna buy some Borm...?"

In an unhurried motion—knowing that his species was one of immortality—, I kinked my head in his direction and returned the shadow of my hood to the face I hid. And though it felt good to kill him, the world did not care nor notice enough to celebrate with me.

If crime is merciless...

BEHIND HALE

THE PROCESS OF WRITING *HALE*:

Before I discuss the representation and symbolism behind *HALE*, I would like to make an effort at briefly explaining the process of creating, writing and publishing this pentalogy's first book:

I began *HALE*'s production in the summer of 2009 while visiting family in California. I was an underclassman in high school during the time I—and my best friend Arlin—decided to write a book in March that year.

I had a girlfriend (In fact, the same girlfriend I am in relation with now), school and its classic agenda, and a vision of becoming a published author before I graduated high school. Little did I know, that would be the most challenging goal in my life to reach.

That fall, I completed the first draft of *HALE*, and felt, with my amateur look on publishing, that its content was worth reading. But I quickly realized, after reading it myself, that it was not a piece of work I necessarily wanted my name on. So I proceeded to rewrite it two more times, and by the summer of 2010 I was submitting my manuscript to many different publishing houses and companies.

Most every company accepted my work, and by that time I was expecting to be published in the fall. With a large laugh, I wasn't. It's the second month, and the twenty sixth day of 2012, and I am just now writing these notes, and submitting the final manuscript of *HALE* to my publisher.

The road I crossed was torn and chinked, there were gaps I had to jump across and barricades I had to break through. But as I sit here, now, writing this, I am more than proud to acclaim the first book, *HALE*, to the Pentalogy of the Becoming as my work! This is just the beginning to my five book, two million word pentalogy, and I assure you, the conclusion to this compilation of literature is more than worth the time it will take to read it. So, with that said, I hope you continue to follow the paths of these books (and all their content) and let them inspire you, as they have inspired me, to become.

HALE:

The first thing you may notice about this book is its size—at roughly 84,000 words, it isn't the largest novel compared to others. But let me begin with saying that everything inside the pages of *HALE* is completely, intentionally intentional.

HALE is, and will always be, the only book in the Pentalogy of the Becoming that will be written in a first-person point-of-view. Alexander Hale is the representation of every human being's ignorance, whether it exists as a tiny sliver in one person, or as a major ingredient in another. And his hood is one motif that emphasizes his representation. Though, the point-of-view itself is a defining element that expresses such ignorance and provinciality seeded in every person on Earth. We wanted this book to write a story from a very narrow sight and a selfish, tunnel-vision angle. You are completely trapped in Hale's perspective, and have no other choice but to see *what* he sees and *as* he sees. There is no room in the book for any flexibility.

I have tricked you!

Based on the words of some old, wise man, you, and your human nature, were convinced (even if the tiniest bit) that Big Rich was guilty of leading the Drug Trade, and that Project Home was a debut to spread his business. And you, just like Hale, placed a glaring perception upon Big Rich. Throughout the entire book, Richard Lucifer only exists as a nominal character, and never once do you see him engaging in the business he is presumed to be part of. And when he was truly innocent, Jay was able to make you think that he was guilty of horrendous crimes, and led Hale to nearly killing his own father, to destroying his reputation, and bringing the death of an entire city.

In the time I was writing *HALE*, I held a very angry, ruthless conception against crime and its criminals. Alexander Hale is an obviously merciless character who believes that crime cannot be tolerated in the slightest way. He believes "if crime is merciless, justice must be to". And so did I until coming to the end of the book and deeply considering such an outlook on morality's defense.

I realized that justice must not be merciless, but must be relentless. Crime *cannot* be tolerated, but justice must keep its shape. So, in the end of the book, Hale's character receives a shine of light, and he, too, realizes what justice must be.

The quote "If crime is merciless, just must be too" is merely a bit of dialogue that is intended on inspiring a thought: *Must* justice be merciless? Its purpose is to question justice's form and its reasoning.

With such an ignorant and blind perception, and a merciless understanding, Hale lost all sight of justice, and, over the course of the novel, forgets what his intentions are, thus leading himself to catastrophe.

Hale (*HALE*) is a reminder to people that they must not approach justice with a narrow mind or a blind perspective. In order for us to beat immorality, we must clutch justice and never lose it. Ignorance is one of our most innate agents, but it is also the blind man's only cure. We must do our best to fight ignorance just as we fight crime.

Don't wear the hood—it will blind you and smear your intentions with blue blood, and will burn away your every sight of justice.

CHARACTERS OF HALE

Alexander Hale:
As mentioned before, Hale is the representation of mankind's igno-rance. He, and his hood, is an example of one's life piloted by blindness. Though, he is also the symbol of mercy in the most con-tradicting form. Because he was merci*less*, you are able to see such a curse's rigor and consequence.

Ed Reel:
In the view of an optimist, Ed represents the world's pessimist, when really he's the symbol of the common person. Though he is very practical and, yes, sometimes very pessimistic, Ed is the common person's perception, conception and perspective.

Conner Barrette:
A fly in the milk. Black on white. The tall from the short and the short from the tall. Barrette is every person who defies practicality and stands out from the herd. Even with the judgment and ridicule of his officers, Barrette stands for what he believes to be right. Barrette, is this world's dying breed.

Raine Waltzer:
Raine—both in her physical (being petite) expression and figura-tive expression—is the representation of morality. She is an angel in Hale's life. Her character is intentionally a minor role, used to

express that there is only a sly amount of morality in Hale's life and world.

Jacob "Jay" Hale:
Jay is our world's deceit, its betrayal and revenge that every living person faces in life. He is a deceiver, a user and a mockery of truth. Jay is the clown who laughs at ignorance after letting it off the leash.

Richard "Big Rich" Lucifer:
The fat lord is the representation of common evil—what most people assume to be wrong at first glance. He is the assumption of immorality, and also the offender of ignorance, for he is not what he is assumed to be.

INTERESTING FACTS ABOUT HALE

- *HALE*'s original title was *Grape Soda*, used to express Big Rich's original way of spreading his drug through grape soda. Other options for titles included *City of the Angel*, *Blue Blood*, and *The Color of Rest*.

- In the original ending of *HALE*'s first draft, Big Rich was indeed guilty of operating the Drug Trade.

- Before *HALE* was part of Pentalogy of the Becoming, it was going to be a series of its own. The second book was called *Vegas Cage*, and was a story about Hale retrieving the last bit of Borm from a mad doctor after being quarantined in Las Vegas, Nevada.

- Alexander Hale's original name was going to be Alexander Just.

- In *HALE*'s very first sets of planning, Hale was going to be fighting both the Sex Trade—led by his mother—and the Drug Trade—led by his father.

- The idea of *HALE* was inspired by a simple text message that read: *Two wrongs make a right*.

- Borm comes from the two combined words, **Big's Form**ula, and throughout the production of *HALE*, an accurate, microbiological formula was equated to create a form of real Borm.

- *HALE* (due to my detail oriented uncertainty) was rewritten three times.

- Jay's gun is loaded with only one bullet, saved for the death of Big Rich.

- Within the text, there are several characters and scenes which allude to the pentalogy's future books and resolution.

- Pentalogy of the Becoming was originally named the Becoming Saga.

SPECIAL ACKNOWLEDGMENTS

Kimberly Waters

Arlin Tawzer

Jeramie Green

Ms. Evans

Robert (Grandpa) Bamford

Robin (Mom) May

Samantha (Sister) Corliss

Ely (Brother-in-law) Corliss

Shawna Sannes

Jacob Sannes

Kyle Rolfe

Julie Piltcher

Melissa Bush

Sabastian Coombs

Paula and Tom (Aunt and Uncle) Florence

Sean Jones

Inkwater Press

Smoky Hill High School

And every person who will ever read this book!

CPSIA information can be obtained at www.ICGtesting.com
Printed in the USA
BVOW012348170412

287786BV00004B/1/P